ADR'

MW01093099

(Never Too Late Book 2)

Aiden Bates

© 2016

Disclaimer

the reader's pleasure. Any similarities to real people, places, events, living or dead are all coincidental.

This book contains sexually explicit content that is intended for ADULTS ONLY (+18).

Chapter One

Pete sat on the floor of the bank vault along with the rest of the hostages. He couldn't think of a time when he'd been less comfortable, or more afraid. Hostage situations tended to end badly, at least for someone. Pete didn't need to be a rocket scientist to figure out his chances.

The six-month pregnant omega couldn't run as fast as the guy in the track team letterman jacket. And the pregnant omega would make a great statement for the bad guys, wouldn't he? "Hey, look how much we mean business! We just shot a pregnant omega in the head! Now give in to all of our demands or we'll take someone else out."

At least it would be quick, he supposed.

The thought was cold comfort as he pressed his back up against the wood of the stand where the deposit slips rested. What had he been thinking, anyway? He shouldn't have come into the bank. It wasn't like banks didn't have mobile deposits, or drive-up ATMs, or ATM deposits, or any one of dozens of other ways to put money from his clients into his account. Hell, Pete could just insist that his clients pay him electronically.

If he survived this, he was going to make sure he did exactly that.

The kid in the letterman jacket leaned over to Pete and whispered to him. "Do you think the cops are here yet?"

One of the robbers took the butt of his handgun and smacked the kid across the face with it. "No talking!" he barked, in a raspy baritone voice. The kid cried out, and so did a couple of the tellers who sat with them.

Pete did not cry out. Pete bit his lip, almost hard enough to bite through it, but he did not cry out. Pete didn't want to give the bad guys any excuses. If circumstances were different, maybe he'd be a little bit more willing to stand up to the robbers. As it was, he wasn't just worrying about himself. He might not have planned to get pregnant, but he loved and wanted this little girl growing inside of him and he was looking forward to being her parent. He couldn't risk them doing anything to hurt her.

So he bit down on his lip and tried to make himself as small as possible so as not to draw attention. It wasn't easy for a guy his height, or with what was basically a basketball sticking out from under his shirt, but he had to try.

The hostage takers were agitated about something. That made sense. They'd come in to rob a bank and something had gone wrong; of course they were agitated about something. Pete tried to think beyond the naked panic that made a cold sweat break out all over his body. What could possibly go wrong in a robbery? Bank robbers didn't like to linger when it came to robbing a bank. Time wasn't their friend. They wanted to get in, get what they could grab, and get out.

They'd been here for half an hour.

That meant that the cops were here. It had to. The thought wasn't as comforting as it should have been.

The robbers were agitated. Their guns were out, and all four of them had a finger on the trigger. Nervous people with their fingers on triggers led to accidents, and the armed cops outside would only hear a gunshot. They had no way to know if the gunshot had gone into the floor, the ceiling, or a hostage.

They were supposed to be looking down, and not at their captors, but Pete risked a glance up anyway. The masks had come off. He looked down quickly. That wasn't good. If the masks were off, that meant that the captors didn't care about witnesses. They didn't plan to leave any behind.

One of the captors picked up the phone. "All right," he said. "You're obviously not taking this seriously. I'm going to prove that we mean business." He slammed the phone back into its cradle. "Grab someone visible."

One of the other robbers, another teenager with a pencil-thin mustache, walked through the assembled hostages. Pete held his breath as the robber paused near the place where he was holed up, but after a moment's consideration the kid moved on.

He grabbed the elderly security guard by one arm. "I think he'll do, Jeff."

"Wait, wait! There's no need for violence." The security guard's voice was reedy and weak. He didn't struggle, but he might not have been able to struggle much. Pete thought he might have been in his eighties. He wheezed as the robber dragged him over to the bank door.

"Put your hands up, Grandpa." Jeff jammed his handgun into the back of the old man's head.

Pete couldn't look away. A different subordinate unlocked the bank door and opened it. From the sound of it, there was a massive police response, because it sounded like dozens of guns came online as the door opened.

Jeff wasn't fazed. He shot the security guard in the back of the head and kicked him out the door. The underling pulled the door shut again and locked it.

A few people screamed. Most of them cried. A few tears escaped Pete's eyes. Jeff had just shot an old man, in cold blood. It could have been any of them. It had almost been him. Oh God, he wasn't getting out of this alive.

Jeff picked up the phone. "Next time it's the pregnant guy we've got in here. You've got fifteen minutes to meet our demands, got it?"

Pete tried not to shake. There was nothing that he could do to get out of this, was there? There wasn't any way that the cops would be able to get three cars there in time, not the kind they wanted, and even if they could the cops weren't going to do it just for him. They couldn't get their hands on four million in cash and no one could get fifty pizzas to a bank in fifteen minutes. That wasn't even remotely possible.

At least it will be quick. At least it will be quick. At least it will be quick.

If Pete repeated that phrase to himself often enough, he might believe it.

He moved his hand over the swell of his abdomen. He knew that it was impossible for his developing baby girl to have any idea what was going on, of course. Her brain wasn't even really formed yet. Still, she moved inside of him with a kind of bubbly joy, like she was trying to reassure her daddy that everything was going to be okay. He wished he could have offered her more. He wished he could have offered her life, and everything that went along with it. First steps, first words, first day of school—everything.

Glass shattered.

Pete wrapped his scarf around his mouth and nose. He didn't know if that would help. He still didn't know what was happening, but he knew the best bet for survival would be to stay down and try not to get caught in any crossfire. He couldn't exactly flatten himself onto the ground, but he got onto his side and did his best to try to protect his abdomen.

Purple smoke filled the room. *Seriously? Purple?* A small section of Pete's brain had time to wonder about that as the rest of him prayed that he'd get out of this alive. Gunfire erupted both indoors and out, punctuated by even more breaking glass and other hostages screaming.

A few of the other hostages started to struggle to their feet. "Stay down!" Pete barked. He didn't know if they could hear him through the scarf, but he had to try. "The cops won't know whose side you're on!"

Most of them got back down on the floor. A couple didn't, staggering off into the smoke.

Pete's heart was somewhere up around his Adam's apple, but he didn't have time to panic. He was on his own. He needed to stay alert and try to find a way to get out of this, and hopefully find a way out for himself and his daughter.

Sporadic bursts of gunfire echoed off the walls. Pete couldn't be sure that the different shooters were even aiming for anyone. He opened his eyes, grateful for the fact that the smoke rose, and found one of the criminals only a few inches away from him, hugging the floor.

The robber winked at him and pressed a finger to his lips. Rage welled up inside of Pete then. He couldn't see the man's gun. That didn't mean he didn't have it, but the idea that he would now try to sneak out with the hostages made Pete ill. He pulled his foot back and kicked the man in the jaw, as hard as he could.

He must have gotten him just right, or maybe the guy had a glass jaw or something. Either way, the robber passed out.

A man in dark body armor, with the words *STATE POLICE* written out in white across the chest, waddled over to him in a semi-crouch. He had a massive gun strapped to his chest, but he reached out a hand to Pete. "Come on, buddy. I'm here to get you out."

Pete almost passed out. The tall SWAT team member was an alpha. He was an alpha who smelled like fresh buttered popcorn.

Pete considered his options. This was not the time to be thinking about alphas. There were still plenty of bullets flying, and one could hit him at any moment. At the same time, the same thing could happen if he stayed in place. He nodded and let the strange cop shield him as they both crouched over to the emergency exit.

The problem with the smoke was that while it hid the cops from the crooks, it also hid the crooks from the cops. By the time Pete and his rescuer made it back over to the emergency exit, Jeff had found his way over there too. His lip curled and he aimed his gun right at Pete.

Just as he pulled the trigger, SWAT Alpha knocked Pete out of the way. Pete fell to the floor and Jeff shouted, turning his gun toward SWAT Alpha.

Pete covered his mouth with his hand. He couldn't let Jeff kill SWAT Alpha. He wrapped one of his legs around Jeff's ankle and slammed his other foot into the thief's knee as hard as he could. Jeff screamed in agony as he went down, firing his gun into the ceiling instead of into SWAT Alpha.

SWAT Alpha stomped on Jeff's wrist, the one that held the gun. Two other cops ran in from outside and helped to grab the robber, and SWAT Alpha turned to Pete. "Are you okay?" He held out his hand to help Pete up.

Pete accepted the help. "I'm a little bruised, but I think we'll make it." He blushed under the alpha's gaze. SWAT Alpha couldn't be this attractive, could he? It had to be the adrenaline rush, the sudden flood of relief of not having died.

SWAT Alpha ushered him outside and over to a staging area, out beyond some barricades the police had set up. "I'd be more comfortable if you got checked out at the hospital. I mean, that was quite a fall you took, and a lot of stress. That's some precious cargo you've got." He licked his lips. "Is there someone that I can call for you? Your alpha, maybe?"

Pete frowned. SWAT Alpha had to know that he didn't have an alpha. He would know that by scent. "There's no alpha." He looked away. Was he trying to humiliate him?

"Oh. I'm sorry." SWAT Alpha shuffled his feet a little. "You never know. Sometimes stuff happens, I don't know. I'm going to shut up now. Anyway. We've got ambulances standing by; you might as well go and get checked out."

Pete sighed. "Yeah. Okay." An ambulance seemed a little excessive to him, frankly, but the SWAT Alpha was right. With the baby, there was no such thing as too careful. He let SWAT Alpha escort him over to a fleet of ambulances, where EMTs buckled him in.

SWAT Alpha handed him a card. "Look, if you need anything at all, even if it's just a ride back to your car, let me know."

Pete looked down at the card. "Detective Osmund Morris, Cold Case Squad?" He lifted an eyebrow. "That's an awful lot of body armor for cold cases."

Morris huffed out a little laugh. "Yeah, well, can't afford to have a whole squad just twiddling their thumbs waiting for stuff to hit the fan, you know? Have to have a day job too." He winked. "Anyway, they're going to want to take a statement, so make sure someone has your contact info."

Pete passed him a card of his own. "Thank you for your help today."

Morris laughed. "Thank you. You saved my life. That guy was going to kill me, but you thought quick on your feet. Or ass, whichever."

Pete's laugh might have had a touch of hysteria to it, but he guessed that he could be excused. "Thanks for that. Dignity is overrated."

"Tell me about it." Morris grinned at him, and looked at him for long enough that the EMTs had to tell him to get a move on.

They took him out to MetroWest Medical Center, where they asked him to stay overnight for observation. Personally, Pete thought that was excessive, but he agreed just to be on the safe side. He didn't want to take unnecessary risks with his daughter.

The next morning, he got a clean bill of health from the doctor, who pronounced him well if bruised and his daughter perfect in every way. Then he called his mother, who sent her driver to come and bring him back to his place in Sudbury.

Cops came by to take his statement after he'd had a chance to shower and change. He told them everything, including the detail about kicking the guy in the jaw. Then they left again, and Pete decided to hide in his bedroom for the rest of the day and quietly break down for a little while.

He'd just witnessed a murder, a near murder, and a violent hostage situation. He'd faced down his own death. He figured he was entitled.

He'd go back to work tomorrow. In the meantime, he could go ahead and let himself get through what he'd just seen.

At least there had been Morris, the hot SWAT Alpha. He'd been handsome and smelled good. He'd been sweet, too. In fact, he could do a lot to make up for the truly awful day. He'd never actually want Pete—no alpha would want a guy who was pregnant with another man's child—but the fantasy was fun.

He settled into a sleep that was much less fitful than he'd expected.

...

Ozzy landed on the mat with a barely audible thump. The staff member on duty in the indoor climbing center looked him over. The guy was a beta, but he definitely had an appreciation for men. "Not bad," he commented as Ozzy stretched his arms out. "We don't usually get a lot of guys free climbing like that."

Ozzy looked him up and down, not making any secret of his intentions. "Yeah, well, I've got to keep myself in form somehow. Not a lot of good ways to climb this time of year, you know? Not around here, anyway."

"Not unless you're into ice, anyway." The blond chuckled.

"I could be up for that sometime." The truth was, Ozzy hadn't ever done ice climbing. It was on his bucket list, but he hadn't gotten a chance to try it yet. "Got any good places to go?"

"I've got a place to go up in the White Mountains. Give me a call sometime and I'll hook you up." The attendant reached into his drawer and pulled out a card.

Ozzy looked at it. "Thanks, Marty. I'll do that." He gave Marty Shaw, Hiking and Climbing Guide, a wink and then headed for the locker room. He'd definitely give Marty a call, and probably a little bit more.

Just as soon as the thought entered his head, the image of the handsome omega from that hostage situation a couple of days ago popped into his head. That had happened every single time he thought of an attractive guy lately. It didn't matter what the circumstances were. He could catch a glimpse of Robles' omega walking down the hall and BAM! There would be the image of Pete Nolan, Photographer. He could be at a bar, talking to a nice and possibly amiable young man and then there he'd be again. Pete Nolan. He could be watching porn in the privacy of his own room and there he'd be yet again, and if that wasn't all sorts of wrong Ozzy didn't know what was.

He washed up quickly, got dressed, and headed into the office. He needed to get his head out of the clouds and maybe call Pete Nolan. If nothing else, it would get his head out of the clouds about the guy.

The ride to work didn't take long, and if there was a little bit more tension in his step than there usually would have been, no one said anything about it. Everyone knew Ozzy got a little tense sometimes. They just rolled with it, just like they rolled with Nick's rigidity or Langer's touchy-feely hippy crap or Nenci's outright assholery. That was why the unit worked so well together.

He logged into his computer, as per usual, and went to go get a cup of coffee while his computer decided to think about warming itself up. When he got back to his desk, he found his supervisor, Lt. Devlin, at his desk. "Hey, sir," he greeted. He looked at the guy beside his boss, Oliver from the lab. "Hey, Oliver. How's it going?"

Oliver straightened his tie. "Not so bad. Not so bad at all. And yourself?" He looked around. "I don't see Detective Nenci here today."

"No, he's out on a case." Devlin didn't smirk at the kid, but he knew. Everyone knew how the poor kid felt about Nenci.

"Oh." Oliver's face fell for a second, but he covered admirably for himself. "Anyway. We've come to talk to you about the bullets used by the ringleader from that gang of bank robbers you fought with on Tuesday."

Ozzy frowned and set his coffee cup down. "Wait. That's not a cold case. That's a very hot case, and one that should be closed considering we have four dirtbags in custody." One of the dirtbags had a broken jaw too, courtesy of the handsome and charming Pete Nolan, Photographer.

That card was still right there on Ozzy's desk, all but burning a hole into it.

"You're right. The bank robbery isn't a cold case. The bullet, though, comes from a gun that was used in a homicide twenty years ago." Oliver's eyes lit up.

"Twenty years ago?" Ozzy shook his head. "If that kid is nineteen years old I'll eat my own shoe."

"Why do you think we're down here?" Devlin rested his fingertips on Ozzy's desk. "That cold case is the murder of a state trooper. Trooper Timothy Harbaugh, to be specific. There's no way that Jeff Balsalmo killed a state trooper three months before he was even conceived. We deal in the real world, here, not in science fiction. Your job is to figure out the connection, and hopefully to solve the case." He bent down and grabbed a box off of the ground.

Ozzy accepted it. "No pressure though." He winked at Devlin. His boss knew him well. The pressure would be no problem for Ozzy; it was his bread and butter. "Let's do this."

"I'll leave you to it." Devlin tapped the top of the box and headed back to his office. Oliver handed him the forensic report, cast a longing look at Nenci's seat, and followed suit.

Ozzy opened the box. There, on the top, was a folder containing the case summary as it stood when the case had been left cold. There wasn't a lot of information or evidence to be seen, even though every stone they could think of had been overturned when Harbaugh had been murdered.

Tim Harbaugh had been middle aged, a family man. He'd been out on patrol one night, doing his bit to keep the state's highways a little safer, when he'd been shot in the head during a routine traffic violation. The bullet had entered his brain through the back of the head, much as the bullet that had ended George Bergeron's eighty-four years earlier this week.

That was interesting. The killer, who could not possibly be the same person, had used the same weapon to kill two apparently unconnected men in uniform in the same way.

It was also interesting that a trooper, who was a trained professional, had been shot in the back of the head. There were minimal signs of a struggle. Dogs on the scene hadn't picked up anything, so the killer had escaped in his own car. No one had bragged to anyone else, or at least to anyone else who spoke about it, about killing a statie. There was no indication about the race, height, or gender of the killer.

Ozzy pulled out a notebook. There were no witnesses to the crime. There had been no real suspects. Harbaugh's line of work brought him into contact with a lot of people, but there hadn't been anyone who seemed to stand out as bearing an exceptional grudge against him. If he'd put someone away for a serious crime, Ozzy could see it, but they didn't tend to get a murderous vendetta over a speeding ticket.

The typical procedure was to make binders for everything, every witness and every suspect. In this case, there was no one to make binders for.

He tapped his fingertips on the desk and blew a raspberry. There had to be something he could do. Harbaugh hadn't shot himself in the back of the head and sent his own ghost to pass the gun to some kid.

Maybe he needed to start at the end and work back to the beginning. The end, of course, was Jeff Balsalmo and the bank robbery. Ozzy started up a to-do list. He needed to speak to the detectives investigating the robbery and murder. He would need to talk to the suspects, of course. And he would need to look into George Bergeron's life, to see if there had been some way that their lives had intersected.

He stared at the card from Pete Nolan, Photographer. Photographers were good witnesses, as a general rule. They noticed things. He picked up the phone and called before he could lose his nerve. "Nolan Photography, this is Pete." The voice that came back was clear and strong.

"Pete, hi, this is Ozzy. Er, Detective Morris, from the other day." Damn it, Ozzy was smoother than a thirteen-year-old asking someone to a dance for the first time. How could he mess up so badly?

"Detective Morris. Hi, how are you?" Pete sounded both relieved and nervous at the same time. "Is everything okay?"

"Me? I'm fine." Ozzy chuckled. "How are you and the baby? I wasn't so gentle when I pushed you out of the way."

"We're fine. Doc said she's perfect in every way. I'll have a bruise for a little while, but better that than the other option, you know?" Pete huffed out a little laugh. "How can I help you today, Detective?"

"Ozzy, please." Pete's voice did things to Ozzy that Ozzy didn't even have words for. "Listen, something's come up about... ah, about what happened the other day. We think that the robbery might be linked to another crime, and I was wondering if you might be willing to go over what happened again in some more detail."

Pete blew out a long stream of air. "I mean, I've already gone over what happened with some detectives, and some guys from the FBI, but yeah. I could do that. I work out of my house in Sudbury. I don't have any appointments until tomorrow. If you wanted to come out here today, that would be okay."

"I could be out there around one. Just email me the address." Ozzy wondered if Devlin would be all that disappointed if he went out and rolled around in the snow or something before he went, just to cool himself down.

"I'll do that. I'll see you at one."

"See you then." Ozzy hung up and took a few deep breaths. Then he called the FBI agents investigating the robbery, and the Department of Corrections to make an appointment to speak to all of the prisoners.

The Feds were surprised by the connection to the cold case, but they were cooperative. "Any help we can give, it's yours," they promised. Ozzy had every intention of taking them up on it.

He did a little bit more digging into Balsalmo's background while he killed time waiting for one o'clock. Balsalmo was a career criminal already, at only nineteen. He'd spent more of his young life in various forms of prison than he had breathing free air, and by the time he was fifteen he was pulling down adult time. Usually Ozzy wasn't a big fan of juveniles doing adult time, but in this case he figured it was justified. There were charges of attempted murder, aggravated assault, armed robbery… the list went on and on.

Something had driven him to that, but Ozzy couldn't be distracted by that now.

He couldn't find much about George Bergeron either. He found a military service record that indicated the old man had served in Korea, and some old employment records from some of the mills in the area. George was survived by children, grandchildren, and one great-grandchild. He would be buried beside his wife, who had been lost to cancer five years before.

According to Agent Newsome, Bergeron had only taken the job to keep himself busy and get out of the house after the death of his wife.

That depressing note impelled Ozzy to get out of the office and head up to Sudbury. February wasn't exactly the happiest month in New England anyway; thinking about Bergeron's fate wasn't going to help.

Pete lived in a nice, good-sized Dutch colonial near the middle of Sudbury with what was probably a decent chunk of property once the snow melted. "I guess photography pays better than I thought it did," Ozzy muttered to himself. He followed the driveway up to the shoveled walk and rang the doorbell.

Pete opened the door. He looked a lot better when he wasn't wrapped up in a coat and trying to cover his mouth and nose. Golden blond hair framed a heart-shaped face, in which huge, dark brown eyes stared out at the world. "Hey," he greeted. "Left the assault rifle in the car, I see."

Ozzy laughed. "Yeah. Well, you know, I'm kind of hoping that it's not going to be necessary out here in the Sudbury tundra."

"You never know. I didn't think I'd need it at Framingham Bank either but here we are." He let Ozzy into the house, which was lovingly decorated. "Can I get you anything? Coffee? Tea?"

"Coffee would be great." He followed Pete into a beautiful gray and white kitchen, where it turned out that coffee had already been made. "So. The reason I'm here is that the gun the ringleader used is the same gun that was used in a cop's murder twenty years ago."

"And you're a cold case detective." Pete grinned. "I get it.'

"You're a smart cookie. So the cops who were speaking to you before, they were looking to prove a case now. I'm looking for clues that might link anything that happened earlier this week to what happened twenty years ago."

Pete shook his head. "Yeah, I mean, I'll try. You'll know better than I would about how useful it'll be."

"I guess my first question is, how into the robbery did they seem to be?" Ozzy leaned forward and wrapped his hands around his coffee mug.

"I'd say they expected to make a clean getaway. I saw how pissed they were that the clerk tripped the alarm." He shook his head. "They killed her too."

"She survived, actually. It's going to be touch and go for a while, but if she's lucky she'll make it." Ozzy squirmed. The poor woman would have problems for the rest of her life, even in a best-case scenario, but at least she was alive. "What about the killing?"

Pete shuddered. "Jeff had one of his underlings choose the victim. He lingered by me for a while, but ultimately chose the security guard."

"Oh." Ozzy closed his eyes. "Oh my God. Pete, I am so sorry."

Pete bowed his head. "It felt very unreal. I don't think that it mattered to Jeff which one he picked. He said I'd be next. He told the underling to make it count. But I don't think he bore the security guard any specific ill will. He wasn't a good guy in a bad situation. He was a cold man, who didn't care about anyone."

Ozzy put a hand over Pete's. "They're going to pay, Pete. They're going to jail. They're not getting out for a very long time, and they're not going to be able to get near you ever again. I can promise you that."

Pete gave him a shy little smile, and Ozzy pulled his hand back. He'd crossed a line, and he knew it. Pete almost certainly had someone else protecting him. He didn't need Ozzy's help.

Chapter Two

Pete looked around the bedroom. He could have painted it himself. He wasn't sure that breathing in paint fumes was going to be the best plan for the baby, though, and it wasn't like painting was exactly fun work to begin with. As a general rule, Pete was a pretty self-sufficient guy. He liked to do things for himself and not spend money if he didn't have to. He was willing to open up the purse strings here and there for some things, though, and one of them was painting while six and a half months pregnant.

He heard the door downstairs open. The security system beeped and then went silent as the new arrival punched in the right code. It had to be his brother. His mother had a code, but never used it. No one else had a code.

Just as Pete expected, Angus's auburn hair appeared around the doorframe just before the rest of him. "Hey, big bro." Angus slouched into the baby's room and stuffed his hands into his pockets. "Looks good in here. You going to let Mom's designer do the interior?"

Pete rolled his eyes. "No, I'm not going to let Mom's designer do the interior." He scoffed. "Come on, dude. Really? It's not like she's going to need much stuff. She's going to need a changing table, a crib, and a diaper bucket. Oh, and someplace to put her clothes." He shook his head. "She doesn't need an antique Venetian glass vase to knock over onto her own head when she starts to crawl, for crying out loud."

Angus nodded at the wisdom of this. "Probably not. But don't you think that will be a little impersonal? Kids need to be free to express themselves and stuff."

"They do. And once she's got a self to express I'll be sure to let her express that stuff. Right now, I know she kicks a lot if I play Shostakovich. I don't know if that means she's super into Shostakovich or if that's her little fetal way of saying *Please make it stop and play Foster the People, Daddy*." He shrugged.

Angus shuddered. "Perish the thought. Mother hates pop music."

Pete shook his head and pulled a tape measure out of his pocket. "Mom thinks that central heating is dangerously innovative, dude."

"I think you're being unfair. I mean, yeah, she's a little set in her ways, but that's just her. She's used to doing things a certain way, and we just have to accept it, you know?" Angus leaned against the wall where the changing table would go.

"I accept it just fine. I also know what I'm dealing with and where to set my expectations." Pete stood up. "So what brings you by?" He slipped out of the baby's room and led his brother back downstairs. He didn't like letting other people into the baby's room, not before she'd gotten here. It felt gross, almost violating in a weird way.

"I just wanted to check in." Angus followed Pete down to the kitchen. "I mean, you went through something kind of scary. That's got to be traumatic, right?"

Pete closed his eyes and pushed back against the memory of the gunman coldly saying that Pete would be next. "Yeah. It was. It's over now, though, and they should be spending a good long time in jail."

"You hope." Angus tapped his foot on the linoleum and watched as Pete started water for tea. "I mean, what if they walk on a technicality?"

"I don't know. The cops on the scene were pretty serious about making sure that all of the i's were dotted and everything." He reached up into a cupboard for two mugs. "Isn't bank robbery a federal crime anyway? You don't see a lot of people walking when they're up on federal charges, not on technicalities."

"I don't know. I'm still uncomfortable." Angus squirmed. "Mother and I were talking it over, and we think you should move back home."

Pete laughed out loud. "Right." The only thing that kept that from being a disaster was his secure knowledge that no one would ever actually want that.

"No really." Angus' pale face got red when Pete laughed at him. "It's obvious you're not safe here. You can't keep yourself safe, and you can't keep your daughter safe. If you'd found yourself an alpha it would be one thing, but as it is you need someone to take care of you."

Pete scrounged through another cabinet for tea bags. "And who exactly is going to do that, Angus? Mom's never taken care of a goldfish without an army of staff, and you have an assistant even though you don't actually have a job."

"That's not the point." Angus jabbed a stubby finger at the table. "Home is more secure. We have a wall, we have a gate, we have security staff. No one will be able to get to you, and you'll be able to raise your daughter in safety."

Pete smirked and folded his arms across his chest. "And when I'm working?"

"Well, you're quitting your job." Angus waved a hand, like he could sweep away everything that Pete had accomplished over the years.

Pete shook his head and turned his attention to the dry dishes in his dish rack. "Like hell I'm quitting my job. It's my job. It's what I actually do. I'm not about to quit it."

"But you were attacked!" Angus' dark eyes were as round as saucers.

"No. I was one of several people who were in the wrong place at the wrong time. I wasn't singled out." *Except when I was.* He took a deep breath and pressed on. "I'm not going to just let myself get locked away because someone else made bad life choices, okay? I like my job, and it's important to me that my daughter sees me working." The kettle whistled, and he poured tea for both of them. "So how are things with you and Keith?"

"Oh. We split up." Angus made a face and looked away. "He wanted us to get a place together."

"Angus, you're twenty-six. It's okay to get a place of your own." Pete knew that he might as well have kept his mouth shut, but it kept the conversation away from him and his own situation so he pushed the issue.

Angus recoiled. "Ugh. No. And who would wash dishes? You might have some kind of a... a sick fetish for used food, but the rest of us are much more sensible about these things. No, no, no. I'm staying with Mother. Love me, love my living arrangement."

Pete sighed and wrapped his hands around the mug. "Someday you're going to regret having given up those opportunities for love. You're going to get tired of waking up cold and alone."

"Okay, but you went after it. You went after it, and you wound up cold and alone anyway. You're just cold and alone with dirty dishes and a baby on the way, whereas I have clean dishes every time and no baby." Angus flashed him a smug look and sipped from his tea. "Damn it!"

"The delicious beverage you're about to enjoy is hot." Pete couldn't dispute his brother's accurate assessment of his life. "I keep up with my dishes."

"With soap, which dries out your hands." He covered his mouth. "Do you have any ice?"

Pete waved his hand at the refrigerator and his icemaker just as his phone started to ring. He pulled it out to answer it, only to see Ozzy's name flash across the caller ID. "This is Pete," he greeted, just in case Ozzy's boss had gotten hold of his phone or something.

"Pete!" Pete could hear Ozzy's broad smile in his voice. "Pete, this is Ozzy Morris. How are things?"

Pete couldn't help but smile in return. How did people work with Ozzy? He just distributed sunshine everywhere he went. "Things are okay. How are things with you?"

"Things here are going okay. I thought maybe it would be okay if we went out and grabbed a bite to eat. Maybe I could give you an update about the case?"

Pete's breath caught in his throat. He knew that he shouldn't read too much into it. It wasn't a date, for crying out loud. Alphas didn't go out on dates with pregnant omegas. Still, he wanted to spend a little time in a handsome alpha's company, even if it didn't mean anything. "You bet. When were you thinking?"

"Maybe tomorrow night?" Ozzy made a wincing sound. "Is that too soon?"

"My social calendar is pretty open these days, Ozzy. I'm free tomorrow."

"Really? I mean—okay. Great. I'll pick you up at six-thirty."

"Sounds good. I'll see you tomorrow."

They hung up, and Pete looked up to find his brother openly staring at him. "What?"

Angus' lip curled. "Did you really just make a date? Right now?"

Pete spread his hands out. "It's hardly a date, Angus. I'm pregnant. No one wants to date a pregnant guy, okay? That was the cop who helped get me out of the bank. He wants to give me an update."

Angus drummed his fingers on top of the wooden table. "Oh really? And are we on a first name basis with all of the members of the SWAT team now or just this *Ozzy*?" He frowned. "Is Ozzy even his real name? It sounds made up. No self-respecting police force would hire someone named after Ozzy Osborne."

Pete flipped his brother off. "Yes, he's a real cop. When he's not charging into a hostage situation, he's a cold case detective. Detective Morris is very handsome, and very smart, and damn good at his job, thank you very much." He sipped at his tea.

"So it *is* a date. Damn it, Pete, don't you learn from your screw ups?"

Pete slapped a hand onto the table. "It's not a date, damn it, and what the hell do you mean by my *screw ups*?"

"Oh, I don't know, the damn basketball you've got under your shirt?" Angus pointed to Pete's baby bump. "Mooning around over men is what got you into this situation in the first place!"

"Oh my God, Angus, having sex with an old and expired condom is what got me into this situation in the first place. Not 'mooning around over men.' I was never emotionally attached to the father; I was horny, which happens with omegas. It's not like you don't have casual sex. Or do I need to remind you of the time that I had to sneak Brenda out of the house for you?"

"Okay, but that was—"

"Six months ago." Pete glowered, and Angus wilted. "Keep your shaming to yourself. It's not a date, I'm well aware that having a baby means that I'm going to be alone forever now, and I don't need you or Mom constantly reminding me. I'm still allowed to find men attractive, and I'm allowed to enjoy their company. I'm pregnant, not dead."

Angus slumped down. "No. You're not dead. I'm sorry. I shouldn't sit here and act like you're supposed to be some kind of a monk." He squeezed out a forced-looking smile. "So. A hot cop, huh? I never realized that you were into the whole *man in uniform* thing."

"What can I say? I guess you had to be there." Pete's whole body softened as he thought about Ozzy. "I kind of feel bad for you. You'll never get the whole experience. You'll never meet a guy and get bowled over by his scent—in a good way, not in a *oh my God this guy hasn't showered in three weeks* kind of way."

Angus pointed at him. "Kip was a wilderness survival instructor. He'd just gotten back from a trip!"

"He could have taken the time to shower before meeting his boyfriend's family. That's all I'm saying." Pete wrinkled his nose. "Anyway, nothing's going to happen, don't worry, but I'm going to go and talk to him. I guess there's something weird about the gun that the leader used in the robbery, and Ozzy's on the case."

"What a coincidence." Angus grinned at him and took a tentative sip of his tea. "He just happens to be working that case when you just happen to be involved with this case."

"I know, I know." Pete shook his head. "I'll pretend you're right for a little while, okay?"

"It's not pretend when it's true," Angus teased in a singsong voice. "Listen, give some serious thought to moving back home, okay? I know it's not something you want to do. You value your independence. I get that. Well, okay, I don't get that, but I respect that it's important to you. You've pulled it off for a long time, but it's different now with a kid on the way. You're not just living for yourself anymore, and you're a witness to a violent crime."

"Ugh, Angus—" Pete sat up a little straighter.

"Seriously. Talk to your hot cop about this. He'll agree with me. If you don't have an alpha to protect you, then you need to take what's being offered, even if it isn't what you wanted when you left home. It's comfortable. It's luxurious."

"It's a prison, Angus. I'm not raising my daughter in a prison." Pete kept his hands around his mug.

"You're risking her being hurt, Pete. And you know it. Are you really willing to risk her safety because you're feeling stubborn?" Angus got up. "You've got time. Give some thought to what I said, and let Mom know when you've decided to come home."

"Have a good trip home, Angus." Pete didn't get up to watch his brother head back out to the car. He knew that Angus hadn't driven himself out there. He didn't want to think about the driver waiting outside in the cold.

He cleaned up from their tea and did his best to clean up the carpets after Angus had tracked salt and snow over them. Once that was done, he retreated to his office. He had a few work leads that he should chase down.

Was he being selfish? He didn't think so. Then again, he wasn't sure that anyone ever really knew when they were being selfish. He had a life, one that he'd built for himself. Sure, he was lonely. He had omega friends, but they'd all gotten claimed by now, and their alphas didn't like them to hang around with an unclaimed omega like Pete. Still, he had the respect and acceptance of his colleagues and two Pulitzers under his belt. He wasn't just some dilettante.

Was he putting his child at risk? Maybe. Was it a different risk than what other parents in a similar situation did every day? He couldn't be sure. He didn't think so. Maybe he should ask Ozzy. He didn't want to end his career—his real life, even though he'd still be alive—but he'd do what he had to for his daughter. He just didn't think that his mother or brother had the first clue as to what was right for either the baby or for Pete.

...

Ozzy looked at the transcript from the anonymous tip line. The state tip line got hundreds of tips per day, and most of them were about as useless as a person might expect for tips that got texted anonymously to a tip line. Apparently Mickey Mouse was responsible for everything from the Boston Strangler's crimes to a meth lab out in Athol. The damned rat with the polka-dotted boxers was a criminal mastermind, and someone needed to get the proof to put him away pronto.

This tip, though, had mentioned the Harbaugh case specifically. They'd splashed a call for information relating to Harbaugh's case on the late-night Saturday news once the connection between the botched robbery and the old murder was known, but they hadn't expected to get much traction with it. It was just something they did sometimes, throwing the request at the wall to see if it would stick.

This time, it stuck. The text consisted of four words: *Check out Dawn Moriarty.*

Ozzy had run a quick check on the name. They had to check out all possible leads, of course. He found a handful of Dawn Moriartys in Massachusetts, but only one with an active arrest record in Central Massachusetts during the mid-1990s. All of those arrests had been for petty crimes: hitchhiking, prostitution, solicitation at truck stops, loitering. Harbaugh was the officer of record for some of those arrests. He hadn't always been the arresting officer, though, and he certainly hadn't arrested her on the night he was killed.

Still, there was enough history there that it was worth looking into. She probably wasn't a suspect. Her record showed that she did know Harbaugh, and that she would almost certainly have some ideas about where to look. He got to work trying to track down her current whereabouts.

He had others he could talk to, as well. Some of Harbaugh's friends were probably still on the force, and he could circle back and find those that had retired. It couldn't be that hard. He'd go talk to the retirees first. He didn't expect to get anything other than full cooperation from friends of the deceased—no one was more eager to nail a cop killer than other cops, for crying out loud—but the case still had to be worked like any other cold case. The guys who had retired would be more likely to share information that could incriminate someone than guys who were still on the force, who could face retaliation.

He didn't work with anyone else on the case, not as an assigned partner. Most of the guys were busy, and Ozzy was no different from anyone else in not wanting to work with Nenci. He did pull in Langer for a little bit of backup, though, as they worked to track down Harbaugh's known associates and partners.

"Know what's weird about this?" Langer shuffled through the stack of files on his desk.

"Other than the fact you've got an octopus-print tie?" Ozzy wrinkled his nose at the tie.

"Other than my octopus-print tie, yes. What's weird is that all of the guys who, logically, should have worked the closest with Harbaugh, they're all retired now. There are a couple of guys from his cohort who are still around, but they don't seem to have worked with him all that often." Langer turned his laptop around to show him. "I mean, all of the guys whose names show up most often on rosters and whatever with Harbaugh's, they're all retired."

"That is weird." Ozzy crossed the room to come look at the report. "Some of those guys would be younger than Nenci, right?"

"Retired. All of 'em." Langer pointed to a few names.

"Huh." Ozzy shrugged. "Well, we'll have to go and see what there is to see. In the meantime, I'm going to go talk to Pete Logan, Photographer, again."

"Really?" Langer smirked up at him. "How many times can you go talk to a witness before you give up the ghost and admit that he doesn't have anything new to add?"

Ozzy blushed. "Look, he smells good, okay? Kind of citrus-y."

Langer stared at him for a long moment. "This is the pregnant guy, right?"

Ozzy stiffened. "Yeah, so?"

"Well, I mean, it's not yours. Who's to say that his alpha won't be back and looking to step in, you know? You don't want to have trouble like that." Langer wrinkled his nose.

"Trouble like what, man? He's a great guy. It's not a crime to go hang out with a great guy, and if the father isn't sticking around then why shouldn't I show an interest?" Ozzy stretched and stood up.

"Because you want to be with a guy who's having your babies, man. Not someone who's having someone else's." Langer just looked up at him. "Are you sure you're not just looking for a fight, man?"

Ozzy scowled and clenched his fist, but let it go. "Probably not." He shrugged. "I haven't given the father much thought since he said that there wasn't an alpha. So. I don't know what his deal is, but it's just dinner."

"Hmm." Langer turned back to his screen. "Well, don't forget, there's quid pro quo here. I helped you with this, you said you'd help me catalogue the different crime scenes for the Anholts case."

"I'm on it like salsa on a chip, man." Ozzy jumped up and grabbed his jacket.

Langer gave him a funny look. "You mean trying to slide off and onto my shirt at the first possible opportunity?"

"Uh, exactly." Ozzy laughed and sneaked out toward his car.

He drove back toward Sudbury and collected Pete, who looked amazing. How a guy could look this good at six and a half months pregnant astounded Ozzy. Shouldn't he be all swollen, blotchy, and uncomfortable?

They went for Thai food. A few people stared openly at Pete, but he ignored them. "Do you get that a lot?" Ozzy asked, as one old woman tried to touch Pete's belly.

"All the time." Pete shrugged and sipped from his water. "It's kind of gross. Like, okay, I brought this on myself, I get that, but I don't... I mean, I got pregnant—I didn't consent to my body becoming public property." He squirmed.

Ozzy made a face. "Your alpha is supposed to be protecting you from that kind of thing."

Pete huffed out a little laugh. "Yeah, well, that's not really an option these days. And I brought it on myself, so whatever, but still." He grinned wryly and took up a forkful of pad Thai. "Whatever. I can live with it for another three months. So what's up with the case, anyway?"

Ozzy tugged at his collar. "Oh, right. The case." His cheeks burned. "Well, the case is proceeding. The case against the robbers is a slam dunk. We're just trying to figure out what it has to do with the cop murder, you know? It's bizarre. I'm finding a few little weird things about that case that are probably nothing. That's kind of the way it is with cold cases. If they were easy to solve they wouldn't be cold, right?"

"I guess." Pete snorted. "Everything probably looks like a bunch of crap until you find the common thread."

"Pretty much. You don't want to hear about pouring over two decades worth of time sheets to figure out who worked the same shifts as a dead cop, though."

"Don't you have software that can do that?" Pete blinked at him.

"Well, yeah, but you have to actually look at them too. You can't just let a computer do your thinking for you. Would you let a computer just do all of your photo editing for you?" Ozzy circled his fork at Pete.

Pete shuddered. "Perish the thought."

"All right then."

Pete glanced off into the distance. "I guess that makes sense."

Ozzy looked over his food for a moment. "So it's really just you? You're going to raise your kid by yourself?" He knew that his question was over the line, that he didn't have the right to ask it at all, but he had to know. It seemed so brave, and so terrible.

Pete shrugged, face unperturbed. "I kind of have to, don't I? I mean, I'm going to hire a nanny and everything—I'm not going to quit my job—but it's not like there's anyone else to help out."

Ozzy's heart gave a twist. "It'll be hard. Can't you track down the father and make him help or something? Or get help from your folks?"

Pete snickered. "The father isn't someone I'd want around my kid, to be honest. I had a moment of weakness. It had been a while, and I'm an omega. I have needs, okay?" He blushed a deep, dark red. "Unintended consequences, but hey, it happens."

Ozzy chuckled. "I guess I'm having trouble believing that you could ever be alone for a while, unless you wanted to be." His own cheeks got hot, and he knew that he was blushing almost as dark as Pete. "Sorry—I don't want to creep you out or make you think I'm coming onto you. I'm just saying, you're an attractive guy...and at a stage when most guys don't look their best, you know?" God, he should just stop speaking. He kept digging himself a deeper hole.

Pete chuckled. "Thanks. I think. But yeah. It had been a while, and I shouldn't have been weak with that particular individual. But anyway. My mother isn't exactly suited to babysitting, and my brother's not someone I'd trust to supervise either. Which is fine." He waved a hand over his dinner. "We'll be fine." He looked up at Ozzy through his long lashes, making Ozzy weak in the knees. "Actually, my mother and brother apparently want me to move back in with them."

Ozzy wrinkled his nose. "Wait, what? Why?"

"They think I'm unsafe out here." Pete made a face. "They've convinced themselves, or at least Angus has convinced himself, that the bank robbers will get out on a technicality and come kill me and the baby in our sleep."

Ozzy nodded. "Ah. I get it." He shrugged. "It's an outside chance, but do your folks get that you literally have a dozen other witnesses? You're not in any specific danger. You have nothing to worry about, and they have nothing to worry about. If you want help with the baby, by all means, move back, but if you don't want to go back then don't."

Pete nodded. "That was my thought, but you know. They wanted a second opinion." He glared off to the side for half a second, before shaking his head a little and turning back to Ozzy. "So what is it that you do when you're not digging into old cold cases or besieging bank robbers?"

Ozzy laughed. "Anything I can."

Pete tilted his head and stilled for a moment. "Well, now, that could be taken so many different ways."

"Right?" Ozzy waggled his eyebrows. "In this case, it means I'm kind of an extreme sports guy. I rock climb, I sky dive, I heli-ski. You name it, I do it."

Pete's eyes widened. "Do you even do the squirrel suit thing?"

"What, the gliding thing or do you mean something a little kinkier?" Ozzy snickered. "Yeah, I haven't done the flying suit thing yet. I want to try it sometime, but I just haven't gotten a chance."

Pete hid his face in his hands. "Oh God. You're an adrenaline junkie."

"Yeah. Maybe a little bit." Ozzy laughed at himself, although something deep in his chest gave a twist. Adrenaline junkie was a good description. At least, it would have to suffice for now. "I like to get my blood pumping, you know? It's not like I get a lot of chances for excitement, sitting behind a desk and counting time sheets from twenty years ago."

"I guess that's true." Pete grimaced. "You'd never catch me jumping out of a plane, though." He shuddered. "Good thing you're not asking me to."

"Aw, I was hoping that was on your bucket list." Ozzy winked. "No, I get that it's not on everyone's list of things to do before they die. As long as people accept that it's on mine, we're good."

"What if you wind up claiming someone though?" Pete leaned back. "Aren't you worried that you'll die and leave them alone?"

Ozzy frowned. "I hadn't thought about it that way. I guess I hadn't thought about claiming someone before." He shrugged. "I've been a live-for-the-moment kind of guy for a pretty long time. I've been around for a little while. I've seen enough to learn to treasure ever moment. You never know when it's going to be your last. Make the most of it. Don't waste them, you know?"

"I guess." Pete gave a little sigh, and then put a hand on his burgeoning belly. "I think those days are gone for me. I'm all she's got, so I have to think about what happens next all the time now."

"True." Ozzy looked down. He'd almost forgotten the baby. "Do you have a name picked out for her yet?"

"Not really." Pete sighed and leaned his head on his hand. "I have a list, but I'm always rejecting things or adding to it, you know? I just have to hope that I fall in love with one name by the time she puts in her appearance. Otherwise she'll go through her whole life just as Baby Nolan."

"Don't do that." Ozzy laughed. "How about Ozzy?"

"For a girl?"

"Osmundia. Osmundia Norris, for the cop whose life you saved." Ozzy clasped his hands over his heart and batted his eyes at Pete, who laughed at him.

Ozzy could spend the rest of his life listening to that laugh, and that was a problem. Since when did he even have thoughts like *the rest of his life*? And Ozzy knew he was no good for a guy like Pete. Pete needed someone who could be there for him and his baby, forever. Not someone who was dancing on a fine line between thrill seeking and a death wish.

At the same time, he couldn't get the handsome, pregnant omega out of his head. Even as he dropped Pete off at his house, he knew that he'd be back.

Chapter Three

Pete packed his equipment into the back of his Subaru and tried not to wince. His back hurt. His hip hurt. He knew it was normal, and that it was just sciatica due to pregnancy, but knowing why it was happening didn't change the fact that it hurt. At least he hadn't gotten to a point where he couldn't do his job anymore.

Today he'd taken on a job to get pictures from a huge demonstration in downtown Boston. People were protesting the governor's stance on accepting refugees, and then some counter-protestors showed up. Things got heated, and then things got violent. Pete was able to get quite a few good pictures of the unpleasantness before riot police broke everything up. He stood to make a good amount of money, and while he was at it the ugly side of resistance to refugee resettlement would be shown for what it was.

In the old days, the pre-baby days, he would have been able to head out and get beers, maybe find some companionship for the night. Now he was so tired he didn't know if he'd make it all the way through uploading the digitals. He'd have to, of course; no one wanted photos of last week's news. Still, the fatigue was different than anything he'd ever felt before. It reached into his very bones.

His daughter didn't seem to be feeling the same way. No, she all but danced in his belly, a bizarre sensation that he couldn't say he was entirely comfortable with. He didn't have the kind of pain some other people talked about. Her kicks still felt fluttery, like little bubbles, and they were almost pleasant. And he knew that they weren't movements with any kind of intent. She had no intent yet. But he still couldn't shake the horror that went along with some kind of alien force inhabiting his body.

Only a few more weeks, however, and she'd actually be here. His body would be his own again.

He headed back out toward I-95, aiming himself toward Rt. 20 and home. Once he hit Rt. 20 his phone rang. He answered it through the Subaru's Bluetooth function. "This is Pete."

"Pete, hey, it's Ozzy. How's it going?"

Pete smiled in spite of his exhaustion. "Better now," he admitted. Was that too much? "It was kind of a long, fraught day."

"Fraught, huh? Family drama?"

"No. Covering the protests down at the State House." Some of the pain left Pete's back. "It was an ugly situation. I'm kind of beat."

"Oh." Pete wasn't imagining the note of disappointment he heard in Ozzy's voice, was he? Maybe he was. Maybe it was wishful thinking on his part. "Well, I guess that means you're not going to be up for Thai food tonight. I was kind of hoping you'd be up for a case update, but I totally get that you're tired. That kind of work, even if you're not in the thick of things, can be exhausting. And that's for people who aren't pregnant."

Ugh. Why couldn't Pete have met Ozzy five years ago, or nine months ago, or even seven months ago? He made a snap decision. "I don't think I'm up for sitting in the restaurant. If you can tolerate hanging around in my house, we could get takeout. Just let me get the pictures out to my editors."

Ozzy was silent for a few moments. Then he gave a little laugh. "Oh, hell yeah! Text me your order and I'll be there at maybe seven?"

"Seven sounds good." That would be enough time for Pete to get home and clean himself up a little bit, in addition to getting the relevant photos out to his editors.

He got into the house and raced up to his office. He'd deal with the film later, but for now he put the rolls into carefully labeled black canisters. In the meantime, he took the digital pictures off of his camera and scanned through to find the best and most relevant images to send to agencies around the world.

He found one that he liked best. The photo was of a woman, protesting to allow refugees into the state, being assaulted by a man in a three-piece suit. A Boston cop stood by and watched the scene play out while a man who appeared homeless—and was homeless, according to Pete's careful notes—jumped to her aid. He sent that one to Reuters. Other photo distributors got different images—the solid wall of blue-clad protestors ringing the State House, or the contingent of elderly nuns on their knees in the snow praying on their rosaries while anti-refugee counter protestors shouted hate at them. All in all, Pete figured he could be proud of the work he'd done today.

Just as he'd finished submitting the last of his breaking news shots, his doorbell rang. He sighed; God forbid that he get any actual rest. It wasn't like he was making a human being or anything. He eased his way downstairs to see who might be there, and did a double take when he saw his mother at the door.

He opened the door. "Hi, Mom."

Cynthia Nolan strode into the house as though she owned the place. Her nose wrinkled, just a little bit, as she took in the scene. "Honestly, Peter, this house feels smaller every time I come over." She took off her fur coat and held it out to him, giving it a shake when he didn't grab it fast enough. "How do you seriously expect to be able to raise a child in a house that's essentially a broom closet?"

Pete hung his mother's coat in the closet and waved to her driver. O'Hara almost never came inside, but Pete never stopped inviting him. "It's not every day that you hear a twenty-two hundred square foot house being called a broom closet."

Cynthia scoffed. "You could fit this house into my house seven times with room to spare. It's a much better place to raise a child, especially a Nolan." She sat down on the couch in his living room and wrinkled her nose again. "How does this cheap furniture even hold you, at the size you are now?"

"Thanks for the confidence boost, Mom." He rolled his eyes and leaned against the doorframe.

"I'm your mother. I'm not here to give you a confidence boost. I'm here to give you much-needed guidance and to keep you on track. Obviously I must have been negligent or you wouldn't be in this condition." She glared at Pete's protruding abdomen. "But you were always willful. You would always go your own way, without regard for anyone else, so maybe this would have been inevitable." She sighed and folded her hands in her lap.

"Maybe." Pete put his hand on his belly. "As it happens, I'm looking forward to being a parent." He felt his daughter kick against his hand. "But come on, Mom. You didn't come all this way to harass me about my many filial shortcomings."

"No. It would be wasted breath, I'm certain. I came out here, Peter, because your brother tells me that you weren't receptive to his suggestion that you move home." She tossed her head. "Peter, this is not the time to be your usual stubborn self. It was irresponsible of you to get pregnant in the first place, but now you're seriously thinking of bringing her up here? In the wilds of Sudbury? You have no one to protect you, no one to keep you safe."

"Oh my God, Mom." Pete pinched the bridge of his nose. "It's not like Sudbury is Harlem in 1968. This is one of the most upscale suburbs in Massachusetts."

"You were a witness to a bank robbery!" she shouted.

"Yes, I was. And everyone involved with the robbery is behind bars now, because the state police are good at their jobs." He considered telling her that he'd kicked one in the jaw, but opted not to. He didn't think that would have the desired effect. "I spoke to the detective on the case and he tells me that I'm perfectly safe and have nothing to worry about."

Her lip curled. "Oh, and they're never wrong."

Pete's doorbell rang again, and he went to answer it. Ozzy stood in the doorway, with a big bag of Thai food. Pete tried to tell himself that it was the scent of the food that made his mouth water. "Sorry I'm early, they just had the order ready early for some reason. Oh—I'm sorry. I'll go wait in the car or something."

"No!" Pete moved aside and pulled Ozzy into the house. "You're not that early. Ozzy, this is my mother, Cynthia Nolan. Mom, this is the detective working on the bank robbery that I told you about, Detective Osmund Morris."

Ozzy stepped forward to offer his hand to Cynthia. "Pleased to meet you, ma'am. I'd come to give an update on the case to Mr. Nolan. He said that he was tired after a long day, so I offered to pick up dinner instead of meeting him out."

Cynthia accepted the hand with her usual public grace. "Delighted. Peter tells me that you tell him that he's perfectly safe here from those hooligans that robbed the bank." She led all three of them into the kitchen.

Ozzy deposited the bag on the counter, and Pete found plates and utensils for them. "I think they gave us an extra broccoli fried rice," he said, turning to Cynthia.

Cynthia inclined her head. "Thank you."

Pete tried to hide his grimace. His mother wasn't known for her enthusiasm about other cuisines. Oh well; she should have called before dropping in.

They sat down around the table and made small talk for a little while, and then Ozzy got into the real reason for his visit. Apparently someone had sent in an anonymous tip that might tie the gun back to the cold case. The tip was just a name, but the name was someone that had been busted by the murdered cop for some petty crimes here and there during her youth. It wasn't anything big enough to kill over, but it was a starting point.

Pete pursed his lips. "If I were to get a name," he suggested, fork poised halfway over his red curry, "I might be able to see what I could find out on my side of the fence. I have some buddies over at the Worcester Telegram. They've been there for a while; they might remember something from back in the day." He thought he saw his mother's eyelid twitch, but ignored it.

"That could be good. See if any of them know or have heard of someone by the name of Dawn Moriarty. I don't think she's really a suspect, but something or someone connected to her might be the key to this case." Ozzy beamed over at Pete, and Pete suddenly felt like he could run a marathon.

They changed their discussion over to more neutral topics, in an effort to include Cynthia in the conversation, and Ozzy left after only a couple of hours. Pete swallowed his disappointment and turned back to his mother, who was watching him with a little smirk on her face.

"What?" he asked.

"Nothing. I mean besides the obvious." She examined her immaculately manicured fingernails.

Pete started to clean up from dinner. "The obvious?"

"Oh come on, Peter. I'm your mother. Do you really think I don't recognize when you're making puppy dog eyes at someone?" She shook her head. "I must say, you have terrible taste in men."

Pete put down the stack of dishes he'd just collected. "Excuse me?"

"Really? Whoever left you pregnant and alone left you, well, pregnant and alone. And then there was that man who convinced you that art school was a good use of your time, instead of looking for an alpha. Look how well that turned out for you."

"You mean besides two Pulitzers." Pete picked up the stack of dishes, mostly so that he wouldn't smack his mother.

"No one cares about those. You're still pregnant and alone." She sniffed. "And now a cop. Really, Peter? Has he even been to college? Is he literate? You're sitting there making sheep's eyes at a man who's probably never read Shakespeare or Hemingway, and who almost certainly can't tell the difference between Stravinsky and Shostakovich."

"Wow. Show your classism just a little bit more, why don't you?" He rinsed the dishes before he put them into the dishwasher, and refused to look at his mother.

"I'm being practical, Peter. Someone has to be. Once the first flush of lust has worn off, what exactly would you have to talk about? Can he debate the finer points of the French

Impressionists with you? Or will you be able to talk about the salient aspects of light beer with him?" She stood up and walked over to him, but she didn't touch him.

"Of course, it would never get to that point with you, would it? It never does, and now that you're pregnant? Forget about it. Let's pretend, just for a moment, that he's not turned off by the fact that someone else's baby is growing right there underneath your skin." She pointed to his belly. "Even people who aren't repulsed by that aren't going to want to do more than sleep with you, Peter. Let's face it. You're not *mate* material, or marriage material, or whatever you call it for you alpha and omega types.

"I don't know why that is. I've done everything that I could do to give you every advantage, in that way. You're wealthy. You were handsome, in your youth. Before you were pregnant, anyway. You were educated, and cultured, and well-mannered when you chose to be. There's no reason under God that you shouldn't have been able to find someone, but you chased them all away. It never got past the lust stage with you, and it never will.

"It's time that you put this silly independence bid to bed, Peter. You've made your point. You tried to live on your own, and all you did was make a bigger mess out of your life than it was when you lived with me. It's time to grow up and come home, and do what's right for your daughter."

Pete stared at his mother. He could feel hot tears building up behind his eyes, but they weren't ready to fall. There was plenty of truth to what she was saying. His personal life was a joke, and he'd never managed to attach anyone beyond a month or two. It was foolish to think that Ozzy would want him. He was just being a good guy, looking out for a vulnerable omega who clearly had no one else.

"My personal life might be a mess," he told his mother, "but the rest of my life is actually pretty good. I'm doing well professionally, and I've got a house that I like. I'm in a good place here. And I'm really not okay with raising my daughter around people who shame her for being born, okay? I'm sorry, but that's just the way it has to be. Anyway, good talk, have a safe trip home."

Cynthia snorted and grabbed her purse. "I'll make sure that there's a room ready for when you change your mind."

He knew that there would be no reasoning with her. He went to the closet and got her coat and watched as she strode back out to the car.

He didn't let the tears fall until he heard the car drive away. As they streamed down his face, he sent a quick text to Ozzy. *Sorry about tonight. I had no idea my mom was coming.*

Ozzy replied within seconds. *It's all good. Parents are like that. Hope you get some rest. Maybe we can get together over the weekend or something.*

Pete grinned. *I'd like that.* Maybe it was all just an illusion, but he was going to enjoy every minute of it.

…

Ozzy's insides quivered as he stood outside the entrance to Abused Persons. He should have had Robles do this, damn it. He should have asked Robles to get this information, and then he wouldn't have had to come down here with his hat in his hand to ask for a favor from Ryan "Pretty Boy" Tran. Okay, so they'd all had that day when they'd gone to the bar and had a few drinks. That was supposed to have cancelled out any bad blood.

If someone, or a bunch of someones, had treated Ozzy the way Cold Case had treated Ryan, a few beers wouldn't have cancelled out squat.

Still, Ozzy was supposed to be an adult. He was a combat veteran. He'd faced down the Taliban in Afghanistan and the men who would go on to become Daesh in Iraq. He shouldn't have anything to fear from a slender, pretty omega whose pregnancy was only just starting to show. Right?

He thought back to some of the stories Nick told, about the things Ryan could do when he decided the time for violence was upon him. Maybe he needed to rethink his strategy. Did Ryan like flowers?

He pushed the door open. It was best to just get things over with.

The department admin looked up from her desk. "Detective Morris?" She pushed her braids back over her shoulder and looked up at him.

Ozzy grimaced. "Does everyone know who I am?"

"You're the only one with an appointment at one o'clock to see Sergeant Tran, Detective. He's expecting you." She gave him a thin, professional smile and gestured to the open door of Ryan's office.

Ozzy thanked her and made his way over to the small office. It had once been a conference room, apparently, but when Ryan had been promoted they'd converted it. He sat behind his desk looking at his computer and drinking what looked like chocolate milk, but he looked up when Ozzy walked in. "Ozzy Morris." Ryan gave a quick grin. "How are things going, man?" He gestured to one of the seats on the other side of his desk.

"Not too bad. You know how it is. The cases are weird. The cases are always weird." He looked over Ryan's desk. It wasn't empty, because that would be impossible. There were piles of paper, and stacks of files, just like there would be on any other cop's desk. Ryan's stacks and piles, though, were neat. If Ozzy didn't know better, he'd think that Ryan checked them with a T-square.

"Ain't that the truth." Ryan chuckled. "They wouldn't be cold if they were easy. Nick said you've got a real puzzler this time around, though." He dropped a hand to his barely-there baby bump at the mention of his partner's name.

Ozzy shifted. Ryan's sandalwood scent did things to him. It had ever since the day he'd walked into the Cold Case office. Now, though, that effect had diminished. Was it because Ryan was pregnant? Ozzy didn't think that could be it. He was pretty sure that he'd still been interested in Ryan after he'd gotten pregnant, and he was definitely into Pete and Pete was very pregnant.

Oh. That had to be it. Ozzy's head was so wrapped up in Pete that nothing else really did it for him anymore.

"Yeah," he said, when he realized that he was expected to speak. "It's a really bizarre case. No clues at all, until we got the gun and then an anonymous tip." He explained the facts of the case to Ryan, and then he mentioned the anonymous tip. He'd sent the name to Ryan before, but he wanted to give the request more context.

"Huh. Okay. Well, your hunch was right." Ryan grabbed a stack of files. "Your girl Moriarty was underage for a lot of these arrests, and that would have gotten her a file in Abused Persons anyway. Her file is pretty extensive." He squirmed a little. "She's had a pretty rough life. And, ah, it kind of shows." He passed Ozzy two files. One was an older file, mostly filled with typed or handwritten forms. The other was a modern file with computer printouts.

Ozzy flipped through them. "Oh, geez. You weren't kidding."

"On the streets turning tricks by the time she was thirteen. Social services got her into care twice, but something spooked her and she ran. Turned up in Providence badly injured back in ninety-eight, and it was the start of a long road even further downhill for her." Ryan tugged at his collar. "She was broke from the medical bills, and she wound up hooked on opiates besides. When she couldn't get the prescription pills…"

"She turned to heroin." Ozzy shook his head. "Geez. You know, I can't even really judge her for it."

"Nah. I mean, it's not the best life choice that she could have made, no, but it happens every day. She's not the first, she won't be the last. If it happens to folks from good, stable families with strong support networks, how is a kid who doesn't have anyone to have her back supposed to resist it?" Ryan turned his face away. "Anyway. It looks like she's made a few attempts to get clean here and there, some of which were court ordered. Fun times." He thumped his hand on the second file. "We have a file for child neglect, and she lost custody of two children on a permanent basis five years ago because she just couldn't take care of them."

Ozzy slumped over. "Sometimes this job is really depressing."

"Right?" Ryan fell silent for a moment, staring off into space. Then he shook himself out of it. "She does have a current job, and no arrests since her last stint in rehab four years ago. She's working at a brew pub in Framingham." He passed Ozzy the notes with her current address and a note from the caseworker who handled her supervised visitation with her children.

"Thanks, man."

"Don't thank me yet." Ryan grinned. It looked a little forced, but at least he was making the effort. "I have here, for your viewing pleasure, the file for one Jeffrey Arthur Balsalmo, age nineteen, and known to our department since the ripe old age of two."

"Geez." Ozzy put the files down. "Please tell me that not everyone who comes through your department winds up coming through as a perp somewhere else."

"Of course not. People make their own choices, buddy. Some of them, like Ms. Moriarty, probably didn't have a lot of options, or didn't see a lot of options for themselves. Others, like the adorable cherub that your bank robber once was, made the choice to be what he was. He was a neglect case, plain and simple. Plenty of other neglect cases wind up fine. Other neglect cases might have their share of problems, but the vast majority of people who were neglected as children do not become homicidal bank robbers." He passed Ozzy the file. "It is something that they have in common, though. They've both been through the system, and through the criminal system, at a young age."

Ryan bit his lip, and then he opened Balsalmo's file again. "And Jeff didn't start out doing bank robberies."

Ozzy looked at the charge Ryan indicated. "Prostitution. Huh."

"Unlike Dawn Moriarty, Balsalmo was working for someone. He had a pimp by the name of Sierzant, Joe Sierzant. Back in the mid-nineties, all he did was pimping. These days, you could get an earful from the guys on the Organized Crime Task Force about him." He made a face. "We've managed to get some of his underlings, but we never did get anything to stick on him."

"Huh." Ozzy drummed his fingers against the top of Ryan's desk. "Thanks a lot for all of this. This is a huge amount of information."

"No problem. I just want to see some justice for a dead cop, you know?" Ryan grinned at him. "Say hi to everyone for me."

"Yeah. I will." Ozzy rose. "Even Nenci."

"Not him. You can toss him out in the dumpster with the rest of the trash for all I care." Ryan glanced back at his screen. "Have a good one."

"You too." Ozzy headed back to Cold Case with the files Ryan had pulled for him and a head full of questions.

Before he could research, though, he sent a text to Pete. *We still on for tomorrow night?*

You bet. The reply sent a little thrill through Ozzy's heart, or maybe it was just the fact that the reply came back so quickly. *You up for a pub? I'm craving nachos for some reason.*

I could do that, I think. Ozzy took a moment to exult over his date with the incredible Pete Nolan, Photographer, before he called up Dawn Moriarty's caseworker.

The caseworker told him that Dawn tended to be somewhat mistrustful of the police, and with good reason, but that she'd probably cooperate if the caseworker came along with him. He swung by her office to pick her up, and they headed over to Dawn's apartment in the hopes of catching her before work.

"I have to warn you," said the caseworker, Mary, "that Dawn isn't necessarily the friendliest of souls. She's got a good heart, but she hasn't had the easiest time in life and sometimes that's reflected in her attitude toward authority figures. Please don't lose your temper if she seems surly."

"I'm prepared for that, ma'am." Ozzy grinned. "I just want to get to the bottom of this case. She's not a suspect. I hope I can make that clear to her."

They found Dawn at home, relaxing a little before work. Dawn flipped out a little when Mary told her that she'd brought a cop over, but Mary managed to get her to calm down enough to come out to a Starbucks near the apartment. She wouldn't let them into the apartment, but she'd meet them in a public place.

Dawn Moriarty's skin showed the effects of her life, with more lines than her years should have allowed. Her brown hair was tied back in a ponytail. The most surprising thing about her appearance was her size. She was short, maybe five feet tall, and solidly muscled. "I don't like cops," she told them both, in a sullen voice. "What do you want from me?"

Ozzy managed a little smile. "Ms. Moriarty, before we start, can I just tell you that you're not a suspect in anything right now? I get that you're suspicious of cops. I get that a lot. I don't blame you. I could wish it were otherwise, but you have your reasons. I'm not here to judge you or go poking my nose into anything, okay? I work for the Cold Case Squad."

Her narrowed eyes didn't relax. Neither did the set of her jaw. "And?"

Ozzy tried not to show his disappointment. "And I'm working on a case that's about twenty years old. We got a piece of evidence that's the first actual, physical evidence we have in the case. It's a gun. Here's the thing. The gun was used in a current case, by a guy who hadn't even been conceived when the old crime was committed. See why that's weird?"

She looked away for a second, and then back up at him. "What's that got to do with me? I ain't got a gun. Can't have a gun. Criminal past."

Ozzy shrugged. "I have no idea what it has to do with you. We put out a call for anonymous tips, like we usually would in a situation like that. Your name is the only one that had any ties back to the original crime."

Dawn slammed her hands down on the table and slid her chair back. "I thought you said I wasn't a suspect!"

"You're not. The gun was used in the slaying of State Trooper Tim Harbaugh. He ran you in once or twice, you probably don't even remember him." Ozzy watched her carefully. Was she going to do something unpredictable? He needed to be ready. "I just wanted to know who might have slipped us your name, and why. That might put us on the right path."

Dawn took a few deep breaths, almost like she was trying to stave off panic. "I don't remember no Harbaugh." She clenched her hands into fists. "I can tell you someone who would want you to come sniffing around my door, though. But it ain't because he wants to be a good little citizen and help the police."

Ozzy did his best to stay still and calm. "Who's that, Ms. Moriarty?"

"Joe Freaking Sierzant, that's who." Her lip curled when she said the name. "I can't prove that he's the one who gave you my name, but he's had it in for me for years. He's always hated me, and it's mutual. Bastard got my kids taken away from me. Bastard tried to kill me more than once, too. This is just one more way that he's trying to bring me down, sending the pigs to my door."

Mary cleared her throat.

Dawn had the good grace to look a little bit abashed. "Sorry," she muttered, shrinking into herself.

Ozzy's mind raced. He needed to play this very carefully. "You think that he would put your name in as an anonymous tip in a murder case just because of an old grudge?"

Dawn leaned back and smirked. She tapped the side of her nose. "Ah. See, I don't know any Harbaugh. I mean, for crying out loud, if I nursed that kind of a grudge against every cop who ever ran me in, that would be, like, serial killer type of stuff, right? And that's not me. I ain't never been violent. You can see it in my record."

"It's true," Mary added, glancing at Ozzy with obvious alarm. "Dawn might have her issues, but she's never been violent."

"No, your record doesn't suggest that you have been." Ozzy shook his head. "Like I said, Ms. Moriarty, you were never a suspect."

Dawn seemed to relax a little. "The thing is, Sierzant is. And he would have found it real useful to have a cop on the payroll. If Harbaugh wasn't willing to play ball, I could see Sierzant capping him, just to keep him from squealing."

Ozzy scratched at his chin. It sounded plausible. He hadn't heard that Harbaugh was having trouble in that area, but he still needed to go through and research Harbaugh's associates. "I see. Well, that's definitely an interesting area to pursue." He held out a hand for Dawn to shake. "Thanks for your help, Ms. Moriarty. If I have any more questions, is it all right if I give you a call?"

She hesitated, and then she nodded. "You're not so bad."

Ozzy gave her a card. "Just in case you need anything." They walked out of the coffee shop and headed over toward Dawn's building.

On their way over, a man came walking down the sidewalk toward them. Ozzy noticed his approach and saw him reach inside his jacket. He was able to intervene just as the stranger pulled out a gun and aimed it at Dawn.

Adrenaline surged through his system as he knocked the gun off target. He pushed Dawn and Mary out of the line of fire before he slugged the stranger in the jaw. The man fell to the pavement, and Ozzy pulled the gun out of his hand and slapped cuffs on him.

He dialed in to headquarters, breathing heavily. "This is Detective Ozzy Morris, calling to report an assault on a witness and an officer. Suspect is down, requesting immediate backup to my location."

Mary and Dawn held onto each other, staring at Ozzy with a mix of admiration and fear.

Chapter Four

Pete slept in on Saturday. He wasn't prone to that sort of thing. He had been once, back when he still lived at his mother's house, but living on his own had kind of rubbed that habit out of him. There was too much to be done. No one else was going to mop his floors or do his laundry. He guessed he could hire someone, but the thought felt ridiculous after so long.

Today, though, Pete wanted to get his rest. The house was in decent shape, and Pete wanted to be as awake as he could be for his date with Ozzy tonight. Not that he should be thinking about it as a date. No, Ozzy was just being kind to a lonely fool. That didn't have much bearing on Pete, though. Whether Ozzy had some kind of actual interest in him or was just being kind, he deserved the compliment of a conversational partner who wasn't falling asleep in his dinner.

Pete had planned to sleep in. He hadn't planned to sleep until noon. He guessed he needed the sleep. When he crawled out of bed, he fixed himself something to eat, keeping in mind his doctor's nutritional guidelines. The first thing he'd do once the baby was out was going to be go out for sushi. Okay, maybe he'd have to wait until he was discharged from the hospital and oh yeah, named the baby. But he was getting into a cab, right there at the main entrance to that hospital, and he was taking that cab to the nearest sushi joint.

After breakfast, he headed for the bath. He took his time there. He wanted to be clean and to smell good, instead of like old sweat and too much garlic. He also wanted to be relaxed. He indulged in a bath bomb, something else that was a rare bit of pampering for him. The soothing lavender scent helped to calm him, to ease his mind and his heart and his aching muscles.

He thought about staying in the bath for a few hours, until just before Ozzy came to pick him up. It was such a tempting thought, to hide out in there and let the soothing scent carry him away. Once an hour had passed, though, he knew he couldn't. There was still too much to be done. He had emails to answer, and dishes to put away. He could stand to clean the toilets, too, because what if Ozzy actually came into the house and needed to use them? It was fine if Ozzy thought that Pete was slutty and an easy lay—in fact, considering how long Pete had gone, a part of him kind of preferred that Ozzy think he was a slutty, easy lay—but he couldn't abide by the idea that Ozzy would think of him as a slovenly housekeeper. A guy had to have his pride, after all.

He cleaned the bathrooms, and he put away the dishes. Then he got dressed in a nice red button-down shirt that emphasized that he was pregnant, not the victim of a beer gut, and went to handle his professional business until the doorbell rang.

Ozzy was on time. Pete liked that about him. He was never late. A lot of guys had a lackadaisical approach to time, but Ozzy took other people's time seriously. "You look great!" Ozzy grinned when he saw him.

Pete knew he was blushing when he let Ozzy into the house. "Thanks. Sorry about the other day. Like I said, she just kind of showed up."

Ozzy shrugged and glanced around. "Parents do that sometimes. Does she make a habit of that? With the baby on the way, I mean?"

Pete grabbed his coat from the closet. "Not so much. Mom was always a little… distant, I guess. Which is fine. She is the way she is, and I love her. It's not like I'd ever change her." He chuckled and shrugged his way into his jacket. "I guess she must have been pretty worried because of the robbery, though."

"Oh." Ozzy followed Pete out to the car and opened the passenger side door for him. "That's sweet, I guess. A little awkward, though." He closed the door once Pete's coat and limbs were clear and circled around to the driver's side. "We had a little bit of an incident yesterday. Nothing for you to be worried about, but I'd probably try to avoid mentioning it to anyone who tended to get all that anxious."

Pete played with the seat belt. "What happened?"

Ozzy sighed. "I went to interview someone, a possible witness in the cold case attached to the gun, and we were attacked. Like I said, it's not something for you to be worried about. You would have been maybe ten at the time of the murder, and that's kind of pushing it. The attacker lawyered up, but we're working on him anyway. There's no connection that we've found to the robbery, so it shouldn't affect you." He flexed his hand, which looked bruised.

"So wait, the guy just tried to punch a witness in the face?" Pete tried to turn to look at Ozzy, but the belt was in the way.

"Er, not exactly?" Ozzy winced. "Look, it was yesterday, and it all worked out. The job can be a little dangerous sometimes, but that's something we all knew when we signed up, right?"

Pete settled back into his seat. It was true, the job was dangerous. And all of the cops did know that when they agreed to the job. Still, the idea of Ozzy putting himself into danger sent chills up Pete's spine. "Doesn't it bother you?"

"What, a little bit of danger?" Ozzy laughed. "No, I've been in worse situations and come out fine. This wasn't even really a blip on the radar." He blinked. "I mean, maybe it should have been, but I didn't even really register that there had been a gun until after everything was over."

Pete shivered. "Wow. I know that the police have dangerous jobs, but I never really think about it until one talks about taking down a gunman like it's just a normal, everyday thing." He forced a chuckle.

Ozzy tightened his grip on the steering wheel. "Yeah, well, maybe not *normal* everyday thing, but yeah, it does happen. But it's still better than what I used to do, I guess."

"What's that?" Pete looked back at his escort for the evening.

"I was in the Army. Infantry." Ozzy swallowed. "Trust me. A bank robber in Framingham, no matter how nasty he is, has nothing on insurgents in Fallujah or the Taliban in Kandahar."

"I suppose not." Pete could see how tight Ozzy's eyes had gotten. The grim set of his companion's jaw didn't exactly speak to a joyful mindset, either. He let the matter drop and instead focused on enjoying a night out.

They weren't going far, only to a tiny little Indian place on Boston Post Road. The host took one look at Pete and seated them right away, which made Pete chuckle. Maybe there were some advantages to his burgeoning belly after all. "So how are you doing with little Osmundia?" Ozzy asked with a grin. "She still doing okay?"

Pete rubbed at his belly. His daughter kicked at his hand. "She's grand. I'm still getting her room set up, you know? It's weird."

"How so?" Ozzy looked into Pete's eyes, and Pete wanted to melt right there into the vinyl upholstery.

"Well, you're decorating for someone who doesn't have any preferences. I know I'm having a girl, right? So everything's pink. Pink as far as the eye can see. Everyone wants you to get pink, ruffly sheets, and to fill her bureau with pink, frilly dresses. But who knows if she'll even like that stuff? It's like you're trying to force that kind of thing on her, the hyper-femininity, before she can even open her eyes." Pete squirmed under the alpha's gaze and reached for his water. "I'm probably overthinking it."

"Maybe a little." Ozzy wrinkled his nose. "What do I know, though? I've never thought about it and I've never had to. I could get her a pink parasail, but I think adding ruffles would affect the aerodynamics too much to make it usable."

Pete glowered. "You said that just to get my goat."

"I did say that just to get your goat. I'm pretty sure that you'd have to be at least fourteen to go parasailing. Maybe sixteen?" Ozzy grinned, a sexy grin that went straight to Pete's gut, and Pete had to laugh.

They enjoyed their meal together as the restaurant filled up. Pete tried to eat slowly, and not just because his stomach capacity was limited by the space taken up by his daughter's growing form. He didn't want the evening to end. Even though he dragged out the meal as long as he could, they couldn't keep the table forever. Ozzy paid the bill—he insisted, which made Pete blush like a traffic light—and then they got up to leave.

As they inched their way through the crowded dining room toward the exit, a thin hand caught Pete around the wrist. He jumped and turned. An older man, maybe in his fifties, had grabbed him. The man's pale face had a few lines, not many, and his brown hair was more faded than gray at this point. It was his hands that betrayed his age more than anything else, with a few brown spots already.

Pete's eyes narrowed. "Can I help you?"

One corner of the stranger's mouth quirked up. "Yeah. Sorry. Your boyfriend dropped this." He pressed a piece of yellow lined paper into Pete's hand, folded so often that it was stiff and the edges sharp. "Better catch up now; don't want to slip and fall on the ice."

"Okay. Um, thanks?" Pete frowned at the man, took the paper, and left.

Ozzy had just reached the exit. He'd turned around and was staring at the stranger with the kind of malevolence reserved for prey animals. "What was that all about?"

Pete passed him the note. "He said you dropped this."

Ozzy stared at the man for another long minute, but then he shrugged and slipped the note into his pocket. "Okay. Come on, let's head out."

Once they were in the car, Ozzy took the note out and read it. "Interesting."

"What is it?" Pete buckled his seat belt.

"According to this note that I *dropped*, we shouldn't operate under the assumption that Harbaugh was some kind of saint. This guy says that Harbaugh got exactly what was coming to him. Interesting." He took a deep breath and folded the note back up. "You know what, though? Harbaugh's not going to get any deader. Tonight's my night off, and I'm spending it with you, not a cold case."

Pete's heart fluttered in his chest. He knew that Ozzy couldn't really mean that, not the way that it sounded, but that didn't change the fact that his words excited him. "Thanks," he murmured as Ozzy turned the car on.

They headed back to Pete's place, and when Pete shyly invited Ozzy in to watch a movie, Ozzy accepted. Ozzy didn't even pretend to keep his distance, but sat right up against Pete and wrapped an arm around his shoulders as the opening credits began. Pete had started a fire in the gas fireplace underneath the wall-mounted TV, just for ambiance, and now sat there letting himself enjoy the comfort.

How long had it been since anyone had wanted to give him this? The politician who had given him his daughter hadn't been about affection or comfort. He'd been about sex, and Pete had been hard up enough to take him up on it. His previous encounters hadn't been much better, not going back for a good long time. He'd contented himself with more or less anonymous sex, because that was all he could get, and he'd more or less forgotten what it was like to be on the receiving end of plain, basic affection.

When Ozzy kissed him, it wasn't desperate. He didn't claim ownership of Pete's mouth or overwhelm him with a sudden surge of passion. He simply leaned in and joined their lips together like it was the most natural thing in the world, and Pete's whole body suffused itself with warmth in response. He held onto Ozzy and opened his mouth, letting Ozzy in and surrendering to the gentle touch.

Safe. It made no sense. That word, that feeling, shouldn't come anywhere near popping into Pete's head when he was making out with a man whose idea of a good time was jumping out of an airplane or jumping off a cliff with synthetic wings attached to his back like Icarus, but here he was. He felt safe in Ozzy's arms, like nothing could touch him or his daughter.

He wanted more, of course. The callused fingers that crept just under the hem of Pete's shirt felt amazing on his skin. They would feel even better on his nipples, or on his hard cock, or deep inside of his body preparing him to receive Ozzy. It wasn't urgent. Pete wanted more, but he could also stay right where he was and be content with Ozzy's kisses until the day he died.

The thought terrified him, just a little. He wasn't used to that kind of strong emotion. He wasn't used to waiting, either. He was used to instant gratification, but Ozzy was different.

When Ozzy did pull away, long after the movie had ended and Netflix's welfare check flashed onto the screen, he licked his lips. "I could do that all week," he said with a sigh. "But I need to get going. I promised my dad I'd do some family time with him tomorrow. Can we get together again sometime this week, or maybe on the weekend?"

"Absolutely." Pete smiled and struggled up to his feet. He kissed Ozzy again at the door, and watched him drive away.

He needed another shower. Now that Ozzy wasn't here anymore, Pete realized that the warmth his date had created had left him with an uncomfortable layer of sweat that he needed to remove sooner rather than later. The hard-on that had been noticeable but not unpleasant when he'd been safe in Ozzy's arms now ached and required attention, too. He could ignore it and hope that it went away, but he didn't feel compelled to subject himself to any more discomfort than strictly necessary in his current condition.

He locked up behind Ozzy and retreated to his room. If nothing else had come of the date with Ozzy, he'd learned one thing. He'd proven, if only to himself, that Ozzy was at least attracted to him, baby bump and all. It was a good feeling, if one he was unaccustomed to, and he smiled to himself as he headed toward the shower.

...

Ozzy gave some serious thought to skipping services the day after his date with Pete. The last thing he wanted to do after spending an evening inhaling Pete's incredible citrus scent was to sit there in an old wooden church and breathe in the much less enticing scent of cheap furniture polish. He went anyway. If he'd torn himself away from Pete—and all of the things he wanted to do with Pete— he might as well go all out.

He sat with his mother and his younger brother in the front row and let his mind wander. He had two things on his mind right now: Pete and the Harbaugh case. The two shouldn't be joined, but it didn't seem to be possible to separate them. Last night some creeper had grabbed Pete—put his dirty little meat hands on Ozzy's omega—and given him a note about the case.

Ozzy knew he shouldn't be thinking about Pete as *his* omega. Not yet, anyway. They barely knew each other, and surely the father of his child would come back into his life once he understood that the most amazing omega on God's earth was going to give birth to a beautiful baby girl that they had created. Ozzy could feel his entire body going soft just at the thought, and it wasn't even his kid!

Before he knew it, services were over and the family was ready to hit the slopes. He extricated his father from a knot of fussy parishioners and herded him out toward the cars. A quick drive back to his parents' place let them change their clothes, and with that they were ready for the half hour drive out to Wachusett Mountain.

"Wanna race?" Ozzy waggled his eyebrows at his brother, Zack.

Zack scoffed and picked up his carefully polished skis. "I'm not racing you, idiot. I have an actual job, with actual responsibilities. I can't take time off for a broken leg."

"Chicken." Ozzy snorted. "That was one time, and it was a hairline fracture that you've been crying about for years."

"There will be no racing." His mother, Linda, elbowed Ozzy in the ribs. She wasn't gentle about it either. "If you can't just be good and enjoy a quiet day on the slopes, Ozzy, then we won't bring you skiing with us anymore. Family day will just be spent sitting around and drinking tea after services."

Ozzy rolled his eyes and grabbed his snowboard. His mother could threaten all she wanted, but she knew exactly how often he would show up to sit around the house and drink tea.

They spent a few hours on the slopes, each enjoying trails suited to their talents and interests. Ozzy liked speed. He found the steepest, fastest, most dangerous trails that he could, and zipped down them as fast as he was able. His brother took more moderate slopes alongside their mother, while their father—who had been skiing for just as long as Ozzy—stuck to beginner slopes.

By the time they were ready to leave the resort, all four had worked up an appetite. They stopped at a little cantina-type place in Leominster for dinner. Ozzy was pleased to note that they weren't the only skiers in the place.

His father smirked over at him across the table. "So, Ozzy. Tell me who has your head in the clouds during what was probably the best sermon I've given in ten years?"

Ozzy had been reaching for his margarita, but he pulled his hand back. "Seriously?"

"I'm your father, Ozzy. And a minister. I know that look on your face. That wasn't some musty cold case you were thinking about. Come on, who is she?" Gary waggled his eyebrows at him.

Linda sighed and pinched the bridge of her nose. "He, Gary. Ozzy's an alpha. He'd only be mooning around after a man."

"My apologies." Gary sipped from his sangria. "So who is he?"

Ozzy thought about lying. It might be a better plan. At the same time, he hated lying to his family, especially to his dad.

Ever since his dad had gotten ordained it felt like he got the double whammy of lying to a man of the cloth and his dad. "His name is Pete. We've had one date, so don't get too excited."

"We'll get just as excited as we please, young man." Linda shook her finger at Ozzy. "You're in your thirties. It's high time you got serious about someone, so the fact that you're mentioning this Pete at all is a big deal."

Zack's lip curled. "Oh my God, Mom. It's one date. Who in their right mind would want to see Ozzy for more than that?"

"Shut up, punk." Ozzy elbowed his brother. He nailed Zack right in the funny bone and gave himself two thumbs up for the accomplishment. "As it happens, we've had one date but we've met up a few times before that. So he knows more or less what he's getting into."

Dad pursed his lips. "That's good, son. Does he know about your service record?"

Ozzy did reach for his drink now, mostly so he would have something to do with his hands. "The subject has come up. Not in depth, but it has come up. Why?"

"It just seems like he should know what he's getting into, doesn't it?" Gary fixed him with a firm stare. "I'm sure he's a great guy, but he should have the chance to decide for himself if he can handle everything."

"I'm fine. Pete knows enough." Ozzy clenched his jaw.

His father looked away. "I'm just trying to help you, son." He looked up with a cheerfulness that seemed forced. "So tell me about this guy. Is he another cop?"

"No. He's a photographer." Ozzy forced himself to rein his temper in. He knew that his father meant well. "He was a witness at a crime scene, actually, and we hit it off."

"Oh my Lord, Ozzy, you don't mean the bank robbery, do you?" Linda put her hands to her cheeks. "I'm pretty sure that it's just not done to pick up dates at crime scenes."

Ozzy had to chuckle at that one. "It's a little unusual, but he's not involved with my current case. I'm not investigating the robbery, so it's all good." He sipped from his margarita.

His brother wrinkled his nose. "Okay. So tell us more about him? Is he The One? Is he going to make you lots of little weird babies, or is he not even an omega?"

Ozzy scowled at his brother. "Oh my God, are you for real? He's definitely an omega, because he's pregnant."

"Already?" Linda had paled, and Gary had to help her keep hold of her drink.

Ozzy shook his head. "Not by me. He was six months along when we met. The father isn't in the picture anymore." He shrugged. "Anyway, he's a pretty well-known photographer, as it happens. I looked him up. Did you know that he's won—"

"Wait a minute." Gary held up a hand. "You're sitting here mooning around over a guy who's carrying a baby that isn't even yours?"

Ozzy froze. A feeling of calm suffused his body. He recognized the tone in his father's voice. He recognized the judgment. "Yup." He picked up his drink, met his father's eyes, and took a long, deliberate sip.

Linda frowned and leaned forward. "Oh my God, Ozzy, what are you thinking?"

"Ozzy," Gary said. He reached out and took Ozzy's hand, and said it again. "Ozzy, I know you probably think there's something very special about this young man, but I'm sure you can see where there's probably something wrong here. I mean, I'm sure that you can see where an alpha with a good job, with good benefits, would be very appealing to a person who was pregnant with no father."

Ozzy's jaw dropped. "Am I really hearing this from a man of the cloth? From the Unitarian church, no less? Weren't you up there today nattering about forgiveness and not judging other people?"

Gary grimaced and sat back. "I guess you were listening."

"It's osmosis." Ozzy glowered. "We haven't talked about the future, or about the baby, or about money, but considering the fact that his mother has enough money to pay some guy to sit in the driveway while we all have dinner together I'm pretty sure he's not after my health insurance. Thanks for bringing that up, though. Very classy."

Linda smacked the table. "Your father is trying to look out for you, Ozzy."

"Look." Ozzy closed his eyes and took a deep breath. Could he hold his emotions in? "I'm very much aware that the kid isn't mine. He hasn't asked me to do anything or take over, or anything like that. We're two guys who enjoy one another's company. It could go further. It might not. I don't see why that's a problem. If I started seeing someone who had a kid that was a couple of years old, that wouldn't be a problem for you. If I took up with an omega who'd just lost his alpha, it wouldn't be a problem for you. The fact that I've started seeing someone who happens to be pregnant—happens to have been pregnant before I met him—is an issue?"

Zack put his napkin on the table. "Would you stop with the histrionics? Seriously, Ozzy, just shut up. You're making a scene. Mom and Dad are right. Think about it logically for once in your life. Sure, he's probably pretty, but let's face it. You've never been great at thinking in the long term. Just shut up and listen to them." His lip curled. "You're not going to flip your lid and go without speaking to them over a guy you had one date with, are you?"

"You do get that I didn't go off in a sulk, right? I was in Fallujah. I couldn't stay in touch. It's not like I could exactly pop in for Sunday services. Or like I was off at law school jerking off and getting kicked off the Law Review."

Linda smacked the table again. "Do I have to come over there and separate you two? I won't hesitate. Listen. You've said what you have to say, and we've said what we had to say. Maybe we should just calm down and talk about something else until Ozzy's had a chance to think things through rationally."

Ozzy pursed his lips, but he took it. He wasn't going to convince them, and he hadn't even come up with a plan to sell them on the idea of Pete yet. It was early in their relationship to think about how he was going to bring their families together.

He forced himself to smile and play along as they switched the subject to Spring Training. He kept his facade up through the ride back to Harvard and his parents' house, where he made a quick excuse and headed home after liberating his snowboard and helmet from the family SUV.

He knew they would talk about him later. Zack, in particular, would have a lot to say about Pete, and babies, and gold diggers, and whatever else Zack's foul and fertile mind could devise. Zack had always been a weasel, and law school hadn't done him any favors.

He knew, too, that staying to reassure his family that he was handling their censure in an approved way might go a long way toward stilling those tongues. His parents didn't trust him. They didn't trust his judgment. He'd done three tours of duty only to be treated like even more of an adolescent than he'd been when he left. He didn't think he could hold his temper if he stayed, so he left. It wasn't so much about Pete, although the hypocrisy of their censure offended him. It was about him, and their attitude toward him.

He returned to his home in Hudson, and he cleaned up before bed. He hesitated for a moment, and then he sent a quick text to Pete. He worried for a moment about whether or not it was too much, or whether he was being too clingy for this early in the relationship, but he decided to do it anyway. He only had one life to live. He'd learned that the hard way; he might as well enjoy it.

Pete replied about a minute later, not with words but with a very artistic black and white photo of the full moon over some barren trees. Ozzy chuckled. Well, what had he expected? He'd taken up with a photographer.

Thinking of you tonight. He smiled as he typed out the text, relishing the thought of Pete in his house. Then he turned his focus toward what would face him tomorrow. He'd ignored the implications of the note he'd gotten yesterday in favor of time with Pete and with his family. A new week was beginning; he needed to get the job done.

And what a job it was. The note strongly implied that Harbaugh hadn't been some poor, innocent victim of a traffic stop gone wrong. Instead, he'd been involved with something he shouldn't have been, and it had come back around to bite him in the end. Had Harbaugh been a dirty cop?

How much faith could Ozzy really put into an anonymous note scribbled onto a legal pad, and passed not even to him but to his date in a restaurant? The question gave him pause, and the reality sent a chill right up his spine. The guy, remarkable only for his age-spotted hands, had followed Ozzy and Pete to the restaurant, gotten a table, and sat through their date just to deliver that note. And Ozzy hadn't noticed him lurking.

Had he followed Ozzy to Pete's house? Had he just lurked around Pete's house, waiting for Ozzy? Either way, the thought was chilling. This man, who knew enough to know that Ozzy was looking into a cop's murder, knew where Pete lived. Knew who Pete was. Pete hadn't been involved with the Harbaugh murder before, but he was now, even if only on the periphery.

Ozzy gnawed on his knuckle. The absolute last thing he wanted was to put Pete in danger. Should he tell Pete to go ahead and move back in with his mother for his own safety?

He moved away from his desk. He wasn't going to do that. Pete didn't need the disruption, and chances were that he wouldn't have any more real safety at his mother's house than he did at home. Unless his mother had an army of bodyguards that she was going to send out to photo shoots with him, it would just be exchanging one house for another.

No, the best way for Ozzy to keep his omega safe would be to solve the case and put Harbaugh's killer behind bars for good. He hopped into bed and pulled the covers up. Tomorrow he would go into work with a renewed sense of purpose. Now it was personal.

Chapter Five

Pete didn't set an alarm on Friday morning. Last night Resist had played in Worcester, and Pete had been there for work. He wasn't necessarily a huge fan of their style of music, but he liked what they stood for and right now he'd take what jobs he could get. He was seven months along now, and Massachusetts in early March wasn't exactly the most exciting place to be.

He'd snagged the job for the Globe, and he'd even gotten permission to sell some of the pictures he'd taken to the band's management for promotional purposes. That was a good deal for him, and it might even translate into more work down the road. More work, that was, assuming he could get someone to watch his daughter. He had a nanny lined up, and she'd agreed to work odd hours due to his job, but Pete was still anxious about the arrangement and would be until he saw how well it worked in practice.

He stretched in his bed and wallowed in the warmth that the covers provided. They hadn't hit a thaw yet; outside everything was still frozen and nasty. Maybe today he'd just stay inside. There was no real reason for him to leave the house. He had food, the walk was clear, and he didn't have any jobs or appointments going on.

His phone buzzed on the nightstand beside him and he groaned. Real, adult life would intrude itself, no matter what he wanted. He snaked a hand out from underneath the duvet and grabbed it. "Hello?"

"Did I wake you up?" Ozzy's voice was soft and intimate on the other end of the line.

"No, I was just waking up anyway." Pete smiled and burrowed into the shelter of the blankets. It would be better if he could burrow into the shelter of the handsome alpha's arms, of course, but he'd take what he could get. "How's your day going?" At first, Pete had been a little startled when Ozzy started calling him every day. By mid-week, though, he had to admit that he liked it. Ozzy's calls weren't overbearing or excessive. They were just nice, touching little check-ins.

"Must be nice," Ozzy teased. "I hope those rock stars didn't keep you out too late. I know that Damian Katsaros is supposed to be pretty hot stuff."

"Mmm. He is very charming. Pretty devoted to Noah Dare, too." Pete sometimes wondered what it would be like to have someone so devoted to him, but he tried not to dwell on it. "How are things going?"

"Meh. You know how it is. We don't get the normal cases, right? That's why they're cold. If they were easy, they'd have been solved right away. Listen, what are you doing tonight?"

Pete considered telling the truth and admitting that he'd just been planning to do some online shopping for the baby, and possibly deep-cleaning the stove. "No real plans," he said instead. "Why?"

"I thought we might be able to get together. If that's okay, I mean. I like spending time with you, and I seem to make more breakthroughs when we've been around each other than when it's been a while." Ozzy laughed. "It's like you're a police work muse."

"I wonder who the muse of detectives would be." Pete rubbed a hand over his belly.

"Agatha." Ozzy's voice was dry. "We have an altar set up to her in the corner of the squad room. We light candles and leave offerings when the cops get one, and we shake our fists in her general direction when some little old British lady solves the mystery."

Pete laughed out loud and hauled himself into a sitting position. "It's a date," he promised. "If only to please Agatha."

"Great. I'll stop by at seven. Do you want me to bring takeout or do you want to go out?"

"I can cook, actually." Pete stretched. "I'm feeling up to it, and it's best to cook at home while I still can, you know?"

"You cook too?" Ozzy's tone was awed. "Awesome. I'll see you tonight."

They hung up, and Pete got out of bed. Now that he'd promised to cook, he was going to have to actually get moving.

He straightened up the house, not that it needed much. Most of his effort was spent on stripping the bed and changing the sheets. He didn't expect much, but he could hope, and he'd rather be prepared for something good than up a creek in case of disappointment.

He showered and changed, and then he went shopping. He decided to make a lasagna for dinner. He didn't know if Ozzy liked lasagna; he hoped that Ozzy liked lasagna. Most people liked lasagna, but sometimes people surprised you. He liked to make lasagna because the leftovers could feed him for days, if he wasn't up to cooking, and the scent warmed the entire house.

While the lasagna baked, he managed to cook a few dishes for later. He could eat them later in the week, or he could freeze them for after the baby was born when he wasn't up to cooking. He had that kind of freedom, and it was kind of awesome. He set the table, with a tablecloth and everything, and even got out the slightly nicer plates.

It did occur to Pete that he was going a little overboard, but he decided that he didn't care. This was probably his last chance to go all out like this. He might as well have some fun with it.

Ozzy showed up at seven o'clock exactly, just like he'd said he would. His dark eyes were ringed with dark-purple circles, and his shoulders had a noticeable slump to them. He smiled, though, low and sexy, when he saw Pete's apron. "You really did cook." He sniffed the air and straightened up. "You cooked, and it smells amazing."

"Come on in." Pete took his hand and pulled him into the house. "Dinner's ready. It's not much, just lasagna and salad, but it should be filling anyway." He took Ozzy's coat and led him into the kitchen.

They sat down and Ozzy's eyes lit up at the sight of the dinner laid out in front of him. "You didn't bake the bread, too?"

"No." Pete ducked his head and sipped from his water. "My talents don't carry me that far, I'm afraid. I'd love to be able to, but I'm kind of intimidated."

"Hey, how many people can't even do this much?" Ozzy grinned at him. "Me, for example." He dug into his lasagna and a positively orgasmic expression suffused his handsome face. "Oh my God, Pete, this is divine. Your mother didn't teach you how to cook."

Pete laughed. "No. No, I'm pretty sure my mother's never actually been inside a kitchen. She has people for that. Ah, when I went to college, I was pretty much on my own. It was sink or swim. I wasn't interested in taking more of my parents' money than I had to, you know? I had to learn to cook really fast, and pretty cheap too."

"Huh." Ozzy swallowed his food, letting Pete see his throat working. "I mean that's good, and I'm obviously reaping the benefits, but why wouldn't you make life easier for yourself? I mean, if you could avoid having to do things like cook, or your own laundry, when you were a kid?"

Pete put his fork down and thought about the answer for a long moment. "Well, for starters, I'd have had to live with my mom. That wasn't... that wasn't ideal. She didn't want either one of us training for a career. College was fine if we lived at home and majored in something suitably useless. I could major in art history, but not art. I had every intention of working, of earning a living. And she wasn't entirely on board with me even going to college at all. She had a whole list of alphas from *good* families, approved families, that she wanted me to choose from."

"I see." Ozzy grimaced. "Not for you, huh?"

Pete toyed with his napkin. He needed to be very careful about how he answered this question. "I wasn't exactly opposed to finding an alpha. It was everything that went with it that I didn't like. I wasn't willing to just kind of end my own life, at eighteen, and go hide in some estate somewhere for the rest of my life, you know? That might have flown a hundred years ago, but I had things that I also wanted to do. I wanted to find a modern alpha, one who could acknowledge that his omega had a life and goals and talents." He put his napkin down. "And I mean, I've done okay for myself, you know? I'm an award-winning photographer. I'm respected. I make enough that I don't generally have to rely on the income from my trust fund, although it doesn't hurt."

"Hey—no judgment." Ozzy reached over the table and took his hand. "You don't have to justify anything to me, okay? Neither of us exactly lives a conventional life, and that's okay. I was just curious. I, uh, I'm not a big fan of living at home myself. I used to do it between deployments, way back when, but after I was discharged it just got to be too much."

Pete squeezed his hand. "Can I ask how so?"

Ozzy let go of his hand and looked up at the ceiling for a second, like he was weighing his options. "I left after the guys in my unit were killed," he said after a moment. "My family seems to think that having survived means that I've somehow reverted to a mental age of ten. I swear, for the first couple of months, until I got into the police academy, my mom was cutting my meat for me."

"Aw, geez." Pete made a face. "That's kind of crappy." He turned back to his dinner.

Ozzy chuckled. "Right? I mean, I know they're trying to be supportive. I do. It's just... I'm a grown man, I'm in my thirties, and I'm a pretty well-respected cop, right? I'm a detective. That usually means that your mind's working just fine, but no. Apparently I need grown-ups to do my thinking for me."

Pete raised his water glass. "To avoiding the well-meaning."

"Amen." Ozzy laughed.

They finished their meal, and then Ozzy started cleaning up the dishes. "What are you doing?" Pete asked him, astonished.

"Well, I've noticed that you don't like to have dirty dishes lying around. I figured that I'd clean them for you. You've been on your feet all day." Ozzy carried a stack of dishes over to the sink.

Pete rushed over to the sink. "How about if I wash and you dry?" he offered with a smile.

Ozzy took the offered dishtowel. His fingers brushed Pete's hand, and Pete gasped.

He got the dishes rinsed and loaded into the dishwasher. When he started on the pots and pans, though, he found a pair of strong hands on his hips and a mouth on his neck. "This okay?" Ozzy murmured into his ear.

Pete closed his eyes and relaxed into the alpha's touch. Ozzy wasn't even doing much, just the slightest little caresses and grazes of his teeth, and it was enough to have him hard in seconds. Pete braced himself against the counter. "More than," he said. He took a deep breath, savoring Ozzy's popcorn scent.

Ozzy moved a little closer, molding himself to Pete's body. Pete could feel the hard line of his cock pressed up against his ass, and he *wanted*. Ozzy wasn't pushing, though. He just stood with his hands on Pete's hips, kissing his neck and nibbling along his jawbone.

His teeth slid up the long column of Pete's neck, and Pete tilted his neck to give Ozzy easier access. He'd give him anything he wanted, and he wouldn't be ashamed of it. He let out a little whine when Ozzy took his earlobe in between his teeth. "You like this." Ozzy gave a dark little chuckle and slid his right hand up Pete's torso.

"You know I do." Pete rocked back, just a little. When Ozzy let out a choked-off groan and gripped his hip even harder with his left hand, Pete knew that Ozzy was just as into this as he was.

"Mmm. Why look, your shirt's gotten wet." Ozzy untied Pete's apron and tossed it onto the counter. Then he slowly unbuttoned Pete's shirt, thrusting his hips ever so slightly as he did so. It wasn't much, just enough to tease, but it still brought a flush of arousal to Pete's skin.

Pete pushed back even more as Ozzy's hand caressed his chest. His nipples were so sensitive now that the slightest touch could set him off; having Ozzy's callused fingers right on the swollen nubs made him moan out loud. He couldn't help but rock back into the hard cock pressing against him now. He needed.

Ozzy ground against him, breathing hard in Pete's ear. One hand inched toward Pete's waistband. "Can I?" he asked. Pete could feel how tightly Ozzy's jaw was clenched, as though he was trying to control himself.

He could have said so much. He could have told the full truth, and said, *Whatever you want, whatever you need,* but he didn't have the words right now. He could have kept it simpler and said, *I'm yours.*

Instead, he just said, "Yes."

Rough fingers fumbled with the button on his fly and slipped into his pants. Even the sensation of someone else's hand on his cock almost threw Pete for a loop. As it was, he didn't last long. He cried out at the first caress against his hot, demanding flesh and thrust into his alpha's hand.

He came with a loud groan. Ozzy wrapped his arms around Pete and shuddered, and then he stilled.

Pete blinked away his post orgasmic haze. "Wow." He turned around and kissed Ozzy on the mouth. He could see, and feel, the wet spot on the front of Ozzy's dress pants. He'd have to have them dry-cleaned. "Thank you for that," he said, resting his forehead against Ozzy's.

"Mmm." Ozzy looked like he was ready for a blanket. "Thank you. That was incredible. You're incredible."

They could have lit all of Sudbury from the glow coming from Pete. Ozzy was probably the perfect alpha. "I know this might have not been your plan, but you're welcome to stay."

Ozzy opened his eyes. "You wouldn't mind?"

Pete let out a little laugh. "Quite the opposite."

Ozzy blushed. "I didn't want to make assumptions. But there might be a bag in my car, just in case. You know."

Pete kissed him again. "Boy scout."

"You know it." Ozzy staggered outside to go and get his overnight bag, and Pete cleaned up the cabinets.

Screw the pots and pans. They could soak.

...

Ozzy had agreed to do a class at the indoor rock wall in Marlborough on Saturday afternoon. He didn't want to leave Pete behind, but he also knew that he couldn't bail. It just wasn't in him, to ignore a commitment like that. When they woke up the next morning, he explained the problem to Pete and left the choice up to him.

Pete gave a little chuckle. "Look, I'm not the kind of omega who needs constant attention, but I'm pretty keen on the idea of spending more time with you. What do you think of the idea of me tagging along with you and bringing my camera?" He blushed, a pretty pink color spreading out over his cheeks like the sunrise. "I mean, I think you'd be an incredible subject, you know?"

"Me?" Ozzy snickered. "I don't know about that. But if you want to take pictures of me, sure. I don't have a problem with that."

And so they showered, together. It would have been fun to explore each other's bodies a little bit more in the shower; maybe they could have drawn out everything they'd done from the night before. They didn't have time, but the promise of more later would keep them going until later.

They had a good breakfast, just eggs and toast and fruit, but it was enough to sate them both. Once they'd gotten through that, they headed out to Marlborough and the outdoor supply store with the biggest indoor rock wall in the state. Ozzy went ahead and got changed, and he introduced Pete. Pete explained what he was going to be doing, and went ahead and got ready to shoot.

Ozzy found it difficult to give the demo, at least at first. It wasn't because he wasn't a great public speaker. No, he'd given this demo at least once per month for years. It was different this time, and it was different this time because of Pete. He couldn't quite shake the knowledge that Pete was there, on site, watching. Ozzy wanted to show off, but he was also desperate to prove himself to his new boyfriend.

Once he got into the rhythm of the demo, though, he found that he was able to get back into the swing of things. He gave his lecture with his usual efficiency, and then he showed the safety equipment that he so rarely used. Then, he demonstrated one of the more difficult paths up the wall and hung from the artificial overhang for a moment before swinging himself up and over the ledge.

His hand slipped before he could get up onto the ledge, and a few of the people down at the bottom of the wall reacted. Most gasped. Some shrieked. Ozzy's own heart slipped into overdrive as he forgot about the safety equipment. It would be so easy to slip and fall. He would fall down, land on something he needed. He'd have to take time off from work. He might even lose his job.

He caught the ledge again, and pulled himself up with a flourish. His limbs still tingled with unspent energy, and he was glad that his shorts were baggy enough to hide the fact that he was half-hard underneath them. He made a halfhearted attempt to will the excessive reactions away. He'd been using all of the safety equipment that the facility required, after all.

There had been no real danger, no real reason for the sudden rush of adrenaline.

It was only a halfhearted attempt. The rush was the whole reason he was here, after all.

He stood up on top of the ledge and waved at the students. Pete stood among them, camera topped by an absurdly long lens. "You all see that?" he said with a grin. "Safety equipment works. Trust it."

And then he rappelled down the side, just because he could.

The next part of the demo involved actual instruction. He couldn't pay much attention to Pete; he had to help these raw beginners with their safety harnesses and their helmets, and help them get started. Some of them didn't get past the first quarter of the wall. Some made it halfway up, laughing wildly the whole time. Two of them made it all the way up, although they took much less challenging routes to the top than Ozzy himself had.

Once the demo was over, Ozzy took another couple of trips to the top before he changed back into street clothes and headed out with Pete. As they sat and had dinner, Pete shook his head at Ozzy. "That was something else, I have to admit."

Ozzy grinned. "Thinking about giving it a try? After Osmundia's born, I mean."

"I'm not naming her Osmundia. And are you joking?" Pete scoffed. "No, I'm not thinking about taking that up after the baby shows up. That's just nuts. Rock climbing with a baby strapped to my back?"

Ozzy rolled his eyes. "You'd leave her with someone else. I'm sure your mom won't mind keeping an eye on her once in a while."

"My mom wouldn't know what to do with a baby, Ozzy. She'd be beyond confused. And my brother would be worse." Pete took a French fry. "And that assumes that I have any interest at all in hanging by one hand from an overhang like some kind of hero in an action comedy. 'Oh, hi there. I bet you're wondering how I wound up in this position.'"

"So leave the baby with my parents." Ozzy shrugged. He'd blurted the words without thinking, and blushed as soon as the words tumbled from his mouth.

Pete just smiled at him and sat back a little. "Your parents aren't keen on the idea of a baby that isn't theirs."

Ozzy wanted to ask how Pete knew that. They hadn't talked about it at all. The subject hadn't been mentioned at all. He knew that pursuing that line of inquiry would be changing the subject more than would ever be acceptable, though. "They'll get over it."

Pete looked away. "Do you want them to?"

Ozzy didn't hesitate. "Yeah. Yeah, I do." He took Pete's hand. "I absolutely do."

Pete looked back at him, fixing him with his amazing dark eyes. "Ozzy, I'm not exactly a catch. I'm pregnant with another man's kid."

"Is he a factor?"

"Well, no."

Ozzy gave Pete's hand a squeeze. He was taking a risk saying this, a huge risk, but he didn't care. "Look, Pete, I'm not going to lie. We haven't known one another long. You've worked your way into my mind like no one else has before, I don't know why that is, and I don't care. We haven't even had full-blown sex, and I can't stop thinking about you. Now, I could sit here and get all hung up about something you did before you even knew that I existed, or I could accept that you are who you are. You're pregnant with your own baby, Pete, and I knew that when we met."

Pete blinked back tears. "Really?

"Really."

They finished their meals and headed back to Sudbury. Pete blew Ozzy that night, taking him deep and sucking him down like it was the single greatest pleasure in his life.

They had a lazy day on Sunday, shopping and dozing together. Ozzy considered bringing Pete to services, but ultimately decided against it. After all of the arguing about Pete last week, Ozzy didn't want to have another confrontation just yet. He'd wait for his family to signal readiness. For now, he'd spend his time doing something he enjoyed, and that was spending time with his lover.

The next day signaled the start of a new workweek. Ozzy had a lot of work to do if he wanted to find a link between Harbaugh and Sierzant, and it wasn't going to be found if he spent his time mooning around over Pete.

He'd already found that most of Harbaugh's close associates were retired. Tracking them down wasn't going to be easy, either. A couple had moved away, and the department was going to dig in for a fight before they signed on to send Ozzy off to Florida or California or the Caribbean to interview a retired cop.

He drummed his fingertips on his desk, which drew a nasty snarl from Nenci. Ozzy flipped him off, but without any heat to it. Nenci was working on a challenging case of his own, and Oliver had gone on a date with a guy close to his own age. Either of these would be enough to piss him off on their own. Together, they'd turn him into an absolute bear.

"What's got you all twitchy today, Morris?" Nenci asked after a moment. "Usually you're pretty calm."

"I'm glad you think that, Nenci. Means I've got you fooled." Ozzy let out a frustrated sigh and gestured to his monitor. "I'm trying to figure out how to trace my vic's associates so I can talk to them, and so far they're all in weird places. This dude here's in La Jolla. This other one's in Fort Lauderdale. I've got another one who's living the sweet life in the Virgin Islands."

Nenci scratched his head. Then he scooted his chair over to Ozzy's side and took a look at the images on his screen. "Huh."

Ozzy turned to look at his colleague. "That's all you've got to say?"

Nenci chuckled. "Well I figured you'd have asked yourself the rest already. Little basics like, 'Huh, I wonder how a cop manages to retire to a multi-million dollar mansion in La Jolla.'" He gestured to another picture on the screen. "I was in the academy with this one, Keenan. Keenan's got two kids in college now. His wife never went to college, never had a job that paid better than a lower end hairdressing place. You want to tell me how he's living it up a few doors down from Donald Trump's summer place?"

Ozzy's jaw dropped. "Holy crap."

"Right? Except there ain't nothing holy about this." He tapped on Ozzy's screen.

Ozzy shook his head. "I… someone suggested that Harbaugh might have been… you know." He dropped his voice to a whisper. "Dirty." He made his voice normal again. "I didn't want to believe it. I mean, there wasn't any evidence and that's not something you want to think about another cop."

Nenci sighed and looked away. "It's sure as hell not something you want to think about a bunch of cops." He turned back to the screen. "But it does happen, you know? Most of us are doing the job for the right reasons, but all of us have a price. Every single one." He pointed at the men on the screen. "I've been around for a good long time, you know? I've seen a lot of things on the force. Sometimes you get more than one. Sometimes you get a bunch."

"If this is true… if this is real… this is going to be ugly." Ozzy swallowed. "I mean. really ugly."

"Well, you know that all of us here in Cold Case will have your back." Nenci folded his lips together. "That goes without saying. I'd be willing to bet that Pretty Boy would be on board, and don't tell him that I said this but he's actually not half bad at finding stuff out. Plus he likes to be a pain when it comes to real cops." Nenci wrinkled his nose. "But you need to make sure that you've got everything in order, because you're going to be a very unpopular man in a lot of departments, brother."

Ozzy rubbed at his temples. He could feel it already, that little hit of adrenaline creeping in. It wasn't like a big rush, not the kind he got in a fight or when he fell from a rock wall. No, it was the kind of low-grade buzz that he got on a long-term mission. "I can cope with that. I've been in worse situations. It's not like these guys have a bunch of IEDs, right?"

"Not usually." Nenci managed a little grin. "You know what my last assignment was before Cold Case, right?"

Ozzy had always figured Nenci's last assignment had been Dour Traffic Cop. "No."

Nenci smirked. "Internal Affairs. I've seen things happen. When cops go bad, no matter what reasons they gave you, the best way to prove it is to follow the money. All this?" He waved a finger at the screen. "All this is reasonable suspicion to look a little deeper into their financials. You shouldn't have any trouble getting a warrant. And you shouldn't have any trouble getting a warrant to look into Harbaugh's either."

Nenci wheeled himself back over to his own desk. "Good luck, brother."

Ozzy stared at his screen. "Thanks, Nenci."

He spent the rest of Monday and Tuesday, digging into the histories of other known associates of Harbaugh's. It all turned out to be more of the same. Some of the cops had moved from the state police to other agencies before their retirements, most notably Worcester.

Worcester, the favorite stomping grounds of Joe Sierzant.

It wasn't proof. It wasn't even close to proof. It was a direction. It was enough to get him a warrant, which would bring him proof. Ed Amos, from Internal Affairs, expressed some concerns about investigating current officers, but Ozzy and Lt. Devlin assured him that at this point they were going after a known gangster, and only in relation to a murder investigation. The most they would do would be to snare some retired cops in their net, but no officers would actually be targeted.

In theory, Amos shouldn't mind if they tripped over a few dirty cops. The fact that he did made Ozzy very concerned.

He started digging into the more complete financial records of those officers on Wednesday. At about two o'clock, he got an email from Pete. The message was small, consisting of a link to a website and the sentence, *I just wanted you to see you the way I see you.*

Ozzy followed the link. It led to a private section of Pete's website, where Pete had posted pictures from Ozzy's demo on Saturday. Ozzy gasped out loud. Some of the pictures were in color. Some were black and white, but they were all breathtaking. Pete had caught his concentration as he made his ascent, and his devotion as he helped the students with their progress. Pete had made him look beautiful.

"I like that one." Langer peered over Ozzy's shoulder and pointed to one photo in particular. Ozzy's hand had just slipped from the overhang, and his face was split by a wide grin. "That one's you, bro."

Ozzy chuckled. Maybe he and Pete hadn't known one another very long, but his omega definitely knew him well. He had the picture to prove it.

Chapter Six

Pete didn't think he would ever get the stink of burning flesh out of his clothes. It probably wouldn't ever come out of his hair, either. He'd done his job. He'd rolled out of bed with the grace of a beached whale when the call had come in, and he'd kept his stoicism and his stomach when he'd gotten to the scene and flashed his press credentials to the cops holding back the crowd.

Now the scene was closed. There was nothing left to photograph. All that remained of the scene—once an old warehouse, then a concert venue, and finally a raging inferno as of eleven twenty-three last evening—was a pile of ash and rubble. He could have taken a few pictures of that, and of the steam rising from it as firefighters kept watch, but it was too dark to catch much of interest.

Now he sat in a booth at the local IHOP, drawing looks of concern and disgust from the waitress. He stank, and he knew it. He didn't have time to wait to get home to edit the pictures properly, and the IHOP had Wi-Fi. He would have to go with the best raw photos for his clients right now and edit for features later.

He found a handful of his best photos and quickly selected three that he could send to the client who had sent him to the scene. Another few went to the usual press wires; that would bring him in some additional income. He added captions of what was going on—the fire itself, emergency workers rushing a survivor to the ambulance, terrified loved ones on the scene begging for help and answers from impotent first responders.

The waitress arrived with his order of eggs and potatoes. It had come with a side of bacon, which he hadn't thought much about at the time. His stomach rebelled at the scent; he had to send it back with his apologies. She made a face until he explained where he'd just been. Then her face just fell and she brought him a free cup of tea.

Pete had covered his share of tragedies. He'd gone to New Orleans after Katrina. He'd covered no end of mass shootings. He'd been to Iraq, to Nice, to Kenya, to Pakistan. It never got easier. He could stay focused and composed when he was in the moment. He had a job to do, after all, and the only way to keep people outside that moment informed about what was happening was to bring them into the tragedy. His job was to make them feel.

After the fact, though, he always fell apart. He fell apart after photographing mass graves, or earthquake victims. He'd caught no end of flak from his editors while on assignment in Flint for jumping in to distribute water, and more flak from his mother for hassling her about donating when he got home.

There wasn't anything that anyone could do in this situation. The fire had killed all but a paltry few survivors, who would have scars on their bodies for the rest of their lives to match the ones on their minds. There was no way that the building had been up to code, no way that anyone should have been able to book the venue, no way that the band should have taken the stage.

Someone would try to play the blame game. They'd sue the band, but the band was dead now. They'd sue the tour sponsors, who certainly didn't go to sites ahead of time. They'd sue the management company, they'd sue the record label, they'd sue the fire department for not putting out the fire fast enough. None of it would bring the victims back.

Pete rubbed at his face. The victims had all been young. Did it hurt more, because the victims had been young? He'd met one parent, a single omega father, who'd lost his only child in the fire. The boy had snuck out of the house to go. He was holding out hope that the boy had somehow escaped, but Pete knew that hope was false. "He was so insistent. 'The world is going to absolutely end if I don't go, Dad.'"

Pete had held the man for a while, before an EMS worker came to lead him away to a more appropriate place. Was this the future awaiting him? He'd given the man a card and asked him to call. Most single omega parents didn't have much in the way of a support network; Pete figured that they needed to stick together.

He felt the table shift across from him and pulled his hands away from his face. A man had slid into the booth and now sat across from him. He didn't look like a remarkable man. Narrow hazel eyes looked out from a pale, lined face under graying brown hair. Pete's guest was short, even sitting down, but otherwise there wasn't anything particularly distinguishing about him.

"Can I help you?" Pete asked him. He hated the way his voice sounded right now.

"You should be careful, Mr. Nolan. You're not just breathing for one anymore. Everything that you're breathing in, your baby breathes in. When you show up to a fire at an old chemical storage facility, it can't be good for your kid." The stranger gestured with stubby fingers in the general direction of Pete's abdomen.

Pete pressed his lips together. Did this guy have any idea how many people gave him "helpful" advice about living for two? "It's not like I'm frolicking in it," he snapped. Then he paused. "Wait—how do you know that it used to be a chemical storage facility? City records say that it stored grain."

His visitor tossed his head back and laughed. Pete had to admit that it was one of the more pleasant laughs he'd heard in his life. "Come on, Nolan. You've been doing your thing for a long time." He gestured at Pete's camera. "You're not really naive enough to think that city records tell the whole story, are you? No, there was a meth lab upstairs from that concert hall. A big one. That's why the fireball was so intense. I'm willing to bet that a lot of the kids would have gone home with some problems from the chemicals anyway. Nothing major, of course, unless they already had a problem. But you know." He shrugged. "These things happen."

Pete's mouth went dry. His palms were cold and clammy, but he couldn't say anything. He couldn't let any of that show. "And you know this how?"

"Oh. The city records have a different name in them, but I'm the actual owner. Joe Sierzant." Sierzant held out a hand.

Pete was shaking the hand more as an automatic reaction than anything else. He knew that name. Anyone who covered any kind of local crime knew that name. He'd heard it from Ozzy's mouth a few times too. "Pleased to meet you. You apparently already know who I am."

"I do." Sierzant grinned and sat back. "You've gotten a lot of attention for your pictures. And that's good. You should get a lot of attention for your pictures. You take good pictures. Went to school for it and everything."

Pete's skin went cold. "I did. It's true. That was a long time ago, though. I'm afraid my college days are over."

Sierzant laughed again and patted his middle. "None of us are getting any younger, that's for sure. I didn't so much come here to talk to you about getting older, though."

Pete made himself grin and duck his head. He'd faced down warlords. He'd faced down armed white supremacists. He could handle one organized crime boss. "I don't suppose you came to talk to me about the meth lab and concert fire?" He kept his voice quiet, so that no one around them would be alerted to their conversation. He wasn't stupid enough to think that Sierzant had come in unarmed, or alone for that matter.

"Not so much, although I'm sure your buddies at the fire department all appreciate knowing what to look for when I leave. Those kinds of operations leave a lot of nasty chemicals behind." He wrinkled his nose in distaste. "I'm not saying that I authorized it, of course, but they'll want to do the investigation and cleanup in bunny suits."

"Thanks for the tip." Pete nodded. "If you don't mind my asking, why seek me out?"

"Well, Nolan." Sierzant folded his hands together and leaned forward, forearms on the table. "It's like this. I like you well enough, and I think we'll probably get along together just fine. I'm sorry about the little incident in the bank, by the way. Balsalmo's young, he's a little unseasoned. He panicked and got sloppy. He didn't mean to scare you, and I can promise you that no one from my organization has ever been authorized to harm a pregnant person."

Pete lifted his eyebrows. "Thanks. That's very reassuring." It wasn't reassuring. It was scary as hell. Pete wasn't about to say that to Sierzant, though. "I'm sure robbing a bank is a very stressful situation. It seems like it would be, especially for a young guy like him."

"That's what I like about you, Nolan. You're reasonable. You can see both sides." Sierzant grinned over at Pete and shook a finger. "Here's the thing. You're seeing this guy."

Icy fingers wrapped around Pete's heart. "Ozzy."

"That's the guy. Ozzy Morris. Tall guy, war hero, likes all of those extreme sports. I think that he and I would probably like each other a lot if it weren't for the whole cop thing." Sierzant scratched his cheek and glanced away for a moment. "It's not that I've got a problem with cops, you know. I've got a lot of cops that I get along with pretty well. Some of them, though, they think it's a conflict of interest to be friends with a guy like me." He pressed his hands to his chest. "I don't have a problem with that. Not really. I could do a lot for them, but I respect that they've got to do things their way. As long as there's mutual respect, we're good."

Pete tried not to be obvious about licking his lips. There was no way that Ozzy would respect a guy like Joe Sierzant. "Yeah, Ozzy tends to have a certain black and white worldview."

"We're not all that different, really. I have that kind of worldview myself. I know what he's trying to do, what case he's working on."

"He's working on a cold case." Pete shrugged.

"The Harbaugh case. I knew who Tim Harbaugh was. That was twenty years ago. I wasn't the player I am today. I was just a pimp. Your boy, he's looking into some stuff that could be very uncomfortable for me now. He thinks that there were a bunch of cops back then who were working for me back in the day. What does a pimp need with a bunch of cops?" He spread his hands wide. "One or two, sure, but not this army that he thinks I had. And definitely no dead cops."

"You think Ozzy's barking up the wrong tree." Pete bit the inside of his cheek.

Sierzant tapped the side of his nose. "I know he is. It wasn't a dirty cop what shot Harbaugh." He stood up. "I'd appreciate it if you could just pass that message along to your boy. I know he wouldn't appreciate a visit from me. Some cops—well, they're not going to take too kindly to a visit from a guy in my line of work."

"No." Pete didn't have to fake his little huff of laughter. "I assume you want a couple of minutes to get out of here before I pass it along?"

"I'd appreciate it, Nolan." Sierzant held out a hand and shook it again. Pete could see the gun stuck into his waistband as he reached over the table.

Pete shook his hand and watched as his uninvited guest left the restaurant.

Once Sierzant was out of sight, Pete let himself relax. He tried to keep himself from breathing too hard as his daughter stirred into semi-wakefulness inside of him. Which should he do first? His hands were shaking and his gorge rising; he wanted to call his lover and take shelter in the safety of his arms.

The only person that Sierzant had threatened had been Pete himself, and even that had been only by implication. Sierzant had also given Pete information that could affect the health of every fire worker that showed up at the concert fire site. He picked up his phone and called his contact from Worcester Fire. "Frank? Hi. I just got a call from a CI. The site of the fire was also a meth lab." He closed his eyes against the obscenity from Frank. "Yeah. Yeah, I know. I'm going to tell the cops in about two minutes. You tell Worcester PD, I'll handle the staties. Just have your guys wear the bunny suits and you should be okay? I guess? I'm just a photographer, man. I don't know. Yeah, I'll call the ME's office too."

Pete called his contact from the Medical Examiner's office and passed along what he knew. While he was at it, he asked about the single omega's son. They didn't have any news of him yet. That was good news, Ozzy guessed. He hadn't passed through autopsy, at least not in an identifiable form.

Now Pete took a deep breath and called Ozzy. Ozzy would still be in bed, but he answered right away. "Pete?" he said, in a voice that was thick with sleep.

"Hey, babe. I just had a close encounter with Joe Sierzant at the IHOP near the fire scene in Worcester. He, ah, he had a message for you." Pete rubbed his hand over his belly.

Well, Ozzy didn't sound asleep anymore. "Don't let them clean anything," he ordered. His voice was little more than a growl. "Don't let them clean anything, and don't move from that spot. I'll be there as fast as I can, and so will a crime scene team. Did he hurt you? Did he touch you in any way?"

"No, Ozzy." Pete couldn't help but smile, despite the fear and nerves warring in his system. "I'm fine. I just want to see you."

"I'll be right there. I love you." Ozzy hung up the phone.

Pete stared at his phone in shock. What was he supposed to do with that?

...

Ozzy should have been arrested for the way he drove to that Worcester IHOP. If he didn't have a siren and a badge, he would have been. He pulled into the parking lot with the squeal of angry brakes, parked across four parking spaces, and didn't feel bad about any of it.

He tore into the restaurant and found two crime scene techs hard at work on the table. One was dusting for prints, while Oliver looked for trace evidence on the seat and the ground. Customers and staff went about their business and tried not to stare, while a clearly exhausted Pete spoke on the phone. "Yes, Dr. Bellamy. I know I'm not a cop. Frank Wollstenholme told me to call you. Yes, that Frank. Because I'm the one who got the information."

Ozzy held out his hand for the phone. Pete handed it over without a word.

The Medical Examiner was in mid-rant. Ozzy wasn't entirely sure what he was ranting about, seeing as how he was coming in on the middle of it, but he was pretty sure it had something to do with civilians not knowing what the hell they were talking about. "Bellamy? This is Ozzy Morris, from SWAT and Cold Case. Whatever he told you, do it. I know what his source was. If he was warning you about something, it's for a good reason." He hung up the phone.

He looked his omega over. Pete reeked. There was a chemical stink that lay over him like plastic wrap. Underneath, he had a pervasive smell of overcooked meat. It almost, but didn't quite, overwhelm his beautiful citrus scent. He looked profoundly exhausted. "Are you okay?"

"I'm fine." Ozzy smiled up at him. "I mean, I'm shook up, don't get me wrong, but I'm fine. Not harmed in any way."

Ozzy closed his eyes and put a hand on Pete's shoulder. "I'm still seeing red," he confessed. "I can't… I can't. That animal came here, he spoke to you, he menaced you—"

Pete rubbed a grubby hand along his arm. "Hey. It's okay. If you want to get me home, maybe we can talk about it someplace a little less public?"

Ozzy seethed, but then he looked into his omega's eyes. "Yeah," he said after a minute. "Let's do that. I'll have someone check your car out and drive it back to your place." He called in his request to some uniformed troopers while Pete gathered his things, and they headed back to Sudbury.

Being in the car with Pete was torture. The stink from the fire was brutal. Ozzy cracked the windows. "Sorry," he said. "It's just—"

"I get it." Pete closed his eyes. "Believe me, I get it. You know how they say you can't smell yourself? Well they lied. And pregnancy gives you a sharper sense of smell."

"Ew." Ozzy shuddered. "I'm so sorry."

"It could be worse. I didn't know anyone in that hellhole." He shuddered. "It would have always gone up, I think. Sierzant told me there was a meth lab on the property. The chemicals made it go up the way it did, or maybe it was their chemicals mixed with something else on site. I don't know. I know darkroom chemicals, not meth labs."

Ozzy opened his mouth to explain.

Pete held his hand up. "And I like it that way, honey." He thumped his head back against the headrest. "I'm very content that my tax dollars go to pay professionals, who are good at that sort of thing, to understand the chemistry of the meth lab so that I really don't have to."

Ozzy closed his mouth again. He chuckled and gripped the wheel a little tighter. The idea that Sierzant had come anywhere near Pete still had his blood boiling, but Pete's presence was starting to calm him down. "So. You've met Suspect Number One."

Pete closed his eyes. "Well, according to Sierzant he shouldn't be your Suspect Number One. He was pretty forthcoming about the kind of guy he is, don't get me wrong. He just wanted me to let you know that while there were dirty cops back in the day, it wasn't dirty cops that were responsible for Harbaugh's death." He held up his hands. "I don't know why he expected you to believe him, I really don't."

"Especially not when he busts in on my omega late at night in a damn IHOP. He must have followed you from the fire!" Ozzy almost broke the steering wheel. Pete's eyes flew open as the car swerved in the lane, and Ozzy knew that he had to get himself under control again. "Sorry. I'm going to need you to come into the station after you've had a chance to clean up a bit."

Pete turned to look at him. "Seriously? I'm wiped. I was honestly going to curl up under the covers and try not to think about everything that I just saw."

"I know." Ozzy put a hand on Pete's leg. "I wouldn't ask it if it weren't important." He left out the fact that he wasn't asking at all, but Pete apparently decided not to say anything either.

They made it to Pete's house, which seemed secure at the moment. Pete staggered into the shower while Ozzy did a sweep of the perimeter. It felt strange to be doing such a sweep in the snow instead of the dust or the sand, but at the end of the day the job was pretty much the same. He found no signs of any unwanted visitors, which settled his mind immensely.

He headed back in just in time to help Pete find some clean clothes to wear. They stowed his camera and then they headed back down to headquarters. Once there, Ozzy could relax. Pete was safe here in the Cold Case unit, with six alphas to protect him.

The guys swarmed around him, eager to meet the omega who'd gotten Ozzy's head "all turned around." Pete seemed almost overwhelmed by them, and well of course he was. They were all strong alphas, and he was unclaimed even if he was pregnant and involved with one of them. The pressure of all of that unbridled testosterone alone would have been intense, but there was nothing that Ozzy could do about it.

By the time Amos from Internal Affairs came in, Pete was all but in Ozzy's lap, and it wasn't in a fun or sexy way. When Kerr from Organized Crime showed up, Pete started to fold in on himself, and Ozzy wondered if he hadn't done a bad thing. Sure, Pete was protected here at the office, but if he melted down was he really safe?

He saw Robles pick up his phone and send a quick text. Not five minutes later, Robles' pregnant omega came striding into Cold Case, with a face like a thundercloud and a spray bottle in hand. He sprayed all of the men looming in and crowding Pete in the face, even Ozzy, with cold water and slammed his hand on the table. "Did every single one of you get hit with a stick from the stupid tree? Can you not see that this poor guy needs his space?" He reached out a hand to Pete. "Look, guy. I've got an office. You'll be safe in there, and I'll only let one person at a time come in. Okay?"

Pete jumped, like the soft voice startled him. "I—can my—can Ozzy bring me there?"

"Of course." Ryan gave him a reassuring smile, one that almost had Ozzy believing that he was a sweet and delicate little flower. "I'll even let one alpha stand guard outside the office, if you want."

Pete nodded. Ozzy helped him to his feet.

"Where the hell do you think you're taking our witness, Pretty Boy?" Nenci stepped forward, pointing a finger at Ryan. "You've got a lot of nerve, coming in here like you own the place."

Ryan brought his spray bottle up again and hit Nenci in the eye with a long stream of cold water. "Bad asshole. No biscuit. Right now my job is to keep this witness safe. Next time you set foot closer to this nice young father it won't be water, Nenci. I don't play nice. Got it?"

Ozzy shuddered and ushered the pregnant omegas out the door.

"Thank you." Pete's shoulders relaxed as soon as they left the room. "I wasn't expecting it to be quite so bad in there."

Ozzy would have shrunk into the walls if he could. "I wouldn't have brought you here if there was any other way, Pete. You know I wouldn't have."

"As it happens, there is another way." Ryan smiled brightly and led them along toward Abused Persons. "My office is very defensible. And I make an excellent bodyguard."

"I noticed." Pete let out a little laugh. "I have to admit that I've never seen an omega be quite so… what's the word I'm looking for?"

"Assertive." The corners of Ryan's mouth twitched. "I like assertive. It has a better sound than *is fed up to here with dealing with alpha BS in that room*." He winked at Ozzy, who hung his head. "Seriously. Never bring an omega in there. Ever." They arrived at Abused Persons and made a beeline for Ryan's office. "So, Ozzy. Since I've got you here, I just happened to do some leg work on your boy Sierzant."

"Because you've got so much free time." Ozzy snorted and helped Pete into a chair.

"Meh." Ryan waved a hand. "The guy's a pimp. Do you really think that he wasn't going to have a file with us or someone related to us?" He indicated the other seat and opened up a drawer. He pulled out a file and a packet of saltine crackers. He passed the crackers to Pete. "Look, it's not much, but you look dead on your feet. You probably want something to nibble on?"

Pete's hands were shaking as he reached out for the snack. "How did you know?"

Ryan's hand found his baby bump. "We get a few omegas through here, in all stages. They've been very generous in terms of making sure that I know what to expect." He grimaced. "Anyway, let's talk about Joe Sierzant. He's not a great guy. The thing is, like a lot of pimps or guys who started out in that oh so noble profession, he can be very charismatic."

Pete nodded, eyes far away. "I can see that. I never forgot who he was, but if I didn't already know, and wasn't already pretty attached, I'd have probably fallen for a lot of things."

Ozzy's heart leaped. Pete was attached to him! Pete's attachment kept him from falling for a pimp's lies! He put a hand onto Pete's leg.

"So, he's got a long history of sweet-talking his way into and out of some interesting situations. His first arrest for pimping was in 1969. He was all of seventeen, and he convinced the judge that it was simply an error of judgment." He flipped to the back of the file. "I'm not entirely sure that it's an *error of judgment* when a guy uses drugs and threats of violence to convince a stable of five young women and one omega to sleep with strangers for money that they then turn over to him, but apparently the Commonwealth felt differently at the time."

Ozzy flipped through the report. "Looks like he did real time for something in eighty-four." He poked at the paper. "Maybe that's when he started to expand outside of pimping?"

"Absolutely. Anyone making a new venture gets caught. He's still got his hand in there, for the record. I had two foster siblings who were caught up in his schemes. One got out. I think she's out in California now. The other one—well, Sierzant was his dad. So they weren't able to get him away completely, and Don didn't want them to." Ryan made a face. "He died fifteen years ago. OD." He sat up a little straighter in his chair.

Ozzy's jaw dropped to the floor. "He puts his own kids out on the street?"

"Oh yeah." Ryan snorted. "Without hesitation. It's all there in the file. Kerr will give you a different file, and it'll show you other things. I wouldn't mind taking a look, just to get a better sense of how guys like Sierzant operate, but you can go ahead and give Kerr this file when you've got what you need. If he's not your killer, Sierzant will do more time for the organized crime rap than he will for anything in here." Ryan ran his finger along the edge of the file, making a sound like shuffling cards.

Ozzy shook his head. "No wonder you're so cooperative."

"I'm cooperative because it's smart." Ryan grinned. "Except with Nenci. Look, though. I am a little bit disturbed by the fact that he decided to go after your omega here." He nodded toward Pete, who had dozed off in his chair.

Ozzy hung his head. "I need to keep him safe, Ryan."

"He is safe, Morris. He is safe. He might be more comfortable if you ask Nick to bring a cot from somewhere, though." He paused. "You really like him, huh?"

Ozzy sighed. He wasn't what he'd call friends with Ryan, but he liked the guy well enough. And Ryan had been the one to come up with a way to keep Pete safe. "I've never felt this way before," he said. "About anyone."

"That's awesome. Hang onto that. Don't let anyone, especially your own fears, talk you out of it."

Ozzy snorted. "You're not going to tell me to steer clear because of the baby?"

"Hell no." Ryan shook his head. "I'm obviously biased, but I think you should do what feels right to you. I mean, hell, you were this attracted to him when you knew he was pregnant. Imagine how you'll feel when he's yours."

Ozzy could almost taste it. He could see the bond between them, as clear as if it were already tangible. "You're a pretty smart guy."

"Right?" Ryan chortled. "Seriously, though. Hold on to this guy. He's pretty special."

"I will." Ozzy wrapped an arm around his sleeping omega's shoulders. "I'll hold him close and keep him safe."

Chapter Seven

Pete hid out in Ryan's office all day. He didn't think it was necessary. His own house was perfectly safe. He'd delivered the message that Sierzant had wanted him to deliver, and no wacky criminal elements should have much interest in targeting him at this point. He should be perfectly safe. At the same time, he had to admit that it was nice to have someone be so very concerned about his well-being.

He mentioned as much to Ryan, who snorted. "Right? It's a little hard to get used to at first, but it's nice. When we've been by ourselves for a while, it can be hard sometimes to adjust. Fitting another person into our lives, even when we really want to, isn't the easiest thing in the world." He put his hand on his baby bump. "I guess it's practice."

"Oh, you don't think he's really going to want to stick around once the baby's born!" Pete blushed.

"Do you want him around once the baby's born?" Ryan leaned back in his chair.

"Of course." Pete looked down. "He's amazing. I've never met anyone like him. But I won't be able to give him as much attention, and alphas like attention, and babies are loud and smell bad."

"Alphas also like family." Ryan put his hand over Pete's. "No one knows the future, not really, but I've spent a little time with Morris. And Nick, my alpha, he's always saying what a solid guy Morris is. If he says he wants to be around, then he'll be there."

All of this was heady stuff, and Pete was still reeling from lack of sleep and everything that had happened the night before. At the same time, he had to take Ryan's words seriously. Ryan knew what he was talking about.

Did he want Ozzy to be part of his life, and his daughter's? He didn't have to think about the answer to that one. It felt like fantasy, but there was no part of him that didn't want Ozzy there with him. He was more than willing for that fantasy to become a reality.

He didn't know how to broach the subject, and he decided as he sat through interviews in a small, crowded office that he didn't need to. If that was something that Ozzy wanted, Ozzy would be there. And if Ozzy changed his mind after the baby was born, then Pete would get over it but he would understand.

At the end of the workday, Ozzy drove Pete home. Pete's Subaru was there in the driveway; apparently the cops had brought it home at some point, after checking it for whatever it was they were afraid of. "I'm staying the night." There was no mistaking his tone. Pete had no choice in this. There was going to be a big, strapping, armed alpha in his house for the night whether or not Pete wanted him there.

Pete wanted him there. He brushed his fingers across Ozzy's cheeks. "Hell yeah you are." He gave his alpha half a grin. "I wouldn't have it any other way."

They headed inside. Pete wasn't up to cooking, and Ozzy wouldn't ask it of him, but he could reheat some of the things that he'd made ahead of time. They ate in silence, and then Pete cleared the dishes away. "All right," he said. "I'm going up to bed now. It's been a very long day, and I don't know how much longer I'll be able to keep my eyes open."

"I'll stay down here." Ozzy looked away. "You'll be safe."

Pete shook his head in exasperation. "Ozzy. I'll be safer if you're with me."

Realization dawned on Ozzy's face, but he closed his eyes. "Pete, I'm supposed to be protecting you. I can't do that if we're fooling around."

Pete took Ozzy's hand. "The neighborhood is safe. And Sierzant has no reason to come for me at this point, all right? I passed along his message, and that's the end of it. Besides," he ran the fingers of his hand along Ozzy's scalp, "I'll be even safer if you're right there with me, in the room. You can keep your gun on the nightstand."

"I should be better at resisting your blandishments," Ozzy grumbled. He stood up, though, and he was already unbuttoning his shirt as he stood. "God, Pete, the things you do to me."

They made their way upstairs. Pete led the way into the bedroom with a fine buzz of anticipation running just underneath his skin. Ozzy wasn't new to Pete's bedroom. He'd slept in this bed before, and more than once. They'd fooled around, explored one another's bodies, and done just about everything short of penetrative sex. This was the last frontier, the final gift that Pete had to give to his lover, and he could not wait to feel his alpha.

The sentiment was new to him. He was no stranger to sex, and sex had always been enjoyable to him, but it hadn't been specific. There had been men he liked. There had been men he wouldn't mind being with for a while, more than a night or two, and there had been men he'd been with for a few months at a time. There hadn't ever been a man he'd *needed* like this, no one whose mere scent could make the rest of the world fade away into nothingness.

He helped Ozzy off with his shirt and rubbed his face against the bare skin now revealed. He loved the feel of Ozzy's skin.

He loved Ozzy's scent, too, the way that his popcorn scent combined with his rising alpha musk to make Pete's mouth absolutely water.

He took one of Ozzy's nipples into his mouth. It was a bold move, he guessed; most omegas would wait to be encouraged. The little groan that his lover emitted, and the way that Ozzy's hands gripped at his ass, were enough encouragement for him. He applied just enough suction to get the point across, while using his hands to trace the lines of Ozzy's cut muscles.

Ozzy disengaged him after a little while. His pants were tented, and his eyes dark with lust. "Are you sure you want this?" he asked, his voice low and husky. He held Pete's wrists in an iron grip.

"I've never wanted anything more in my life." Pete wasn't kidding, either. Every fiber of his being wanted the man in front of him. He barely registered the room, or the temperature. His body thrummed with need—the need to please, the need to be filled. "I need you."

Ozzy let out a noise that was half moan, half growl. "Too many clothes," he told Pete.

Pete understood the implications of that statement. He stripped quickly and tossed his clothes over a chair. He'd deal with them later, maybe tomorrow. It was a matter of seconds before he stood before Ozzy, bare before his gaze.

Ozzy licked his lips, just once. "Look at you," he said and stepped into Pete's space. This close, his scent was almost a physical thing. He touched his lips to Pete's in reverence, and then with a guttural moan he claimed Pete's mouth with a searing kiss that almost made Pete forget his own name.

Pete let Ozzy herd him backward toward the bed. "I'm going to take such good care of you," Ozzy promised, as Pete sat on the edge of his bed and watched. "I'm going to make you feel better than you ever have before. That's a promise, baby. A promise, and an absolute fact. I'm going to blow your mind."

Ozzy put his service weapon on the nightstand and rummaged around for lube. He must have gone through Pete's things at some point, because he knew exactly where to look. He pulled out the lube, and then he pulled out a condom. "Do we need this?" He licked his lips again. "I'm clean. I've been tested."

"They test you when you get pregnant." Pete took a deep breath. "I'm clean." It would be more responsible of him to insist on using the condom, he knew. They hadn't agreed to be exclusive, and while Ozzy might be clean now he wouldn't necessarily stay that way. Right now, Pete didn't care. He trusted Ozzy. "Put it away. Please. I want to feel you, Ozzy. Alpha."

Ozzy made a half-feral sound and grabbed the lube. He slicked up his fingers and urged Pete to lie back. Ordinarily, Pete would want more foreplay than this. This was different. He could feel Ozzy's urgency, and it matched his own.

He relaxed when the first finger breeched him, looking up at the alpha he already thought of as his mate. He couldn't see much below Ozzy's sculpted upper abs, not with his own belly in the way, but that didn't matter. He'd seen Ozzy's magnificent cock. He'd held it in his hands. He could feel it brushing against his leg now as Ozzy slipped another finger inside of him, stretching him out so that he would be able to take him. His brain could put all of the pieces together just fine.

When Ozzy knew he was ready, he slicked himself up again and met Pete's eyes. "Are you sure that you want this?"

"Absolutely." Pete wrapped his legs around Ozzy's waist and pulled him closer. "Please, Alpha. Don't make me wait."

Ozzy grinned, a dark look full of promise. "Say it again."

"Don't make me wait?"

"Not that."

Pete pouted. "Please, Alpha!"

"That's it." Ozzy worked his way into Pete with short, shallow thrusts. "I like the way that sounds."

Pete smiled, but he didn't say anything. Ozzy wasn't a small guy, and letting him in took concentration even with adequate prep and plenty of desire. Once Ozzy was fully seated, though, Pete smiled up at him. "That feels amazing, Alpha." He gave a happy sigh. "I wish you could feel what I feel, having you inside of me like this."

Ozzy's face seemed to be suffused with a kind of inner light when Pete addressed him as Alpha. He gazed down at Pete in naked wonder until Pete told him to move. Then he snapped his hips back and took Pete on the ride of his life.

Pete wasn't a clock watcher, unless the sex was truly terrible. Sex lasted as long as it lasted, and as long as they both had a good time that was all that there really needed to be to it. He would much rather lose himself in the rhythm that his alpha set up for him. Ozzy set up an easy pace, not quite gentle but not as vigorous as Pete had expected. Pete didn't mind; not only did that show consideration for his condition and his exhaustion, but it allowed Ozzy to hit his sweet spot more reliably than if he were just jackhammering away like so many men.

When Ozzy lost the rhythm, Pete snaked a hand between his own legs and gave himself a few tugs. They came more or less together, and Pete might have been driven to it without the help just by the sight of Alpha's face alone. His head was thrown back as he released into Pete, the flush of exertion and arousal going from his face right down to his collarbone. He looked like he was lost in ecstasy.

Ozzy stood there for a moment, collecting his breath. Then he staggered into the bathroom to get a washcloth, so that he could clean them up. When he came back, he carefully moved Pete over to the other side of the bed, so that he would be closer to his service weapon, and wrapped himself around Pete.

"I love you," he murmured into Pete's ear.

"I love you too," Pete told him, murmuring words thick with sleep. "You're my Alpha."

Pete felt Ozzy's smile against the back of his neck. "Damn straight I am."

Pete drifted off to sleep in his lover's arms.

The next day, Ozzy went back to work. He declared himself to be uncomfortable leaving Pete alone, but he knew that he had to get over it. "The alpha in me wants to keep you where I can see you until the threat is past," he explained over coffee. "The sensible human being in me knows that you're right. The neighborhood is safe, you're a grown man, and I've already asked Sudbury PD to keep an extra eye on your house for me."

"Seriously?" Pete chuckled and blushed. He could still feel everything from the night before, but it was a good kind of sore—the kind he would have gotten after a workout. It had been a while since he'd moved his body in quite that way, after all.

"Well yeah. You were a witness to a violent crime, man. That's even before one of the biggest crime bosses in Worcester came to chat with you about an investigation into a dead cop, that looks like it's going to involve dirty cops. Like I said, I want to keep you safe." He squeezed Pete's hand. "You're the most important person in my world, Pete. Never doubt that, even for a minute."

After he left, Pete sat down to get back to work. He didn't exactly doubt his alpha's words. He knew that he was important to Ozzy. He couldn't disbelieve the evidence of his own eyes, after all! But he couldn't bring himself to believe that this magnificent alpha would feel the same way once the baby was born.

Well, he would find out. There was nothing Pete could do either way to influence his lover's decision, so he would have to accept whatever Ozzy chose. In a way, it was kind of freeing. Pete would do what he always did, go about his life in the usual way, and if Ozzy chose to remain in it then he would be delighted.

He went through his checklist of preparations for the baby. Her room was almost ready. He just had a few more things to get, and they were probably things that he could live without. He had plenty of clothes, and cute little toys, waiting for her. All that remained was for her to get here.

And he needed a name. Osmundia was right out. He did wonder if there would be another way to honor Ozzy with the name. Would that be pathetic, naming his child after a guy? Would it only be pathetic if he named the baby after Ozzy if Ozzy bailed?

Marissa. It wasn't a name that had a lot of resonance within Pete's family, and no one would ever know that he'd chosen it because it sounded vaguely like Ozzy's last name. Maybe it was ridiculous to name his daughter after his new boyfriend—*his Alpha*—but the name itself wasn't obviously related to Ozzy at all.

"Marissa." He put his hand on his baby bump and smiled as the baby kicked back at him. Apparently she liked it. Marissa it was.

...

Ozzy spent Friday morning trying to come down from his high. There weren't words in the English language for the way Pete made him feel. The sex had been incredible, of course. He'd known that it would be, whenever they got around to actually doing it. What he hadn't understood was the way that being there, being buried deep inside Pete, would cement his feelings so thoroughly.

He'd known that he wanted to be with Pete. He'd known it for a while now. He'd suspected it since their first kiss, and he'd been pretty sure since he'd had that fight with his parents. Now Ozzy knew for sure. His life would never be complete without Pete's presence.

And if Pete was calling him Alpha, Ozzy could be fairly certain that he felt the same way.

He tried to hunker down at his desk in the hopes of dimming the joyful glow that he knew had to be coming from his person. They could have lit half of Framingham from his happiness, but he couldn't do anything about it right now. He couldn't claim his love now. He had to wait until the baby was born, and until Pete had recovered. And he had to get Sierzant off the streets.

Once he'd come down from his buzz, he forced himself to focus on the problem at hand. He had people researching the dirty cops, which was good. Ozzy wanted to focus on Sierzant's side of the equation. He wanted to know every place he'd been, and everything he'd done, during the whole of 1996.

He had a lot of digging to do. The first link between Sierzant and Harbaugh that Ozzy could find was tenuous at best. Harbaugh was the arresting officer when Sierzant was arrested on a procuring charge back in 1995, but that didn't mean anything. Ozzy had arrested dozens of pimps, and he knew plenty of other guys who had done the same. Sierzant had, moreover, been arrested several times, on the same charges no less, and not once had the cop in question wound up with a bullet in the back of his head.

One was dead, but that had been ruled to be a result of "lifestyle factors." His liver gave out back in 2002.

Still, the connection existed. It was the only link, and Ozzy was going to have to go with it for now.

He spent the weekend with Pete, of course. He didn't want to leave him alone and unprotected, and he didn't want to spend much time away from him either. He did take a little time to take his bike out on the Assabet River Rail Trail, because he couldn't make himself stay indoors the whole weekend. The ride wasn't exactly thrilling; the trail was asphalt and lacked any serious test of his mountain biking abilities. It still got him outside and let him move around a little.

Maybe after the baby was born he'd put a child seat on the back and take her out there.

The idea gave Ozzy something to think about as he sped down the former rail line. Would Pete let him play a paternal role? Would he actually be allowed to treat the little girl like his own? He didn't care that his own genes hadn't gone into making her. All he cared about was making sure that the baby and her father had the best possible life.

What would Pete want, though?

It would be best to iron out all of these things before the birth, and before the claiming. That way, the claim couldn't influence

Pete's feelings, or interfere with his ability to give consent. The absolute last thing Ozzy wanted to do was interfere with Pete's ability to give consent.

He went back to work during the week with a new approach to take with regards to Sierzant. He couldn't go after Sierzant directly, of course. He had no real evidence, and he certainly didn't want to send Sierzant after Pete again. What he could do, though, was talk to someone who almost certainly knew him.

He paid a visit to Ryan, who pretended to grumble but already had the pages printed out. Then he went and called up Jeff Balsalmo's lawyer. He explained himself quickly: he wasn't looking to implicate Balsalmo in the case he was investigating. He simply wanted to follow up on how the gun had gotten into his hands, none of which would affect the outcome of his trial.

The lawyer, MacDonald, admitted that he was uncomfortable with it but agreed to the meeting anyway. "I get that there isn't a lot of likelihood that Jeff's getting out of this unscathed. I just want to minimize the damage."

Ozzy called over to the Middlesex County Jail, where Balsalmo was being held until his trial, and made the half hour drive up to Billerica. Once there, he went through all of the arduous procedures in place to keep the inmates, staff, and visitors safe, and then followed a guard into the interview room to wait for Balsalmo and MacDonald.

Balsalmo had been locked up for close to a month now, and it hadn't done good things for him. His hair had gotten downright greasy, and his skin had gone from pale to waxen. He sneered at both Ozzy and at MacDonald before submitting to the shackles that kept him in his seat. "To what do I owe the pleasure, boys?"

Ozzy raised an eyebrow. "You're not even old enough to shave yet."

"Doesn't matter." Balsalmo leaned back in his seat and smirked. "Way I see it, we wouldn't be having this conversation if I didn't have something you needed. You're my boys, until I say so. Maybe I should put it in words you can better understand." He cackled, low and dirty. "You're my bitches. Now dance, monkeys. Dance for me."

Ozzy exchanged glances with MacDonald, who shrugged. Ozzy guessed he could see why the lawyer wasn't making much progress with his client. It was a crying shame, though. "Mr. Balsalmo, I came here to talk to you about the gun that you used in the robbery."

"There's no proof that I used a gun." Balsalmo folded his hands together.

"Dude, I was there. I saw you. A bank full of people saw you. The video camera saw you." Ozzy blinked his eyes in disbelief. Had he stepped into the Twilight Zone or something?

No, he was here in the real world. MacDonald bowed his head and pinched the bridge of his nose. "Jeff, we've talked about this. Pretending that those witnesses weren't there, or that the evidence doesn't exist, isn't going to make it go away. Your best bet—"

"Is to fire your ass and find me a lawyer who's going to get me out of this dump." Balsalmo slouched in his seat and crossed his arms over his chest.

"Is to be honest, emphasize your youth, and admit that you've never knocked over a bank before," MacDonald continued, as though his client hadn't spoken. "Everyone saw you with the gun. *Everyone saw you.* Your prints are on the gun. The bank robbery by itself is a federal crime, genius. The murder during the commission of a federal crime? My goal here is to keep you away from the needle." He glowered at his client. "Talking to the cop about the gun will actually help your cause."

Balsalmo pouted. "But I hate cops!"

"It's okay." Ozzy managed to grin. "I hate teenage bank robbers, but I think we can all put our differences aside and come up with a win-win that works for everyone. That's why we have lawyers, right?" He forced a jovial laugh, when inside he was screaming. This guy was still only nineteen years old, and he was already looking at serious federal time. He didn't seem to recognize it, either. Maybe he just didn't care.

"What do you know about the gun?"

Balsalmo squirmed. "Look, that's one of those things that I feel like I probably shouldn't answer. On account of the Third Amendment."

MacDonald closed his eyes and palmed his face. "Fifth Amendment."

"Fifth? Are you sure?"

"The Third means that you aren't required to put soldiers up in your home without your consent during peacetime. You're homeless, Jeff. It doesn't apply to you anyway. Trust me, it's the Fifth. I'm your lawyer. I know things." MacDonald had a little twitch, right under his left eye.

"Oh. Okay. Then I'm not answering that because of the Fifth Amendment."

"Fine." Ozzy huffed in frustration. "You do get that I'm not on that case, right?"

"You're not?" Balsalmo tried to scratch his head and failed, thanks to the shackles restraining him to the table.

"No. That's the FBI, man. I'm working a case that went cold before you were born. The gun you used killed a cop." Ozzy showed him a picture of Harbaugh.

Balsalmo looked at the picture. "I mean, it's one less cop on the streets, so awesome, but it's nothing to me. It's a gun that gets passed around sometimes, okay? I use it, other people use it, and it's all good." He mustered a cocky grin. "I don't suppose I'm getting it back? It's something of a family heirloom."

A hunch made itself known to Ozzy then. He opened up Balsalmo's file. "Family heirloom, huh? That's interesting. I noticed that you were removed from your family at a young age, Mr. Balsalmo."

Balsalmo twitched. "We stayed in touch."

"That's good. It's good for families to stay as close as they can in this day and age. Of course, that didn't exactly keep you out of trouble, did it? I wonder if anything would have. I think we have that in common, at least. Of course, I let it out by fighting and a bad attention span. You... well, you did your fair share of fighting, it looks like. And you had a few run-ins for prostitution, too."

Balsalmo stiffened. "So?"

MacDonald turned to Ozzy. "I don't see where it's relevant. That was a long time ago."

Ozzy held up his hands. "Hey, no judging. I mean, yeah, it's illegal, but a person does what they have to. No, what interests me about the whole... thing..." He circled his hand, since the kid was obviously bothered by the old record. He might loathe this guy, but he still needed him, and he had plenty of real sins to shame him for. "What interests me about that particular period of your life is that you were working for someone."

"Most of us were." Balsalmo's words were clipped and harsh. His eyes were as hard as stone.

"According to the records, you were working for a guy by the name of Sierzant." Ozzy leaned forward. "As it happens, Sierzant and that gun are the only two parts of my cold case that link back to the modern era."

A bead of sweat ran down Balsalmo's face. He froze for a moment, and then he curled his lip. "What, you think that out of all of his stable he confided in me?" His words were brave, but his tone was quiet.

"Did Sierzant give you the gun, Jeff?" MacDonald watched his client through hooded eyes. "You're a smart guy. I don't have to tell you that it would be in your best interests to say so."

Balsalmo slammed his hands down on the table. "Dude, this goes way beyond some kind of Fifth Amendment crap, all right? We're talking about how you could put me in solitary, for the rest of my life, in a bulletproof vest, and I still wouldn't be safe. I go giving up Sierzant and there's no cell, no safe house, no hiding spot in the world that can keep me safe. You think he'll cut me a break, give me an easier time of it just because I'm his kid? Nah. He might make it faster. Then again, he might draw it out, just because he expected better."

Neither Ozzy nor MacDonald said anything. They didn't have to. Balsalmo's harsh, angry breaths said enough. The buzz of the fluorescent lamp made a perfect counterpoint—irritating, and inexorable. Then Ozzy spoke. "He sent you into that bank."

Balsalmo huffed out a little laugh. "So what? I said yes. I planned it. I cased it out, I picked the backup. It was my job."

"Your old man is going to let you rot. He put you out on the streets, and he sent you in to rob a bank, and now he's going to let you rot. For him. Tell me, Balsalmo, has he ever done anything for you, anything good, to make you so goddamn loyal that you would take a needle for him?" Ozzy met Balsalmo's eyes and held them. "I mean, did he take you to a game at Fenway, or down to Foxboro at least? Help you with your homework? Save you from drowning? What?"

"You don't understand!" Balsalmo shook his head. "You don't understand what happens to snitches."

"We can keep you safe, Balsalmo." Ozzy leaned back.

Balsalmo closed his eyes. His whole face was covered in a sheen of sweat, glistening in the bad lighting like glitter. "He gave me the gun," he said, after several minutes. "He gave me the gun, and he told me that it was a *lucky* gun. That's what he called it. *Lucky*." He snorted and shook his head, rattling his chains. "Have you ever heard of a gun being lucky? I mean, that's got to be one of the dumbest things I've ever heard in my life."

Ozzy privately agreed. "I'll tell you what—that gun was hugely lucky for you."

"How?" Balsalmo held his hands up. "I'm in a jumpsuit, in jail, waiting for a trial that even Crackerjack here thinks I can't win."

Ozzy stood up. "Well, for starters, you could be looking at a needle. We'll get you an affidavit, you'll sign it, you'll testify in court, and you'll be looking at a safe life with health care and three squares a day instead of hoping that the docs didn't go for off-brand drugs. The rest, I guess, is kind of up to you."

MacDonald followed him out of the room. "Do you really think that he'll escape the death penalty for this?"

Ozzy sighed. "I'm not a prosecutor. I'll talk to the feds; I'll talk to the prosecutor if I can. I think it should certainly count for something, right?"

MacDonald blew out a breath. "Yeah. Normally. Not when the guy he shot was a defenseless old man."

"He gave us evidence against a cop killer. I have to hope that it counts for something."

"Me too." MacDonald returned to the interview room to talk to his client.

Ozzy commandeered a workstation to type up an affidavit, and Balsalmo signed it that day. It would be best if he testified in open court, of course, but things had a way of happening in organized crime cases. This way, if Balsalmo were suddenly no longer available to testify, they would still have his words to present in court.

Ozzy felt pretty good as he headed into the rest of his week. Soon, Pete would be safe.

Chapter Eight

Pete liked Sunday mornings. He loved to linger over breakfast. In the two weeks since he and Ozzy had finally made love for the first time, lingering over breakfast had become even more pleasant. They could sit and stare at one another over pancakes, or they could discuss newspaper articles over eggs and toast. The important thing was being together and alone, and in peace.

When he heard a car pull into his driveway, he was less than enthusiastic about visitors. He didn't think that reaching for a gun was necessarily the appropriate reaction, though. "Oh would you put that away?" he asked, shaking his head. "It's probably my mother or my brother."

Ozzy scowled in the direction of the driveway. "You're joking, right? They'd have called before they dropped in on a Sunday morning." He lowered the gun, but didn't put it away. "What if you weren't wearing any pants?"

Pete chortled. "Then it would serve them right for showing up unannounced, now, wouldn't it?" He heaved himself out of his chair and waddled over to Ozzy's seat, brushing a kiss across his cheek. "Especially now. I'm the size of a house."

"Hey. You're growing a whole new human being. She needs space to develop. Pretty soon you'll get your body back, and it's all going to be good." Ozzy pulled him down for a loving kiss that Pete would have loved to deepen, if it weren't interrupted by the doorbell.

"I'll get this." Ozzy set his features into a grim sort of scowl as he jumped up and headed toward the door.

Pete frowned. Was loving a cop always like this? Or would it get better once Sierzant was behind bars?

He stayed behind Ozzy, and a little behind the door, until Ozzy answered. He didn't think that there was any cause for alarm, but he wanted to make Ozzy comfortable. When the door opened, though, he rethought his plan of coming out and greeting his guest.

"Can I help you?" Ozzy kept his gun hidden behind the door.

"Who are you?" Angus didn't have the good grace to be afraid, or even concerned. He just scoffed and tried to push his way in. "Who are you, and why are you in my brother's house? Pete? Pete!"

Ozzy blocked his way. "You're not going anywhere until you tell me who you are and what the hell you're doing here."

Pete stepped in. He didn't want Ozzy to shoot his brother, whatever they'd said to one another as children. "Ozzy, it's okay. This is my brother, Angus. Angus, this is my alpha, Ozzy."

Ozzy put his gun away while Angus looked Ozzy up and down like a piece of meat. "Well. Hot cop stuck around, I see. That's sweet, I guess. Anyway, go put on something more suitable, would you? You're late for your baby shower."

"My what?" Pete wrinkled his nose. "There's no baby shower."

Angus rolled his eyes and gave an affected sigh. "Don't be ridiculous, Pete. Of course there's a baby shower, and it's today. Come on, you don't want to keep Mother waiting."

Ozzy turned to Pete. "Who throws a baby shower and doesn't consult the person having the baby?"

Angus scoffed and stuffed his hands into his pockets. "It isn't like he had anything better to do with his time anyway. Go and get dressed, Pete. Now!"

"Hold up." Ozzy frowned. "He's not going anywhere without me. Not someplace I don't know." He glanced at Pete.

Pete met his eyes, and Pete read his mate's real intent there. Ozzy wasn't that kind of possessive, controlling alpha. Not by a long shot. He was, however, defensive of his omega. More than that, he could see that Pete's family might not be the friendliest right now. He wanted to give Pete his options, whether it was to stay at home or to go into hostile territory with backup.

A wave of adoration swept over Pete. What kind of man put himself out there like that, volunteering to suffer through a baby shower with a bunch of people who definitely didn't care for him?

"Let's go get changed," he said after a moment. "It's not how I planned to spend my Sunday, but if people want to give Marissa things, I suppose that I should be there to accept them. What about you?"

"With everything going on, I'm not comfortable having you at an insecure site full of strangers when it takes you five minutes to get up off the couch." The corners of Ozzy's mouth twitched as Angus' jaw dropped in outrage.

"Our house is perfectly secure! It's gated, for crying out loud!"

"It's also going to be full of people, any one of whom may be compromised. There's a lot going on right now, stuff that you don't necessarily know about, Anus—"

"Angus," Angus corrected, flushing red. Pete tried not to laugh.

"Angus." Ozzy kept a straight face. "But I'm not just his alpha, I'm a cop, and I'm going to keep him safe while he can't do it for himself. Good talk." He patted Angus on the shoulder, closed the door behind him, and followed Pete up the stairs.

"Don't go messing with my stuff," Pete called as they climbed, an echo back to their childhood.

"Bite me," Angus retorted, from somewhere closer to the kitchen.

Once they were upstairs, Ozzy closed the door behind them and turned to face Pete. "You get this isn't normal, right? Normal people don't decide to throw a baby shower and forget to invite the parent." He rummaged through the closet until he found one of his suits from work. More and more of his things had migrated over to Pete's house over the past few weeks, but that just made sense. He was over here more often than not.

Pete grabbed for a suit of his own. He'd gotten a couple for pregnancy, just in case he needed them. "Welcome to Clan Nolan. They honestly think I spend my days sitting around eating bon bons." He started to change. "You don't have to come if you don't want to. I know you weren't necessarily impressed with my mom the last time you met; I don't think it's going to get much better in a house full of her clones."

"Then I'm absolutely coming." He huffed out a laugh. "She thinks you're slumming it, doesn't she?"

"Well, you're not the old-money CEO she wanted me mated to, so kind of." Pete shrugged. "But you're the one I want, so I guess she'll have to get over it." He gave his alpha a quick peck on the cheek. "I'm sorry if you'll be uncomfortable there; I can't do anything about them."

"I know. And trust me. I've been through worse."

"But not for me." Pete looked away. "I mean, not for me specifically. But we'll get through it."

Ozzy grabbed for his hand. "Did you really decide to name the baby Marissa?"

Pete blushed. "Well, Osmundia sounds dumb."

Ozzy's eyes widened. "But Marissa sounds like Morris." He nodded, and then he blushed a deep red. "That's the sweetest thing anyone's ever done for me." He wrapped Pete up in his arms. "I don't suppose we can tell your brother to go screw off and maybe stay up here all day?"

Pete laughed. The temptation was certainly there, and the desire strong. How could he really say no when it was all he'd wanted all morning? "We should go," he sighed, hand lingering on Ozzy's chest. "Otherwise my mom will come here, and she won't be nearly as easy to get rid of."

Ozzy shuddered. "Not the moment when I really wanted to see her face." He chuckled and moved away, and they both got dressed.

Angus tried to force them to ride in the car he'd secured from their mother, but Ozzy was adamant. No one was driving Pete around but him, or Pete himself. Once they were ensconced in Ozzy's Jeep, he openly admitted that he'd done that just so they could make a hasty retreat if they needed to. "Every day I love you a little bit more," Pete told him.

They headed to Weston, a twenty-two minute drive that was actually very pretty if Pete didn't let himself think about where they were going. Trees were just starting to show their buds, and the forsythias had started to turn yellow. The world was coming to life again after a long winter, and it felt good. Maybe the shower wouldn't be so bad. Maybe there wouldn't be so much judgment, or blame. Maybe it would just be a nice, small get-together.

"Did you even register for anything?" Ozzy asked him as they crossed the town line into Weston.

"No." Pete leaned his head on the glass.

"I see."

"I wasn't thinking about a shower." Pete winced. "It just never occurred to me." He thumped his head against the headrest. "I'm going to get fifty-seven silver spoons and not a single diaper pail, aren't I?"

Ozzy grabbed his hand. "Sweetheart, you already have two diaper pails."

"I know." Pete waved a hand irritably. "It's the principle of the thing."

They pulled up into the circular drive in front of Pete's mother's house, followed closely by the car carrying Angus. "I feel like I'm in a fire lane," Ozzy grumbled, and tugged on his collar. "Is this really the house where you grew up?"

Oh. Crap. "Uh, yes?"

"Like, the whole thing?" Ozzy's eyes dragged across the front of the house.

"Well, yeah." Pete blushed. "I don't live there now, though."

"No. No you don't." Ozzy shook his head, as if to clear it, and then gave Pete a peck on the cheek. Angus made gagging sounds that Pete could hear through the window. "I guess we'd better go inside before your brother makes himself throw up for real." He got out of the Jeep, circled around it, and then helped Pete out of the car. Angus led the way into the house and into the Blue Parlor.

To his credit, Ozzy showed no awe at the furnishings, nor at the size of the house. He nodded at the occasional staff member who looked at him or greeted Pete and stayed by

Pete's side. When they got into the Blue Parlor, he offered Pete his arm and met Cynthia's eyes squarely.

Pete's mother rose from her chair near a marble-topped side table. She wore a pale blue pantsuit with a hat set at a jaunty angle. "Peter," she said, striding forward to give him a cool hug and air kisses. "Glad you could make it to your own shower."

Pete just smiled and shook his head. "If I'd known in advance, I might have been a little better prepared. I might have even had a registry."

"Hah!" She turned to look at the two women with whom she'd been conversing. "A registry. As if we've ever used such a thing. Please. You remember Laura Sienkiewicz, of course, and Agnes Legrand."

Pete smiled at them. "Of course. How could I forget? Ozzy, these are dear friends of my mothers. She knows them from her work with the horse sanctuary up the road. Laura, Agnes, this is my alpha, Ozzy."

Cynthia wrinkled her nose, just a little. Pete probably wouldn't have noticed if he hadn't been looking.

"Charmed." Ozzy shook hands and shot Pete a look of confusion.

People started to trickle in, and hired catering staff circulated with hors d'oeuvres and mocktails for all. Everything, from the drinks down to the last crumb of food, was pink. For a moment, Pete almost regretted having told his mother that he was having a girl.

Then Ozzy touched his arm, and he got over it. The food, while pink, was exquisite. He enjoyed his strawberry smoothie so much he had another one. His mother had enough good sense not to have tried to force party games onto everyone, but then again that wasn't really Cynthia's style anyway.

None of the guests were people that Pete was all that close with. He knew some of them. Most of them were unknown, friends of his mother's through one organization or another. The shower was less a celebration of Marissa's impending arrival than an excuse for Cynthia to throw a themed party for all of her friends, and the knowledge stung just a little bit.

Pete tried not to take it personally. After all, Cynthia was Cynthia, and he wasn't about to change her at this late date. At least he and Ozzy got some free fancy food out of it, and he got a picture of the adorable cake with the mouse topper to show Marissa when she was old enough to be interested in that sort of thing.

Some of the guests were people that he knew, of course. His aunts on both sides put in an appearance, although Pete wished they'd stayed home and polished their hair or whatever they did. One of them, Pete's father's Aunt Isabella, made a point of approaching Ozzy. "So. Cynthia tells me that you're supposed to be Peter's new alpha, hm?"

"That's the plan." Ozzy gave her a polite little smile, and Pete knew that this encounter was only going to go downhill.

"Hm. And you're a policeman."

"Yep. Detective, to be precise about it. Also a retired captain in the United States Army. And you are?" Ozzy kept that polite smile on his face.

"My ancestors were on the Mayflower." Isabella drew herself up to her full height, all four foot ten of her. "Which means that *his* ancestors were on the Mayflower. He could have had the son of a President!"

"Oh, Isabella." Cynthia sailed over before Isabella could cause a scene. "Are you on about that again? Dear me, that's so fourteen years ago. His father would never have allowed that; the age difference was too great. I may not be thrilled about the whole pregnancy outside of a claim aspect of things, but I'm quite content that he didn't wind up with that dried up old pervert anyway." She waved a hand. "Things happen for a reason, dear."

Isabella narrowed her eyes at Cynthia. She couldn't attack Cynthia on pedigree; Pete knew that his mother could claim descent from Queen Victoria. "Be that as it may," the older woman drawled, "I find it difficult to believe that you, of all people, would ever accept a policeman into the family."

"My dear, if he takes care of my son and my granddaughter I don't care if he's a detective, a garbage man, or a stripper." Cynthia sipped at her drink. "I certainly wanted him to choose from a family that we knew when he was younger, but he decided to go his own way. Tearing our hair out because he didn't elope with a man old enough to be his father seems a little counterproductive, doesn't it?"

"Hmph!" Isabella went storming off, and Pete picked his jaw up off the floor.

"Thanks, Mom," he said, staring after his aunt.

She grimaced. "The old bat had it coming. She's trying to fix Angus up with a woman who's my age."

Pete winced. "Well, if it's love…"

"She's a lesbian, Peter. Isabella's a busybody." Her eyes snapped over to Ozzy, whose eyes had gone a little wild. "Look, it's not going to get any better than that for a lot of people. Some people can't let go of their prejudices, I'm afraid."

Ozzy straightened up. "I don't care about that. I care about Pete, and about Marissa."

The vaguest of smiles crossed Cynthia's features, and she patted Pete's arm. "There now." And she walked back to the gathering.

...

Ozzy wasn't entirely sure how to feel about the events of Pete's baby shower. He knew that Cynthia didn't like or care for him, and had known it since they'd met. To have her spring to his defense like that seemed just a little bit like flipping a switch. He couldn't help but suspect that it had less to do with himself, or with Pete, and a lot more to do with scoring points against the old bat who thought they were still living in the 1920s.

He'd known that Pete came from money, too. At least he'd known it intellectually, although it was hard to reconcile that vague, theoretical knowledge with the reality of a guy who worked hard, lived frugally, and dressed in cheap and sensible clothes most of the time. What could Ozzy possibly offer Pete?

Pete was more than happy to reassure him of his place in Pete's life. "You offer me you. You protect me. You make me smile, and you make me feel more complete than anyone ever has before. If I wanted that kind of life, or even that kind of house, I'd have it. I chose to live here, like this, long before I met you, my love. Believe me, I'm not about to start pushing you to bring me home a Benz."

They had a good laugh together over some of the gifts that Pete's mother's friends had given Pete and Marissa. Some of them were very thoughtful, like the diaper bag that looked like a laptop bag and wasn't covered in flowers or other "mommy" crap. Others were the more typical clothing sets, some more practical than others. In the privacy of Pete's house, they could share a chuckle about how people who bought dry-clean clothes for babies had probably never had to do laundry, or manage their own baby, in their lives.

Some of the gifts were generous, if not particularly of interest to an infant. Some guests had given the baby various financial products, like shares in exchange traded funds or long-term bonds. The sums involved weren't inconsiderable—Isabella the Old Bat had put ten grand into bonds for Marissa—and Ozzy figured that she would appreciate them someday. Of course, that day was far away, but whatever.

The spoons, though, those were bizarre. "Is the silver even safe for her?" he asked Pete, as they looked down at the array of silver spoons that had been given to Pete's baby girl. "I mean, what exactly is she supposed to do with them? Has the metal been mixed with something dangerous, like lead? I don't know."

Pete grinned at him. "We'll just put these aside. I guess if we find that Sudbury is being menaced by werewolves we'll know exactly how to handle it, right?"

The jewelry, too, struck Ozzy as distinctly odd. A baby didn't need a string of pearls, damn it. He supposed that it was a very nice, high-quality string of pearls, insofar as he knew about such things, but a baby would just chew on it and probably wreck it. Those had both men shaking their heads, but they just agreed to put the jewelry into a safe deposit box once it had been put onto the insurance and moved on.

All that laughter would have to carry Ozzy well into the new week at work. He arrived on Monday morning to find himself summonsed to a meeting with Lt. Devlin. When he got to the meeting he found himself at a table not only with his own supervisor, but with Ed Amos from Internal Affairs and with a tall, thin, fairly butch-looking woman in a dark red pantsuit.

"Detective Morris." Lt. Devlin showed him to a seat near his right hand. "Have a donut. You remember Lt. Amos, of course. I want you to meet Lt. Eliza Ryley, from Worcester PD's Internal Affairs department."

Ozzy shook Lt. Ryley's hand before sitting down and helping himself to a donut. "Worcester Internal Affairs. I see."

"When you noticed the pattern about questionable finances with some former state troopers, I did a little digging." Amos squirmed. "And some of those former troopers wound up transferring over to Worcester PD before they retired. I gave Lt. Ryley a call, and we had a little chat."

"Then I did some digging." Ryley made a face. "It's not good."

Ozzy paused with the donut halfway to his mouth. "To be honest, it was Nenci who pointed out the money. I just noticed that everyone who was associated with the deceased was no longer on the force."

"Well, it's your case. You're still the one who noticed something was wrong." Devlin grinned. "The thing is, because you noticed that, because you picked up on the pattern, the case has blossomed beyond a cold case murder of one man and moved into a large scale investigation of corruption of two law enforcement agencies. I don't have to tell you what that means."

"Internal Affairs officers aren't popular cops, Detective." Amos took a sip of his coffee. "I've been threatened. I've been attacked. I had a guy from the bomb squad try to blow up my car because I was investigating claims of sexual harassment against him. If we pursue this, it's going to get very ugly for you."

Ryley cleared her throat. "This corruption… I have no reason to think that it's ended just because Harbaugh's dead.

Sierzant's power and reach has only grown, and he couldn't have done that without some collusion."

Ozzy groaned. "No. He couldn't have." He hung his head. "I'm not going to lie. I'm nervous. Not for myself—I've faced down worse—but for my omega. He's going to have a baby in maybe six weeks. I'm worried about him." Then he picked his head up. "I'm worried about his safety, but the best way to keep him safe is to put this scumbag away. Put them all away, really."

"I told you he was smart." Devlin winked. "Now. Let's come up with a plan of attack. If we can cut the head off of the snake before your handsome photographer brings his bundle of joy into the world, that would be super."

Amos grimaced. "Man, I hate this. I get that it has to be done. I do. I just—I get that sometimes a cop or two steps out of line and needs to be reminded of what he's supposed to be here for. Sometimes the stresses of the job get to him. We don't see anyone on a good day, you know? Even when we show up to help them, it's not like they're in a state to be appreciative of that. You're not able to sit there and think, *Oh, I'd better be nice to this guy* when your arm's off, right? And that's fine. That's part of the job. But dirty cops—that's something I hate even thinking about, you know?"

"I hear you." Ryley gave a heavy sigh. "Everyone has their price, though, right? If you know what their breaking point is, and you have the means to reach it, it isn't that hard. And Sierzant is good at that. We see it in his dealings with civilians in organized crime all the time. They think they'd never do x, or y, and he makes them an offer or he puts the pressure on just the right way and *bam*. Next thing you know they're just as dirty as everyone else. I met a priest who became a fence of stolen goods because Sierzant promised to keep his church open." She shrugged, hands spread wide. "Who knows what it would take to make someone break like that?"

"You know, I try not to judge." Ozzy shuddered. "You know that Sierzant put his own kids out on the street?" He snapped his fingers. "We can try to talk to Balsalmo again. I don't know if it would work. He's got a thing about snitching, and he's more terrified of Sierzant than of anyone else alive. Maybe now that he's already snitched once he'll be more willing to open up."

"It's worth a shot." Ryley nodded, hazel eyes alight with respect. "I'll get my people to work looking for proof about the transfers in from state, and see how far the contagion spread. I want to know if it kept going once that initial crew retired or if it's still a problem."

"Like an apprenticeship." Amos made a face, like he'd just bitten into something unpleasant. "I'll work on it on my end. We'll meet up here in another week and see what we've come up with."

"Sounds good." Devlin shook hands with his counterparts, and everyone was dismissed. The other Cold Case detectives fell on the donuts like starving men, and Ozzy got to work.

It took until Thursday before Ozzy could get in to see Balsalmo, time that he spent fretting worse than he had since the eve of his first deployment. He'd been in danger before. He sought danger, chased it in the hopes of getting that high that he craved so badly. This was different. This was that moment of fear, the terror of standing on the cliff just before the jump, without the safety harness or the hang glider or the parachute.

The difference, of course, was Pete. Ozzy wouldn't pay the consequences if this went bad. If Sierzant or his team decided to try to bring Ozzy to heel, they wouldn't go after Ozzy. They'd go after the "soft" target of Pete or Marissa. He'd meant every word he'd said, about taking down Sierzant, but that didn't mean that things couldn't go sideways in a heartbeat.

Ozzy had no idea how to process these feelings. He wasn't sure he wanted to know, either.

He went to the prison on Thursday and met up with MacDonald. Together, they went to visit Balsalmo. The teenaged murderer looked a little better than he had the last time that Ozzy had seen him, although his pallor still made him look waxen. "Well well well, if it isn't the finest piece of fuzz that the state has to offer." Balsalmo's swagger was back, and so was his sneer. "What can you possibly have to ask little old me?"

Ozzy rolled his eyes. "We've got some questions for you about Sierzant's operation."

Balsalmo chuckled. "Buddy, even if I were of a mind to talk to you about the inner workings of his operation—which I am not—I couldn't. He doesn't confide in guys like me, okay? He gives orders, and I take them. Because I know my job."

Ozzy snorted. "I'm not looking for trade secrets here. We already know that he had cops on the payroll."

"Yeah, so?"

"What did he do with them?" Ozzy spread his hands out wide. "Come on, man. Answering that won't get you into any kind of trouble."

MacDonald acknowledged this with a nod of his head. "It's true. It's got nothing to do with you."

"Maybe not in court. That's like hardcore snitching." Balsalmo's face twisted. "He uses cops for all kinds of things, okay? Uses them for research. Uses them to get info about his rivals, who might be planning something. Uses them to move stuff around the city, because no one's going to pull over a goddamn cruiser and search it, right?" He chuckled, a dark note coming into his voice. "Sometimes they'll do jobs for him, too."

Ozzy's mouth went dry. "Like… like a hit?"

"Sure. Not often, though. More often, though, it'll be like… say he's got a ho who's trying to get away. Or say there's a girl who's out on her own, not working for nobody. He'll send a cop out to go get her. She gets a choice. She can work for Joe, or she can take a dirt nap. The cop will pick her up; the cop will get her things. If she chooses option B, the cop will usually do something about the body, too. Cops will protect Joe's girls, too. I mean, he's got his fingers in a lot of pies. He can't be going out to take care of all the girls, so he has the pigs do it. They get paid well, and the girls give 'em a cut on the side too. I know I did." He glared at the Plexiglas window.

"Can you give us any names?" Ozzy swallowed hard. "Did you know any names?"

"Oh sure. There was a guy named Bannon. Worcester cop. Had a big scar on his left hand, was really free with both hands if you know what I mean. There was another one, Bishop. I think he was a statie. He was a real bastard. All the girls were afraid of him." Balsalmo massaged his temples. "Look. I'm sure he used them for other things too. All of these guys, they were greedy. They wanted money before they wanted sex or anything else, you know?"

"Okay. That's a good place to start. Thanks for your cooperation." He blinked. "I'm sorry they did that to you. Cops are supposed to be better than that."

Balsalmo waved a hand, rattling his shackles. "A cop's just a man, no different from any other. He's got to get his, just like I've got to get mine."

Ozzy and MacDonald left the interview room. As soon as they were outside prison walls, MacDonald turned to Ozzy. "Tell me you're doing something about that. Tell me that the kid isn't ruined just so more cops can just do whatever to whoever."

Ozzy hung his head. "I can't talk about it. It's a big operation, okay? Multiple agencies. But you don't think that I dragged you all the way up to Billerica for the pleasure of Balsalmo's company, did you?"

"Well, no. As a matter of fact I didn't." MacDonald sighed. "I guess with everything I hear in the news, and now what I just heard from him, and stuff I've seen from other clients, I'm discouraged."

"Me too." Ozzy ran his hands through his hair. "I'm not going to lie. What he just told us turns my stomach. But look, one thing that he did say, that I agree with, is that cops are just people. There are going to be bad cops out there. There hasn't always been a great commitment to dealing with them in the past, but right here and right now, that's going to change. Folks like he was describing—they make it worse for all of us, you know? We want to help people, do the right thing, and then those guys are out there being worse than the people we put away." He took a deep breath. "We're going to do all we can."

"Good." MacDonald clapped him on the arm. "Give me a call if you need anything."

"You too, my friend." Ozzy headed back to Framingham, so he could put everything he'd just heard down into a report.

Chapter Nine

Pete had passed the point where sex was permitted.

This wasn't exactly a surprise, although it was a serious disappointment to him. He'd gotten big enough that most positions were uncomfortable for him, although he was willing to put up with it for Ozzy's sake. The thing was that he'd started experiencing contractions as a result of orgasm. The first time that happened Ozzy had rushed him to the hospital, where the doctor had assured him that this was comparatively normal but that it meant that "marital activities" needed to cease until after the delivery.

Ozzy had just nodded, his eyes as round as saucers, and promised the doctor that they would be as celibate as two monks until Marissa put in her appearance. The doctor harrumphed at them. "Better make it two monks living on opposite coasts, alone," he muttered. "I lived in a monastery once."

Pete made a conscious choice not to think about that and put his clothes on. Ozzy drove him home, face frozen into an expression that told Pete that he'd made the same choice.

The past couple of weeks had been both blissful and challenging. He had stopped taking jobs that required travel or much physical exertion, which meant that he rarely left the house. Victorians had called this time, the time just before and just after the birth of a baby, *confinement*, and it seemed to Pete like a perfectly good word. Nothing was confining him to the house but fatigue, pain, and the necessity of preparing for Marissa's arrival, but he was confined nevertheless.

He napped, a lot. When he wasn't napping, he was putting things away in Marissa's room. She would be the best-outfitted baby in the world for the first six months of her life at least, and Pete wasn't about to lie to himself and claim that the stacks of little pink onesies and little dresses and diaper covers weren't too adorable for words. His mother seemed to have hit a breaking point and accepted the girl, too, because a new package with a new outfit appeared in Pete's mailbox every day.

Pete wasn't sure that Marissa needed pantsuits just yet, but it wasn't his money.

Ozzy was fabulous through the whole thing. He helped Pete with the heavy lifting, and with the not so heavy lifting. He came by every day to make sure that Pete didn't need anything, hadn't fallen down, and hadn't gotten sick or hurt. Some of it was the paranoia. Pete knew that Ozzy was still worried about that Sierzant guy being out there. He was worried about Sierzant possibly coming for Pete, and that was part of what had him stopping by.

He also knew that Ozzy was stopping in because he loved him.

Ozzy stopped by over the last weekend in April, and Pete knew that he'd be there for the whole weekend. They curled up under one blanket on the couch and flipped channels for a while on Friday night while Ozzy unwound from his long day, and Pete carded his fingers through Ozzy's hair. Maybe they couldn't be sexual for now, but they could be intimate. "This is nice," he murmured.

"Mmm." Ozzy all but purred as he leaned into Pete's touch. "I wish we could do this every night."

It was the opening that Pete needed. "We could, you know."

Ozzy's eyes fluttered open. "Seriously?" He sat up. "I mean, would you want that? I know I told you that I wanted to stick around. And I do. But do you really want me underfoot while you're raising your daughter and everything? Especially when she's new?"

Pete's insides churned. He was taking a big risk saying anything, especially given how delicate everything was right now. "I'm worried that I'll be emotionally weird, because of hormones," he said after a moment. "That happens to some people, and I'm afraid that it will damage our relationship. But Ozzy, I call you Alpha. I'm naming my daughter after you. If you're willing, then yes. I want you here. I love having you here, and I'd love to have you here when I have my body back and can better keep up with you."

Ozzy's response was to gather Pete up in a big hug and plant a massive kiss on his lips. "We can start this weekend," he promised. "We'll start by making room in here for your stuff."

"Awesome," Ozzy said, with a sunny smile. "This is fabulous."

They went to bed early, so as to get an early start.

Part of Pete felt badly about the house. This wasn't them moving in together; Ozzy was very much moving into Pete's space, which had been decorated according to Pete's taste. There was nothing about it that testified to Ozzy's presence here at all. Ozzy assured him that he understood, though. They hadn't decided to just get together and start up a household; they were coming together as adults, with established households of their own. As time went on, the house where they lived would take on characteristics that would be suitable for them both.

"We might want to move into a bigger place eventually anyway, depending on how you feel about giving birth," Ozzy pointed out, dropping a kiss onto Pete's bulging belly. "I mean, if you wanted to have more kids, someday, I'd be game." He blushed. "I'm going to love Marissa—I already love Marissa— but I also want to watch you grow, you know?"

"I don't know. I think I've already grown plenty since I've known you." Pete rubbed at his belly. "But we'll see how I do during birth. I won't lie. I do like the idea of growing someone together." He liked that idea a lot, a little too much, and he peeled away from his alpha so that he could go and work on the bedroom.

They spent all of Saturday working on the bedroom and the kitchen, until Pete couldn't stand up anymore and had to go lie down. The next day, Ozzy drove the twenty minutes back to Hudson and started packing up his things.

He didn't bring everything over at once. He brought his clothes and the kitchen things he liked best over in that first run. Then he went back for the sports equipment he treasured. Two trips was enough before they were both ready for dinner; they were both exhausted, and settled for a pizza. Then they spent a little time unpacking before Pete fell into the bed—their bed, now—to go to sleep.

It felt great to have Ozzy come home the next day, come home to him. He hadn't gotten out of bed much, but he roused himself to heat up some of the stew he'd made weeks ago. He couldn't wait until he was feeling better, so they could really settle in and build up a rhythm. He wanted to cook fresh food for his alpha, and get to know all of the things that he would like and dislike.

Ozzy told him about the investigation, or at least about part of the investigation. Pete knew that his alpha wasn't telling him everything, and he didn't expect him to. Sierzant was still out there, and what Pete didn't know couldn't hurt either one of them. "Would you believe that the guy put his own kid out on the street?" Ozzy asked him. "Not just that robber, either. It turns out that a lot of his kids were out on the street. Under his control. He didn't see them as being any different than any of the other kids that he controlled, and that's just... I mean, how do you react to that?"

Pete shifted his position, trying and failing to get comfortable. "No idea. I've seen some terrible things, you know? Terrible parenting, just terrible people in general. I can't guess at what goes through some people's heads or why they have children in the first place, but there has to be some way that this is relevant to the case. Some way that it's going to help you to break the case wide open."

Ozzy went quiet for a moment. "I think you're right. Hell, I know you're right. I know we're going to nail this son of a bitch to the wall. I just want to do it sooner rather than later. I want to have it done before Marissa gets here, you know? I want to have it done so she doesn't have this hanging over her."

Pete rubbed at his belly. He did it so often these days that it felt like a reflex action, something over which he had no control at all. "I don't know if you've got that kind of time," he said after a moment. "She's going to be here soon."

"I thought you weren't due until the first of June." Ozzy laid his hand out flat on top of Pete's belly. It felt warm and good, like something pleasurable.

"I'm not. You do get that those due dates are rough estimates, right? I mean, I know the exact date when she was conceived, but that doesn't mean she'll pop out exactly forty weeks later. She'll come out when she's ready."

Marissa had moved inside of him, and his whole body was uncomfortable now no matter what he did. He didn't think it would be long now before everything came to a head. It seemed kind of early yet; his due date wasn't until June first, and today was only the first of May. As long as Marissa was healthy he'd take it; he'd had quite enough of this discomfort, thank you.

When he went to his doctor's appointment on Tuesday, Dr. Baxter agreed with him. "I wouldn't start any long books," he warned with a little smile. "And I'd pack a bag if I were you. I can feel that your daughter has dropped. You could go at any time, although I'd be happiest if you could put it off for at least another couple of weeks. I'm going to recommend that you stay in bed as much as you can. It might not put things off for all that long, but if it can put things off at least until we cross that thirty-seven week mark, I'll be satisfied.

Pete wasn't all that thrilled about bed rest, but he took it. As long as he got a healthy little girl at the end, he'd do anything.

He explained the situation to his alpha when Ozzy got home. Ozzy made a face. "Well that's not going to be much fun for you," he said. "What can I bring you?"

"Right now? Just you. Maybe my laptop before you go to work in the morning. We'll see what I can find. It's only for a little while. There are some people who have to go through this for months." Pete sighed.

"I can see if your mom or brother wants to come by. Or that wacky old bat, Aunt Isabella. I'm sure they'd all love to keep you company."

"Just what I need," Pete groaned. "They'll love to sit and look at my stretch marks."

"Hey. I love your stretch marks, every last one of them." Ozzy kissed one, just to prove a point. "Listen. I want to be here tomorrow night, but I called my parents to give them my new address and they want to talk."

Pete rubbed his hand along Ozzy's cheek. "Okay. We're in love, not chained together at the ankle."

"I know, I know." Ozzy blushed. "But I hate having to leave you alone when you're not supposed to be getting up or anything, so I asked Pretty Boy if he'd be willing to come by and help you out."

"You mean Ryan?" Pete raised an eyebrow.

"Yeah. Sorry. It's just what we call him in the department." Ozzy's blush deepened. "At first it was because of him, and it was mean and everything. Now it's mostly to bust Robles' chops. Anyway, you two seemed to get along okay. He's a good guy, and he's pregnant too so you two can talk about pregnancy stuff and what a pain alphas are."

"His might be a pain. Mine is perfect." Pete chuckled and kissed Ozzy's scarred knuckles. "I'll be fine, but it'll be good to have someone here to talk to besides Marissa. She's not the best conversationalist."

Pete wasn't under any illusions about Ozzy's family. Ozzy didn't speak about them often, but he knew that they weren't exactly accepting of him or of his presence in their eldest's life. He could accept that. He didn't need to be their favorite, as long as he was Ozzy's.

He did feel badly, though, about separating a son from his parents. He knew that Ozzy loved his parents, and that he'd made the effort to connect with them before Pete had screwed everything up. It was outside of his control, of course. He couldn't control their reactions, he couldn't control how he responded to Ozzy, and he couldn't control how Ozzy responded to him. They loved each other, and they were going to love each other forever.

What made parents think they could decide their child's love life like that? Okay, so Ozzy'd had a difficult time adjusting to civilian life when he came back from war. Lots of guys did. That didn't mean they surrendered their right to make decisions for themselves, for crying out loud.

Of course, the way that Ozzy's parents went about it wasn't all that much different from the way that Pete's mother went about it. Cynthia used different methods, because people from Cynthia's world just didn't take a hands-on approach like the Morris family did, but they each had the same goal. Both wanted "what was best" for their sons, through control of their romantic choices.

Cynthia had never known what was best for Pete. Pete was willing to bet that the Morrises had never known what was best for Ozzy. He trusted that Ozzy would stay strong in the face of his parents' resentment and hate, and keep his back when there wasn't anyone else around to do it.

He and Ozzy went to sleep that night in their nice big bed. When they woke up, Pete made extra sure to give his love a good-bye kiss. His parents might not trust him, but Pete did, and Pete wanted him to know it.

He drifted off back to sleep as his belly grew even larger.

...

Ozzy met up with his parents in Stow, which was about halfway between Sudbury and Harvard. They'd agreed to meet up at a place that billed itself as selling Asian cuisine, because of course there was only one type of food served across the entire continent of Asia and it was Crab Rangoon.

Whatever. Ozzy wasn't going to make a fuss about it. He wasn't here for fine dining. He was here to hear his parents out. He didn't expect to hear anything good, and his low expectations were met as soon as he found his parents at their booth. "Son." His father looked up at him with soulful eyes. "Glad to see that leech would let you away."

Ozzy ground his teeth together, but managed to keep his hands from clenching into fists as he took a seat next to his brother. "There aren't a lot of leeches in Sudbury. You're welcome to go try to find one." He smiled up at the waitress, who showed up as soon as he sat down to take a drink order and asked for water, then took a look at the menu.

"You know who your father means, Ozzy." Linda leaned forward and spoke in a stage whisper. "That boy. The one trying to foist a cuckoo bird on you."

"Is this 1950? Because it's starting to feel like 1950." Ozzy sat back in his seat and tried to look at the situation like a cop instead of like a family member. "Pete's not after my pension. He's not after my money. He grew up in a house that's bigger than state police headquarters. His baby girl got jewelry worth more than your house, just as a baby shower gift. Okay? Quit worrying about him being out to take something from me and start worrying about why you think that about a single pregnant omega."

Zack rolled his eyes. "Look. No one's saying that he shouldn't be allowed to keep his baby, but why do you have to get involved here? We just don't trust him. There's something about this all that's very fishy. I mean, you come on the scene and all of a sudden this guy who was supposedly perfectly okay with raising his kid alone is all gung-ho for you?"

"We're gung-ho for one another." Ozzy kept his tone light. "You'd recognize that if you'd ever had a relationship with someone who wasn't your own right hand."

"Ozzy!" Linda banged her hand on the table.

"I'm sorry. I forgot that Zack is left handed." Ozzy smirked. "Now look. Yes, we're moving quickly. I think you need to do some research on what it means to have the alpha or omega gene. There are hormones you can't hope to understand, senses you'll never experience. We do move quickly, for the most part, once we've acknowledged that sense of attraction to the other. It's just our way. We can't help it. Hell, I'd have claimed him already if it weren't for the baby."

Gary drew back. "Ozzy, you're in your thirties now. You're a grown man. You can't just go around making snap judgments based on hormones! You've always been impulsive, but this just takes the cake. You haven't even known this… person… for three months yet and you're moving in with him. That doesn't make sense by any sensible or rational assessment of the world. That completely lets out the fact that you haven't gotten our approval—"

"Because I don't need it."

"I'm going to have you committed." Gary gave a massive sigh. "You've left me with no other choice. You're not going about this rationally."

"Oh, get over yourself." Ozzy pushed his menu away. "This isn't 1847 anymore and you can't actually do that. I'm a grown man, and I'm not just a grown man I'm a grown man who's heading up an actual important investigation. You don't get to decide that I'm incompetent just because I'm choosing a partner you don't like."

"We don't know him to dislike him," Linda pointed out. "We don't need to. It's not about him, although the fact that he's more than willing to take a man who he barely knows when he knows he doesn't have the in-laws' approval is a little suspect, don't you think? If this were one of your little cases, what would you tell the people involved?"

Ozzy restrained a growl. "You do get that my cases are murders, right? People died, and other people couldn't solve it, and that's how they wound up on my desk. It's not… it's not a game. You have to understand this. It's not like some kind of role playing game. We're literally talking about people's lives." He glared daggers at both of his parents. "And I would tell the interfering parents—I have told the interfering parents—that when they're dealing with an adult in his thirties, they have no actual authority. If they haven't managed to imprint whatever their issue is on that kid by now, they can't force it."

"Mm-hmm." Gary put on his best "understanding" face, the one he used when he was counseling parishioners. Ozzy had seen him use it a hundred times. "But if that adult has a long history of impulsive decisions, and a history of trauma, that changes the game, doesn't it?"

"No. Because now you're putting judgments in place that aren't valid. The fact that I was impulsive in middle school, like most twelve-year-old boys, has no bearing here. The fact that I got caught more often than Zack here is only slightly more relevant." Ozzy shook his head in disgust. "What, you think you know something that my commanding officers and now my superiors on the force don't? That they were all willing to put plenty of responsibility on my shoulders but you—you know, deep in your heart of hearts, that I can't be trusted to reason my way through a dinner selection, never mind choosing a life partner?"

Linda pointed her finger at him. "Let's not forget the whole heaping helping of trauma that you served up for yourself over there, buddy boy. That does things to a man. We know. He knows." She jerked her head at her father. "Do you know how many of his parishioners he's had to counsel through PTSD?"

"And do you know how many of his parishioners he hasn't? Yeah, it was hard when I came back. I saw my entire unit die. That leaves a mark on a guy. It doesn't somehow damage my ability to make a decision, and by the way? It's super ableist, and shows your abysmal attitude toward veterans and survivors, that you think it does. Yeah, I survived something. Yeah, I've had some problems with it. That doesn't mean that I cede all control over my life to my parents, okay? I'm doing okay, and I've been doing okay. You're just upset that I'm not submitting. Stay mad." He got up and threw some money onto the table. "That's for the tip."

"Where are you going?"

"I'm going home, to my omega. Have a nice life. I love you, but I won't be in it." He left the restaurant, got into his car, and drove back to Sudbury. He shook with anger as he drove, but he kept the car on the road and moving in a straight line.

Ryan was still there—of course he was there; Ozzy hadn't been gone for very long. Ozzy sprang for a pizza for all three and explained the encounter with the parents. It did occur to him that he probably should have kept it quiet, but maybe it wasn't a bad thing to get an outside perspective on things.

Ryan frowned when Ozzy got to the end of his recitation. "Wait a minute. Hold up. I'm confused. Isn't your dad, like, a minister?"

Pete laid a head on Ozzy's shoulder. "Yeah," Ozzy said. Just inhaling Pete's scent made everything seem better. How could one person, one aspect of one person, have such a profound effect on him? "You'd think he'd be a little more Christian about things, but nah."

Pete nuzzled into Ozzy. "Hey. I'm sorry it came to this. I'm sure they're great people. They raised you."

"Yeah." Ozzy let himself sigh as the enormity of the breach crashed over him. "But it is what it is. As long as I have you, I don't need them or their interfering."

Ryan took off after dinner, saying that he'd see Ozzy tomorrow, and Pete and Ozzy retired to bed. Ozzy wouldn't have minded staying up for a little while longer and puttering around for a while, at least under normal circumstances. Tonight was different. Tonight he wanted the comfort of his mate.

The next morning, he headed into the office and stopped in to see Ryan. "Thanks again for coming out last night. I know it wasn't long, but it really put my mind at ease."

"Any time." Ryan grinned. "Pete's a nice guy. Smart, too. For his sake, I hope the baby comes soon. The whole bed rest thing has got to be murder. I hope it doesn't come to that with me." He shuddered. "But he told me that you thought you might have an idea as to ways that would get your conviction."

"Ah, yeah. I did." Ozzy played with the stapler on Ryan's desk. "Listen. We've noticed how Sierzant's kids aren't immune to being put to work."

"No, they aren't." Ryan hunched in on himself a little. "Wish we could do more for them."

"There might be a way. I mean, not the ones who've been put in that situation already; I'm not sure there's anything we can do for them. But we can get justice." He repeated Balsalmo's story about the dirty cops to Ryan. He knew that the whole investigation was supposed to be secret, but Ryan was trustworthy. He knew that for a fact. "If we could find a way to correlate the arresting officers with pimps for kids picked up during the time that Sierzant was a pimp, that would be a good place to start."

Ryan nodded. "That's a really good idea. And we could take it a step further by looking into kids brought in either DOA or severely injured. Their pasts really only get looked into if foul play is suspected, but we have an excuse now." He winked. "It'll give some of our rookies something to do. They won't even know they're working on anything related to Internal Affairs."

"Thanks, Ryan. I owe you one." Ozzy shook Ryan's hand and stood up. "How are things going with you and the baby, anyway? I've been so caught up in Pete's baby that I haven't asked about yours."

"Well, Pete's baby seems a little larger than life right now. I swear, the poor guy seems so uncomfortable! But yeah." He put his hand on his baby bump. "We're doing good. What I can tell you for sure is that he doesn't like court. I'm pretty sure he bruised a rib when we had a court date for the case I worked with Nick. I'm not sure if it was all the noise, or just my stress levels at being in a court room, or what the hell ever, but he doesn't like going to court."

"Sensible little guy. No one likes to go to court." Ozzy chuckled. "So you're sure it's a boy?"

"As sure as they can be without invasive procedures." He shrugged. "I mean, we'll both be happy as long as he's healthy."

"Yeah. Same." He blushed. "I keep forgetting that she's not really mine."

"I'm not in the same position you are." Ryan smiled at him and let his cheeks pinken up. "But if you're around from the beginning, and you love her, I'm pretty sure it counts. I'm around a lot of families, in a lot of different circumstances, and believe me when I tell you that it's the love that counts. The rest will come later."

The love wasn't a problem. The love could never be a problem. Ozzy knew that he would love Pete until the stars fell from the sky, and Pete would love him until those same stars cooled. What about Marissa, though? Would she someday want to know about her biological father? What would Pete tell her?

They would cross that bridge when they came to it. For now, Ozzy resolved to focus on building their loving little family.

Information poured in from different sources. Lt. Ryley in Worcester was making some headway with teasing out the older information. Apparently no one had thought it all that odd that a cohort of state troopers had decided to transfer over to become city cops, and then had all stayed on as beat cops without ever seeking to transfer into another department or get a promotion. Discussions with other officers showed that while one or two had seemed to drive personal cars that should have been beyond their reach, most of them hadn't lived visibly ostentatious lives.

Amos in the Troopers' Internal Affairs division turned up similar information, and transferring those guys to Worcester hadn't stemmed the tide. It turned out that the troopers involved had lived somewhat more ostentatious lives than the troopers who had transferred, but still no one had raised any eyebrows or done any digging.

Ozzy slapped his hand down on yet another file, this one for a trooper named Meyrick. "Look at this one. One month he's looking at foreclosure. Next month he's out of foreclosure, by the end of the year he's paid off his house, year after that he's got a damn Ferrari. No one asks a single question?"

Nenci sniggered at him. "Maybe he just found himself a sweet little sugar omega."

"Suck it, Nenci. I swear to God." Ozzy turned around to glare furiously at the elder statesman of the department, who blew him a kiss in return. "Seriously, no one asked a single question?"

"No one wants to see it." Tessaro flipped a pencil up into the air and watched it stick into the ceiling tile. "If one of us was dirty—and we're not—every single one of us would make every excuse possible to justify why he was actually a really good guy and hadn't done anything, it was all a misunderstanding. We don't want to think anything is truly wrong with the people we spend our time with day in and day out. I mean Nenci over there is very clearly a tree troll, but we keep telling ourselves he's a cop because we don't want to admit that we were sharing space with a tree troll."

No one said anything for a long moment. Then Robles spoke very slowly. "Tessaro, did you get into the evidence locker again? Cause that's bush league."

"Yeah, everyone knows that Nenci's a bridge troll, not a tree troll." Langer bent his head to his work again.

"You know what I mean though," Tessaro said, laughing as Nenci flipped them all off. "Really. No one's going to ask questions, specially not when their buddy still seems to be getting his work done. You can't turn this into a witch hunt."

Ozzy wrinkled his nose. "There's not turning it into a witch hunt and deliberately turning a blind eye to corruption. I mean, this makes it so much harder for the rest of us." He rubbed at his face in exhaustion. "But you know what? I can't do anything about it. All I can do is trace the money and hopefully nail Sierzant to the wall."

His phone rang, and Ozzy jumped. Pete wouldn't usually call during the middle of the workday. "I need you to come home," Pete told him, without waiting for him to say anything.

"Okay. Wait, did Sierzant show up?"

"No. But Marissa is about to."

Chapter Ten

The hospital was a place of contradictions. It was hard for Pete to concentrate on much. He was in pain, and all of those websites that said that labor would be more *discomfort* or *pressure* instead of real pain were full of crap, thank you very much. He was filled with shame, because his water had broken and he was still leaking like someone had stuck a pin into a water balloon. And he was afraid.

He was afraid of what was happening. He was afraid that the pain would get worse—hell, he knew the pain would get worse, that was what he was afraid of. He was afraid that Ozzy would have to leave and there would be no one here to help him. He was afraid that something would happen to Marissa. He was afraid that the doctor would slip and fall on some unseemly bodily fluid, hit his head, and not be available to help him. Worse, he might sue Pete!

Not all of his fears were rational, and on some level Pete knew that. He fought to stay calm and not show anything to the nice, mellow health care professionals that were trying to check him in. He restricted his outward display of anything to gripping Ozzy's hand tightly and squeezing as hard as he could when another contraction hit.

Admissions seemed to take forever. Maybe it just felt like forever because of the pain, and the anxiety, and because Pete's humiliation at coming in all wet and uncomfortable was so all encompassing. None of the nurses in the triage area seemed to be in much of a hurry. They laughed and joked with Ozzy as he helped with the insurance and answered their questions about medical allergies and the like.

It was only when one of the nurses asked how far apart his contractors were, and Pete replied by holding up his free hand. It shook from the pain, and her eyes widened when she saw the three fingers Pete held up. "Three minutes apart?

That's moving fast! You should have come in a while ago!" She stood up and came around to the other side of the desk. "You poor thing, you must be in a world of hurt. Let's get you right up to the birth center, okay?" She glanced at Ozzy. "Your alpha can come, of course."

Pete didn't correct her, and they all headed up the elevator. The nurse grabbed Pete a wheelchair so that he didn't have to be on his feet, which was fine by Pete. As long he got to hold on to Ozzy's hand, he didn't care what they did.

They got him right into a delivery room, where more nurses helped him change out of his sodden pajamas and into a johnny. Then they helped him get onto the bed and get his feet up into the stirrups.

"Do you want a mirror?" a nurse asked him.

Both Pete and Ozzy looked at her. "A mirror? What the hell for?" Ozzy asked.

"So that he can watch the crowning!" she told him, her eyes bright and sparkling.

Pete covered his mouth and Ozzy hugged his head to his chest. "Thanks, but I don't think that we need to do that."

"Oh." The nurse looked at them both like they had two heads and walked away. "Okay, then."

Other technicians came in to test Pete's blood. They hooked him up to monitors that beeped, and they taped things to his belly to keep track of his contractions. A doctor popped in to check on his progress and declared him to be "much farther along than expected," and then felt along his abdomen.

The pain was so intense that Ozzy cried out from how hard Pete grabbed his hand. "Did that hurt?" the doctor asked, eyebrows drawing together.

"Just a bit," Pete panted out, trying to get himself back under control. He could see and hear exactly how fast his heart was beating, thanks to the heart rate monitors. "It's not like there's a tiny giant trying to claw her way out of my body or anything."

"He's got a point." Ozzy petted Pete's hair. Pete watched as his heart rate slowed just a bit.

"Hm. Well, we can certainly get you an epidural, if that's something you want. Are you in a lot of pain in general, or is it just affecting you when someone touches your abdomen?" The doctor peered into his eyes.

"Everything hurts," Pete admitted. "It's like a stabbing and burning pain, everywhere. Yeah, the belly's more than tender. It's my back, it's my hips, it's everything. I feel like I'm being pulled apart by horses, honestly."

"Well, it's like I mentioned. Everything is moving very quickly, and your body doesn't have time to adjust to it like I'd usually like to see. I'll call someone from anesthesiology down to get you that epidural, and then you shouldn't have anything to worry about." The doctor touched his hand. "You're going to be all right, Mr. Nolan. It's all going to be all right." He stepped out into the hall.

"Is it really that bad?" Ozzy kissed the side of his head. "Why didn't you tell me?"

Pete panted his way through another contraction and smiled up at his mate. "It's not like there's anything you could do about it. I didn't want you to worry."

"Not true. I could raise a ruckus, get someone in here to give you an epidural." He used his sleeve to wipe the sweat off of Pete's face. "There's nothing that I wouldn't do for you, babe. Nothing."

The anesthesiologist came in to deliver the epidural. When Pete saw the size of the needle he almost passed out, but he rolled over and let the doctor do what he needed to do. It didn't feel good going in, that was for sure. He bit through his lip trying to hold back a shout, even though the pain from the needle was more of a minor note compared to the pain in the rest of him.

It took about twenty minutes for the medication to kick in completely, by which point Pete thought he must be cracking teeth. "What the hell is wrong with me?" he whispered.

"Nothing's wrong with you, babe." Ozzy stroked his face. "You're having a baby. That's perfectly normal."

The doctor returned to the room. "That's the thing," Pete said, ignoring the doctor. "Thousands of guys every year have babies and they don't sit here and complain, and they don't crack their teeth from trying not to scream. They're fine. They do their thing, and they come out on the other side with a baby. Why am I the pathetic snowflake who needs an epidural and extra attention?"

The doctor was an older man, and he reminded Pete a little bit of his father as he sat down on the edge of the bed. "Mr. Norris, plenty of guys have had babies every year since the dawn of time. And do you want to know what happened before modern obstetric practices? They died a lot, Mr. Norris. It's a normal and natural procedure, of course, but lots of things are normal and natural processes that can still kill a person. Male hips, for example, are not designed to widen as female hips are. The pain you're feeling right now is a combination of normal childbirth pain, and your hips trying to essentially dislocate themselves. It's okay to admit that it hurts, okay? Also, your body has to rip itself a whole new orifice, which by the way, is not comfortable.

"I get that it's presented to omegas, and to some extent to the outside world, as something beautiful and wonderful and amazing. And to some extent it is, because you're bringing a new life into the world. But it's excruciating, and it's dangerous. Don't let anyone tell you different, okay?"

"Okay." Pete closed his eyes and forced himself to relax.

"Good. Because it's time to push." The doctor got up and moved over to the foot of the bed, where all of the excitement was. "Press that button, would you?"

Ozzy pressed the button for Pete, who went ahead and pushed. Pushing with the epidural still didn't feel great, but everything felt better than it had without the medicine.

Nurses rushed in, and it was show time. Pete tried not to focus on them. He tried to focus on his breathing, and on pushing. If he stopped to think about all of the people looking at his bits, he'd probably die of shame right there on the gurney.

"Push again, Mr. Norris. There we go, just a little bit further, I think."

Oh good Lord, did they really want more from him? He let his head fall back into Ozzy's lap and bore down as hard as he could manage. He didn't know if it would be enough, but he had to try.

"Got her!" the doctor crowed. There was a vague tugging sensation, and then the doctor was holding an angry little baby up for his viewing pleasure.

They whisked Marissa away to be checked and cleaned up and weighed. Pete lay on the gurney for a little while, while the doctor checked him for ill effects and waited for him to expel the afterbirth. Pete tried to relax, but he couldn't when he heard his daughter's angry cries. Whatever they were doing to her over in the corner, she didn't like it one bit.

When the doctor brought Marissa back over, this time clean and swaddled, they handed her directly to him. She quieted down when Pete took her into his arms and held her close to his chest. When he brushed his little finger against her tiny hand, she grabbed it with a surprising grip. "You're perfect, Marissa," he told her, and kissed her little cheek. "You're absolutely perfect."

Ozzy loomed over his shoulder, eyes enthralled. "Hi, baby girl. Welcome to the world."

Pete rested his head against his mate's chest. "Hello, Marissa. This is your daddy. He loves you too. And he'll get to hold you just as soon as I can let you go." He chuckled. "Which won't be soon because you're amazing."

He wasn't allowed to hold her forever. He got a few minutes of cuddling, and then it was time to make room for another new parent. Nurses came to put Marissa into a special, clear plastic bassinette with wheels. Other nurses came to clean Pete up, at least somewhat, and to get him into some scrubs. Then they put him onto another gurney and brought him to a small but private room where he was going to be allowed to recover.

The room had a pullout chair for Ozzy to sleep on. Pete's own bed was ready for him, and he climbed into it gingerly and pulled the covers up. He let Ozzy put Marissa into his arms and give him a bottle from the samples provided by the hospital; he'd decided a long time ago that breast feeding was not a practical option for someone like him, so he wasn't going to try.

Marissa drank down a little bit of her bottle—not much, but some, and even that much was impressive—and then she hunkered down for a nap right there against Pete's chest. Pete had to smile. There was no feeling in the world as beautiful as this.

Ozzy used his phone to snap a picture. "How do you feel now?" he asked, stroking Pete's forehead.

"Honestly?" Pete chuckled. "Sore. Like someone's stretched all of my limbs out of my sockets and they haven't quite gotten all the way back in. And, ah, I feel foul. Gross, you know? And there's shame, because I just had a bunch of strangers looking at me basically naked and touching my bits, which isn't high on my list of fun." He let out a contented sigh. "But I've got you, and I've got her. We're all together. I'm exhausted, but it's like… I'm in a good place, for all that."

"Will she be Marissa Morris?" Ozzy asked, staring into Pete's eyes.

"Yes." Pete blushed. "If that's what you want, something that you want to claim, then that's what I want too. Just… Ozzy, be sure."

"I am perfectly sure. I might not have put her there, but I was there when she came into the world. And I'm going to be there every step of the way, from here until my last breath." Ozzy's jaw twitched.

Tears sprang to Pete's eyes, and he knew that it wasn't just the result of hormonal fluctuations. "You are, without a doubt, the most amazing thing that's ever happened to me."

"I think we've been pretty good for each other." Ozzy bent down and dropped a kiss onto Pete's forehead. "Sleep now. I'll hold her. You get your rest."

Ozzy lifted Marissa off of Pete's chest and carried her over to the chair. The last thing that Pete saw before sleep claimed him was the image of his alpha and his daughter, curled up in the chair. Marissa seemed perfectly content to grab onto Ozzy, or at least didn't wake up and start howling.

It was the same sight that greeted him two hours later, except his daughter was awake and being changed by Ozzy. From the looks of things, he was pretty good at it, too. "I had no idea that you knew how to change a diaper," Pete murmured from the comfort of his bed.

"Oh honey. Wait until you see all of the things that I know." He waggled his eyebrows up and down. "I learned in the service. You never know what you're going to be called on to do. I've changed babies, I've delivered babies, I've fed them, and I've carried them out of combat zones. I'm your guy." He winked and gave Marissa a kiss.

Marissa made a grumpy sound and waved her little fist at him.

"I know, I know. You want to get back in your nice warm blanket. Here you go. Now that you're all clean and dry again, maybe your papa can give you something to drink while I go clean up.

Pete took the baby and the bottle. He let himself smile as he watched Ozzy wash up at the sink. It might not be a big family, but it was his, and it was enough.

...

Ozzy got a week of family leave time to spend with Pete and Marissa. They spent two nights of that time in the hospital.

There was no part of Ozzy that didn't feel as though Marissa was his, not from the moment she emerged from Pete's agonized body. He had no biological children of his own, so he couldn't say for sure that the feeling was any different, but she'd always been part of the package with Pete. He felt the same kind of fierce need to protect her that he felt with Pete, that same kind of sense of family and pack and kinship.

When the registrar from the hospital came to fill out the birth certificate, he kept a perfectly straight face when Pete identified him as the father and listed Marissa as Marissa Nolan Morris. It was technically illegal, but it was a literal fact. He was the baby's father in everything but genes, and that was what mattered.

Pete recovered from the birth slowly but surely. He was able to take a shower that same night, with the help of a nurse. Ozzy would have preferred to be the one helping him, but Pete wanted him to stay with Marissa and keep an eye on her.

When they got home from the hospital, Pete still moved a little stiffly, and of course he was still exhausted. He was better than he'd been in the days before the birth, though, and that was the important thing. They got settled back into the house, got Marissa adjusted to her new surroundings, and then they made their announcements.

Once the announcement was made, the stream of visitors began. Cynthia was the first, in a surprise to both Ozzy and Pete. She didn't have a lot of interest in holding Marissa. She seemed to be almost afraid to hold her, as though she thought she might drop her. Angus seemed fascinated by his little niece, though, and was happy enough to hold her if he could sit on the couch and not be expected to move much.

Of course, Angus struck Ozzy as the kind of guy who was usually content to sit on the couch if he wasn't expected to move much, so maybe there was something to that.

Pete didn't have a lot of close friends. His job and the hours he kept made him a little bit of a loner, something to which Ozzy could certainly relate. He did have a lot of friendly colleagues, though, and a lot of them wanted to see the new arrival and wish her well. His most reliable local editors stopped by, which was how Ozzy wound up meeting the managing editors from the *Globe,* the *Herald*, and even the *New York Times*. Other local photographers stopped by too, and Ozzy was pretty sure that Cynthia was going to have a heart attack when her granddaughter grabbed the beard of a biker named Bruce and tried to swing from it.

Bruce didn't seem to mind. In fact, he seemed to love it.

The house all but crawled with cops, too. The guys from SWAT showed up with bags upon bags of gifts. They brought clothes (*Trust me, Morris, you can never have too many clothes, these kids, they will burn through every stitch*) and they brought towels. They brought bibs, and sink top bathtubs. They brought toys, too, the kind that would stimulate Marissa's baby brain into flights of fancy.

They brought gifts for the new parents, too. They brought self-care baskets for Pete, with soothing creams and aromatherapy candles. They brought parenting books for Ozzy, along with baby bike seats and an extra sturdy baby carrier for the kind of hiking that Ozzy liked to do.

And they brought a series of baby SWAT onesies, in progressive sizes. Everyone had a good laugh about that, except for Marissa, who slept through most of the visit.

The guys from Cold Case all stopped by, although they came separately. Langer brought an offering of books for Marissa, which she wouldn't get so much benefit from now but would as she grew, and some decent bottles of wine for the parents. Nenci showed up with a box of thirty-one bibs, because sometimes people can't get to laundry the way the mommy blogs say, and two huge jugs of high quality rum for the parents.

Ozzy decided that he didn't want to think about Nenci reading mommy blogs. Not now, not ever.

Tessaro brought more toys, along with a beautiful set of cocktail glasses and some fine gin and vermouth to go with them, "since there wasn't a housewarming or anything." Lt. Devlin, ever the practical soul, brought a gun safe for the house, which would absolutely be necessary as Marissa became more mobile. He also got a lock for Ozzy's service weapon, because "kids are grabby."

Robles came by with Ryan in tow. Ryan embraced Pete like an old friend, and looked so honored to be allowed to hold Marissa that it even brought tears to Ozzy's eyes. They disappeared to Marissa's room to gush over the new arrival in ways that only omegas could, leaving Robles and Ozzy alone.

"So. Fatherhood, huh?" Robles said with a grunt and a nod. He spread out, as though asserting his masculinity and then he leaned toward Ozzy. "Does it suck?"

"I'm still pretty new at it, buddy." Ozzy chuckled. "Ask me in five years. But... I mean, she's up every couple of hours, like clockwork. And there are aspects that smell really bad, so far. But then she looks at me and touches my face, and she cuddles up on my chest and makes this little face, and it's both incredibly imperious and impossibly cute at the same time, that my heart just melts. No, it doesn't suck. It's the most perfect thing in the world. I love my baby girl almost as much as love her daddy, and life couldn't be better with her."

Robles smiled then, a small, shy smile. "I'm so glad to hear that." He glanced over at the stairwell. "It's good that they're such good friends. Gives Ryan someone to call if he gets nervous, you know? Someone who's been through it before."

"Right? Well, Ryan's been so helpful with Pete. It's good for them to have each other." Ozzy chuckled.

Lt. Amos came by with flowers, and with a wooden place setting that he'd turned himself in his own workshop for Marissa. It seemed much more practical than the silver spoons that Pete's relatives had given. Lt. Ryley also came by with an afghan that she'd crocheted herself, in the short time that she'd known Ozzy. "Everyone needs a hobby," she said, blushing. "This one is mine."

Of course, Marissa was too small to use a blanket when she slept, but she was old enough to have one draped over her when she was being held.

MacDonald, Balsalmo's lawyer, sent a gift of books as well. Even Balsalmo sent something. It was ramen, which threw Pete for a loop, but Ozzy was able to calm his mind. "He's buying from his prison commissary account. The number of things they can buy in there is pretty limited. I guess he's not irredeemable after all; he wanted to send something to celebrate, and he sent what he could."

Pete's eyes shone with unshed tears when he heard that. "I'm not sure how to feel. I mean the guy was ready to kill me, but I guess it truly wasn't personal after all." He sniffed. "We're not feeding that to her, but we can explain it to her when she's older. It can go in her keepsake box."

"That's right." Ozzy wrapped an arm around his mate.

The weirdest gift was an absolutely massive teddy bear that arrived on the Friday of Ozzy's week of leave, along with a huge bouquet of flowers, for Marissa and Pete. The card simply read *from Joe*.

There was no doubting who "Joe" might be. Ozzy called in to the office, and they sent a team out to check out the offerings. There was a bomb-sniffing dog that drooled a lot and wanted treats, but found no explosives. A tech team found no hidden cameras or recording devices. Another dog came out to look for drugs and found nothing. The gift was just what it appeared to be: a giant teddy bear, nothing more.

After some discussion with Pete and with Lt. Amos, they decided that it would be acceptable for Marissa to keep the gift. The gifts had been given not to Ozzy but to Pete and Marissa, and Pete was not yet technically Ozzy's omega. There was no legal issue at this point, and it made sense to avoid offending a criminal of Sierzant's reach until absolutely necessary.

After all, it was entirely possible that Sierzant had given the gift out of sheer exuberance. These things happened sometimes.

"That's some Al Capone level stuff right there," Ozzy grumbled as he wrestled the bear up into Marissa's bedroom. It would live in a corner until the little girl was old enough to play with it.

Pete shrugged. "Organized crime is organized crime, right? I mean, a guy like Sierzant probably tries to model himself on Capone. Didn't Capone even start out as a pimp?"

Ozzy stopped, and turned to stare at his omega. "Yeah. That's actually really helpful. But why do you know that?"

Pete flashed him a quick grin. "Oh come on. Didn't you see my coffee table book about organized crime?" He winked. "It's on the shelf over there. I still get royalties, you know."

"Seriously?"

"They sell it at Alcatraz, in the gift shop. That plus a version of what I did to Capone's mug shot on a tee shirt. I could get a copy for Joe, if you wanted."

Marissa waved her little fist. Ozzy agreed with her. "Let's not go giving gifts to crooks, okay?"

He went back to work on Monday. There was a marked patrol car from the state trooper's office sitting across from his house. The patrolman in the car lifted his cup of Dunkin at him in a kind of salute. Ozzy waved back as he pulled out, and kept his appearance friendly, but he couldn't help but wonder if the cop watching his house was a friend or a foe. After all, Sierzant's fingers reached far.

Devlin was waiting for him when he got in. What was it about Devlin anyway, with the early-morning lurking? He led Ozzy into a conference room, where Lt. Amos waited with another familiar-looking state trooper. "Ozzy. Good morning. You're well acquainted with Lt. Amos. I want you to meet Lt. Roger Nervetti. He heads up our Organized Crime division. Lt. Nervetti, this is Detective Morris. He's heading up the investigation into Harbaugh's death."

Nervetti shook Ozzy's hand. "Detective Morris, it's good to finally meet you. I think our investigations might be running along the same lines here. I hadn't planned to reach out."

Ozzy raised an eyebrow. He was exhausted. He'd been up for a long time; Marissa had been unusually fussy last night, as though she'd known he was going back to work, and all he wanted to do was to crawl under his desk for a nap the way he knew Langer sometimes did. "Seriously?"

"It's not personal. We cover organized crime all over the state. Sierzant's a pig, don't get me wrong. He's just not quite as aggressive as, say, the Russians over in Brighton and Brookline. Or the Vietnamese gangs up in Lowell. Those guys will mess you up without breaking a sweat. Sierzant is on our radar, but we have a pretty limited budget. We were more than happy to let another department have at it; it wasn't as if we had all that much to add." He sighed. "That was before he started going after a cop's family."

"I see." Ozzy could see, actually. He understood the need to direct resources where they would do the most good. He didn't know much about gangs in Lowell or in Brighton. He knew about cold cases. It still infuriated him that Organized Crime could have helped at any point and had just hung back.

"I've put a uniformed cop outside your house. He'll be there until the case is closed. And I've pulled two detectives back from working on drug running gangs in Springfield to help out with this. I figure they've got the most expertise in operations similar to what Sierzant's doing."

Amos cleared his throat. "The detectives are a little on the young side, but that's good. I checked them out while you were on leave. And I've been checking out the cops who've been put on duty outside your house, too. No unusual transactions or suspicious activity. Pete and Marissa will be perfectly safe."

Ozzy relaxed, just a little. "Okay," he said, with a grin of relief. "Okay. You can imagine how wound up I've been since we got that enormous freaking bear."

"I'm kind of wound up about the bear, frankly." Nervetti wrinkled his nose. "I mean, come on. That's straight out of Capone's playbook."

"I said the same thing." Ozzy drummed his fingers on the table. "It was Pete who seemed to think that Sierzant was modeling himself on Capone. And it makes sense, you know? I'm a little weirded out by the fact that my omega apparently did a coffee table book about organized crime, but he definitely knew what he was talking about."

"He's *that* Pete Nolan? Oh, hell, we've got that book in our department! He's got some great shots in there." Nervetti grinned. "Awesome. Well, listen. I'll share information with you if you share it with me, okay?"

"Sounds like a plan. Let me know if anything comes up." Ozzy shook hands with Nervetti and watched him leave the office. Then he turned to Devlin and Amos. "What do you think?"

Amos sighed. "Three of his most senior detectives tripped red flags. I haven't told him yet, but he wanted to assign all of them to this case. I vetoed them on general principles. I'm nervous, but I'm keeping a tight rein on everyone from that department right now." He shook his head. "For what it's worth, I think he's honest. I just think he's got a lot of trust in his men. Like most supervisors, you know? He feels like he knows them."

Devlin grimaced. "That doesn't make me feel good, man. I feel like I know my men."

"Tom, I check your guys every six months. You're clear." He chuckled, maybe a little bitterly. "Apparently I should be more focused on other departments. I didn't say anything because these detectives aren't in Sierzant's territory." He sighed. "Temptation, or pressure, can come from just about anything. I busted a cop once who definitely came up dirty, but he never took a dime. It turned out that a crime boss arranged for the guy's wife to get a kidney, got her bumped up on the transplant list." His mouth twisted. "The courts were lenient with him. No jail time, but he lost his job. The wife is still around, though, so he says it was worth everything. They're living down in Florida now. The guy does analysis for talk shows."

Ozzy squirmed. "I know I shouldn't judge. I know. He still... I mean, it's hard enough to get people to trust us, you know?"

"Oh, don't I know it." Amos slouched in his seat. "That's why I'm here. But anyway, that's the story. Do with it what you will."

Chapter Eleven

Ruth, the nanny, moved in two weeks after Ozzy went back to work. Pete wasn't starting back up with work so soon, not entirely, but he wanted to be around during that early transitional phase and make sure that everything was going smoothly. Marissa would be Ruth's primary responsibility during normal working hours once Pete went back to work, although if he wasn't out and working he'd certainly be around as a backup.

Ruth was a rare soul among the nannies he'd interviewed in that she understood the need for flexibility. On the one hand, she was going to have a lot more free time than many of her contemporaries. On the other, she was going to have a lot of time on nights and weekends when Pete got called to a scene and needed her to step in. The possibility of travel was there, of course, but she'd be towing a child around while she took in the sights.

Ruth was an artist. Part of the appeal of the job was that she would have the time and the freedom to practice her art. Pete could respect that; not everyone was as lucky as he was. And she would have even more time to work on her own projects given that Ozzy was likely to be home most weekends.

She didn't take long to move in. She only needed her supplies and her personal effects. "I don't often keep my finished projects around a house where I've got kids I'm taking care of," she explained with a wry grin. "Learned that one the hard way. All of my inventory is stored off-site."

"Smart woman." Pete grinned at her and gave her the tour.

He didn't have a hard time getting used to having another person around the house. At least, he didn't have any more difficulty than he'd expected to have. He'd been alone for years, and that had been okay, but he was an omega. Omegas liked contact, they liked connection, and Pete was no different. It couldn't be a coincidence that he was healing from childbirth faster than he'd healed from that big old bruise he'd picked up during that bank robbery.

The hard thing to get used to was giving up his time with Marissa. She was so tiny, and so affectionate. Maybe *affectionate* wasn't the word at three weeks old, but she was getting there. She had decided preferences, that much was certain. She liked long cuddles, fresh air, and Chopin's nocturnes. Things that she disliked, such as bright light, loud and jarring noises, and bad smells, got squalls and waves of her little fist.

He loved spending time with her, even though she didn't do much at this stage beyond eat, sleep, cry, and crap. He absolutely hated the fact that someone else was going to be there for the big milestones. He had plenty of money, thanks to his grandfather and his father. He could afford to just stop working if he wanted to.

He'd already signed a contract with Ruth, though. And while his heart burned with jealousy every time he saw his daughter in Ruth's arms, he had to admit that he was going a little stir crazy. All of his time on bed rest—an insubstantial amount, compared to what many people endured, but too long for his restless spirit—had worn on him and he longed to get back into the field.

He practiced by taking as many pictures of Marissa as he could. She was a great subject, in that she didn't have enough control over herself to pose or to turn away. She just kind of moved, and it was up to him and his camera to keep up.

He started to get his body back. He hadn't fully healed yet, of course. Something that no one had warned him about—that no one warned most expectant parents about, whether female or omega—was that there was bleeding after birth, and it went on for a while. It had become less terrible by the third week, but it was still going on as his body worked to heal the wound it had made to expel Marissa from inside of him. Still, he could see that he was visibly starting to look like himself again, not a bowling ball with arms and legs.

He made a point of going for a walk with Marissa and Ruth every day, preferably in the morning before he could psyche himself out of it again. It was June by now, and he wanted to make sure that he was active as soon as he could be. Ruth was on board, although Pete wasn't sure if she was doing it for the exercise or to get a better sense for the neighborhood.

She was pretty freaked out by the presence of the patrol car on the other side of the street. Pete felt pretty much the same way, but he couldn't do much more than roll his eyes. "Apparently Ozzy is working on something that's gotten him to be a little more paranoid than he was before. I don't know. It's weird. If it makes them feel better to have a guy sit in a car for a shift, I think it's a waste of tax dollars, but I'm not going to tell them no, you know?"

Ruth shuddered. "If whatever it is makes him feel that jittery, maybe he should transfer the case to someone else. I wouldn't want to risk my mate and my baby."

"I think he's the best one for the case, you know?" He stretched a little. It was a fine line to tread, between doing too much and not doing enough. He didn't want to hurt himself, but he didn't want to get complacent either. "What do you say we push just a little bit farther today?"

They did push a little farther than their usual boundaries, moving just past where they would normally have been and circling back. Everything was in full bloom now, and the days were starting to get a little bit warmer. "You know, at least half of my mother's friends gave me coats in newborn sizes." He shook his head. Marissa had kicked off the light blanket he'd thrown over her to keep the sun off of her delicate skin again. "Can you believe it?"

"They come from a generation that was always told to keep the baby wrapped up and warm, and not to trust their own judgment." She shrugged. "Thinking has changed, but if they don't have kids or grandkids they can't be expected to know about it."

"I can't imagine that any of them actually raised their own kids." He sighed. "I'm sorry. I'm having trouble with all of this. It's not you."

"No, it isn't." Ruth laughed. "I'm good at my job and we get along just fine. It's you. You've never asked anyone for help a day in your life, have you?"

"I—well, I must have. Once, I'm sure." Pete blushed. "Am I really that bad?"

"Oh yeah. But it's not necessarily bad, it's just different. I see the way that you are with Ozzy, and how he basically has to intervene when you're too tired or are overdoing it. You yourself told me that you're used to doing things for yourself. And that's okay. I need you to not undermine me with Marissa, and I won't undermine either of you, but I think that we can reach consensus. We'll get there, Pete. Our arrangement isn't traditional, and we'll keep that up as long as it works for Marissa. You're a good dad. You'll do what she needs when she needs it."

Pete couldn't argue with that. Everything was for his daughter, everything in the world.

Ozzy was showing himself to be an amazing father already. As the weeks went by, he took on an equal share of diaper changes and feedings, just as though he'd been doing it all his life. Marissa preferred Pete, but that was only natural. She'd been hearing his voice since her ears developed. Ozzy was her dad, but he wasn't the same warm, safe space as Pete was.

That made no difference to the fact that Ozzy and Marissa had a very special relationship. Ozzy liked to cuddle his daughter right up close. If he lay down on his back, she would wriggle and scooch herself up until she lay just under his chin, with her hand on his cheek. It was an adorable image, one that Pete photographed more than once. He hung prints from the wall in his office and on the wall in the front entry, and gave Ozzy a copy for his desk at work.

By week four, Pete was willing to take a few local jobs. He covered a controversial condo development on the site of the old state hospital in Waltham. He got some fantastic wildlife shots at the Assabet River National Wildlife Refuge, and he went deep into some Sudbury conservation land to do some work on local ties to Metacom's War. They weren't exactly hard-hitting photojournalism projects, but they were fun and they got him out of doors. He got to be home at a reasonable hour and got to take care of his beautiful little girl.

He got back into the swing of cooking, too. He didn't do fancy meals, not yet. There wasn't time, even if Ruth was there to take care of that now. He liked to make good, hearty and healthy meals that would keep all of them satisfied for a good long while. The day would come when Marissa would reject good, hearty, healthy food in favor of chicken nuggets and swill, but until then he wanted to make sure that she had only healthy examples in front of her.

They made an effort to visit with Cynthia and Angus a little more often, just because they were family. If anything ever happened, they both wanted Ruth to know where to go and who to contact. Cynthia was her usual distant self during these meetings, and she would usually insist on keeping Pete late for a *chat* afterward to talk about either Ozzy or Ruth.

"Are you sure that Ozzy's such a great partner, Peter?" she would ask, chin stuck out in defiance. "In addition to his lack of education, you have an armed guard outside your door."

Pete scratched his head. "Why do you know that?"

"I'm your mother, dear. It's my job. Also, Veronica Dinsmore saw him on her way to check up on a horse. Don't avoid the question, Peter. Why is there an armed guard?"

Pete sighed and pinched the bridge of his nose. "Ozzy's working on a case that has some sensitive implications. He just wants to be sure that I'm safe. That's all. I'm pretty sure that it will all be over soon, you know?"

"Hmph." She sniffed and turned up her nose. "I'm sure that any little old country lady from Maine could have solved this weeks ago."

"Mom, that's *Murder She Wrote.* Not real life. Country amateur sleuths don't face down actual gangs in real life, or if they do they die a lot." He had to laugh at his mother's attitude.

Another time she confronted him about Ruth. "Are you absolutely sure that she's a good choice to help out with your daughter? She seems a little loosey-goosey to me. She's going to try to, I don't know, Montessori that daughter of yours and you'll come crying to me."

"Montessori is an educational philosophy, Mom. And we might put her into a Montessori school, if that seems like the right choice when she's older. Right now, I'm not worried about her educational philosophy. I'm just worried about her health and safety. I need to make sure that she's getting fed, changed, and held when I can't be there."

"Nonsense." His mother stomped her little foot. "We always hired the best, the smartest, and the best educated nannies. You speak Chinese because we hired Yaling."

"I understand a little. I was also nine when you brought her on. Not four weeks old, Mom. Right now she's still kind of loud and smelly luggage." Pete squirmed. He missed his loud and smelly luggage. "I brought you a picture of her."

"Oh yes. The one of her in that large pillow thing. It's very cute. Baby girls look adorable in all black, I must say. Does Marissa like this hippie?" She raised an eyebrow.

"As much as we can tell. She gave us a smile the other day, because we did something that made her happy."

"What was that?"

"We kissed."

She let him go after that.

All in all, life was working out fairly well for the little family now that they'd all settled in. If Ozzy missed his family he didn't say anything about it or them. He just went about his day. Sometimes he spoke about his progress on the case, and sometimes he didn't.

They hadn't gotten back to a point where sex was a possibility yet. Pete had tried to make up for it with some spectacular hand jobs, which Ozzy certainly appreciated, but they both knew that it wasn't the same. Pete couldn't wait to get clearance from the doctor to resume his normal activities.

Would Ozzy even still want him? He knew that he wasn't losing the baby weight as fast as he wanted to. Maybe Ozzy would prefer someone slim and handsome, someone who hadn't gotten pregnant at the drop of a hat. Pete had known that would be a possibility, just as he knew that Ozzy was too good to ever say anything.

Then again, Ozzy was still giving him plenty of attention. It wasn't sexual, but it was as romantic as he could want it to be. He never failed to touch Pete whenever he walked by, or to put his mouth on him and gave him a kiss. He would wrap his arms around his omega for no readily apparent reason, and he wouldn't let go.

"How did I get so lucky?" Pete shook his head as he watched his mate playing with his daughter. He didn't know what he'd done to deserve this, but he was never going to let it go.

...

Ozzy liked being a father, for the most part. He loved living with Pete. He loved waking up beside his omega. Even though they still couldn't have sex, not until his postpartum checkup, Pete's citrus scent was enough to keep Ozzy warm and sated and happy. Of course, the occasional hand job—or, less often, blow job—didn't hurt.

He loved waking up when Marissa needed something. He knew that it had been a hard decision for Pete not to breastfeed his little girl, but it truly hadn't been a practical solution. Not when he was getting called out to cover events at all hours of the day, or might have to travel. The upside of bottle feeding was that both parents could enjoy this special time with their little person, just them in the quiet room. He didn't even mind diaper duty, although it was more onerous for alphas and omegas than it would be for betas.

He loved the weekends spent together, all three of them wrapped up in each other in search of adventure. These weren't the adventures he'd chased in his youth. No, these were tamer adventures, the kind he could chase with an omega still recovering from the rigors of childbirth and an infant in a carrier. They went for beautiful, if sedate, hikes. They visited some old historical sites. They had picnics and just enjoyed the outdoors. Marissa, in particular, seemed to take particular pleasure in any kind of fresh air, so they indulged as much as they could.

It wasn't Ozzy's usual cup of tea. He wasn't racing down a hillside hoping he didn't wreck, or jumping off a cliff with a pair of nylon wings attached to his back. No, he had an entirely different kind of adrenaline pumping through his veins right now, and it wasn't the fun kind. The implicit threat to his loved ones had Ozzy on edge almost all of the time, and he wondered if he'd ever reach a point when he'd feel secure enough to seek out a good thrill again.

Pete suggested, once, that they could go to the beach for a little while. Ozzy was doing pretty well, all things considered. He knew a lot of guys who were in a very delicate condition, and had a long list of things to avoid while they got back on their feet. Ozzy wasn't like that, hadn't been like that in a while, and he thanked whatever deity or spirit looked over guys like him that he'd been able to get on with civilian life pretty quickly because it wasn't like that for everyone. He also knew that putting him around dust and sand, when he was already this keyed up and on edge, wasn't likely to end well for anyone.

Pete didn't encourage that again. He only encouraged excursions to woodlands or historical sites, and the whole family was happy with that.

At work, progress on the case moved at the approximate speed of a glacier. He moved along and tracked down every lead he could. He found plenty of dirty cops, which made his stomach cramp every time he noticed. He didn't work for Internal Affairs. He worked for Cold Case, and he had a job to do. Tim Harbaugh was still dead, and his death was still unsolved. He couldn't let Harbaugh's murder get swallowed up in such a large, and apparently long overdue, investigation.

He pulled back and tried to refocus. He knew he was missing something here. If past performance was any indicator, he was probably missing something that had come into play early in the investigation. It just wouldn't have made enough sense to follow up on, not with so many other things that made perfect sense just falling into his lap. Did he have any leads that had fallen by the wayside?

The only thing that sprang to mind was the line that had sparked it all. *Harbaugh got what was coming to him.* It had been some stranger saying it, some guy in a restaurant on one of Ozzy's first dates with his omega. He hadn't taken it all that seriously at the time, but now the words cried out like a beacon across his brain. *Harbaugh got what was coming to him.* Ozzy had only heard that when he'd already been turned onto the organized crime connection, and the link to Joe Sierzant.

When Dawn Moriarty had turned him onto the connection.

He'd only interviewed her once, and he hadn't felt strongly about interviewing her again. She'd been a scared creature, unwilling or unable to trust a cop as far as she could throw him. And ultimately she'd been right. They'd been attacked by a thug, who had promptly lawyered up and refused to speak a word even in his own defense.

Correct that. They hadn't been attacked by a thug. Dawn had been attacked by a thug. The attacker would have been perfectly happy to leave Ozzy and the probation officer out of it.

Acting on a hunch, Ozzy sought a meeting with the attacker and the attacker's lawyer. They showed up, but Ozzy didn't get very far with them. Unlike Balsalmo, the attacker—Oriol?—had something to lose. He would get out of prison, even if the judge threw the book at him. He wasn't willing to talk, even in exchange for leniency.

That left the source herself. Ozzy wasn't willing to go in without ammunition. He went to Ryan first. Ryan was into his third trimester now, and confined by policy to desk duty. He hated it, even if he was better at it than his boss. Things hadn't run this smoothly in Abused Persons in years. Ozzy privately suspected that people were just afraid to run afoul of Ryan's ill opinion, even though they all seemed happy and relaxed enough when he stopped in.

Ryan smiled at him. "Hey, it's my second favorite daddy! How's it going?"

Ozzy considered. "It'll be going much better once I clear this case off my plate."

"Yikes. Well, since you're here in my office and not waiting for me to show up and play with that adorable bundle of joy you call a daughter, I can only assume you think I can help you with that." Ryan raised an eyebrow.

"Well, yes, actually." Ozzy sprawled across one of Ozzy's visitor chairs and ignored the undercurrent of sarcasm. "A few months ago you looked into a witness for me, Dawn Moriarty."

"Right." Ryan nodded and folded his hands on top of his belly. "I remember. Sad case. No real hope there, probably for a long time before we knew about her. What about it?"

"Well, we only really talked about her record before Harbaugh's death, and then as an adult. We didn't look much at her record after Harbaugh's death." Ozzy looked at Ryan and gave him the best puppy dog eyes that he could manage.

"Don't do that, Ozzy. You just look constipated." Ryan swiveled his chair to type into his computer. "Okay. We have five arrests between Harbaugh's death and when she showed up at that hospital in Rhode Island. All for solicitation, all as an independent worker. After she leaves that hospital—and by the way, this part is not admissible as evidence, nor is it something you can act on to get a warrant—she's no longer independent. She's got a higher-up."

"Let me guess." Ozzy closed his eyes. "Sierzant."

"Oooh, got it in one, even with the sleep deprivation. How does he do it?" Ryan held out a pen as a phony microphone.

"Blowjobs, man. Anyway, thanks. I think I need to go talk to our little girl lost again. I think here are some questions that I should be asking." Ozzy slouched down in the chair. "The last time I interviewed her someone tried to kill her."

"So don't let it happen again." Ryan shrugged. "Blowjobs, huh?" His gaze shifted toward the wall and became speculative. Ozzy fled the room before he could hear more than he wanted to.

He reached out to Dawn's caseworker, Mary, and explained the situation. Mary was reluctant to be part of arranging a meeting. After all, the last time she'd done that someone had tried to kill her client. The thing was, Ozzy wanted to talk to Dawn about exactly that incident, among other things. He didn't want her to lie. He didn't want her to hide the truth. In fact, he wanted her to be very open about it. He needed to meet with Dawn Moriarty, and he was going to get his way. He just wanted to give her the opportunity to do it on neutral ground, someplace that Dawn went on a regular basis.

According to Mary, when she called him later, Dawn initially balked. She gave in a little while later, though, and agreed to come in and meet. When Ozzy saw her, though, she didn't seem to remember that this had been a voluntary move on her part. "So now that I've come all this way," she said with a scowl, "what's some scumbag going to try to kill me for today?"

"You tell me, Dawn." Ozzy kept his tone as soft as an alpha could. He knew that it could still be intimidating. "I think there are still a few things that we need to discuss, don't you?"

Dawn's back stiffened, suddenly, like she'd been wearing a corset and someone had suddenly pulled on all of the strings. "Hey now. I told you everything."

"You didn't tell me that you ultimately wound up working for Sierzant."

Dawn slumped. "Everyone winds up working for Sierzant." Her lip curled as she turned to look at Ozzy. "You think you won't? Just you watch. They'll make you an offer, and it will be something that means more to you than your life. More than your badge. And you'll hate yourself, but you'll do it.

"And once you've taken that little step, he owns you. Because yeah, maybe you did it to save your great aunt Sally, I don't know, but he's still got that to hold over you. You'll bow down to anyone, lick any boot, suck any dick, pull any trigger, because once you've said yes once, you won't stop."

"Seen it happen a lot, have you?" Ozzy tried not to be affected by her words. The most he could do was to avoid outward displays.

"Sure. He's got a guy working for him now; Sierzant pays for his health insurance. He's got a kid that needs round the clock care. Sure, it started out with, *Oh, this is a one-time deal, and I won't do this or that or the other thing*. That same cop has killed twenty-three people for Sierzant. He's also supervising other patrolmen. Sure, he's all about the sick kiddies." Dawn snorted.

"So he recruited you." Ozzy wiped his mouth with his left hand. He couldn't imagine the horror.

"He'd been trying to suck me in since I was maybe thirteen? Fourteen? I managed to avoid it for years. He's got cops, you know?" She closed her eyes against a bad memory, and Ozzy fought against the urge to wrap her up in his arms. "Sierzant wants what he wants, and there's nothing you can do. If he wants food, he takes it. If he wants something that can be moved, he takes that too. And if he wants a person for his stable…"

"He takes that." Ozzy nodded. He'd heard that sort of thing before.

"Right." Dawn nodded, eyes on the ground. "Except he's got cops. So if a girl, say, didn't want to work for him but wanted to stay solo, a cop would pretend to arrest her. And then he'd drive her to some secluded location and try to make her see the error of her ways."

"God." Ozzy put a finger to his lips as his gorge rose.

"Yeah. It was about as much fun as it sounds. Your buddy Harbaugh was one cop who was really into that. Like up to his eyebrows deep. After I got away from that dirtbag, I moved to Providence and tried to get better. Instead, a whole pile of Sierzant's goons attacked me and tried to kill me, and here we are." She shuddered. "They caught up with me, and I haven't been the same since. My children are gone, out of reach. I have no family. There ain't much else to tell you."

Ozzy rubbed at his face. "Was Harbaugh one of them?"

"Of course he was." She tossed her hair over her shoulder. "I thought that went without saying. I'll never forget that creep's mustache, right over me. You know? I'll just never forget that. I wasn't the only one, either. But I got away. That happened sometimes. It just made Sierzant mad, though. He wants what he wants, and what he wants he gets. Eventually."

"What was it that he wanted?" Ozzy gripped the edge of Mary's desk in an attempt to keep the room from spinning. "I mean, his stable was plenty big by that point. Why did he need to expand it by so much?"

"Why not?" She shrugged, eyes on the ground. "I was pretty successful, as streetwalkers go, so he wanted that. And then he just hated the fact that someone was telling him no." She looked up with a wry grin. "I've had a chance to get to know what makes him tick, you know? He hates not getting his way."

"I can see that. Dawn, I have to ask. Why did that man attack you, the last time we spoke?" Ozzy leaned forward, elbows on his knees. "I've been trying to make some sense out of it and I just can't do it. Why would Sierzant try to throw you under the bus in the first place? He fed you to us, and put you on our radar in the first place, right?"

She shuddered. "He did. He's not going to stop until I'm in the ground, is he?" She buried her face in her hands for a moment. "He got me under his control, back after Rhode Island. Made me a slave, more or less. He took everything I had, and there wasn't much I could do to stop him. But that wasn't enough. I got to be older than he wanted to have on the payroll. He wants his girls nice and young, and twenty was definitely too old to turn in the kind of profits he wanted. At least it was for the kind of business he was running. There are girls out there, you know, who can keep bringing in the cash for years and years, but I'm so not at that level.

"The thing is, I know too much. He didn't like to let me out of his sight, and even when I was high as a kite or half passed out from pain I still knew what was going on around me. So I paid attention, you know? And he hated that more than anything else. He can't stand that I know any part of his business, and he'll do anything to try to get rid of me." She smirked. "Especially if I'm talking to cops about a twenty-year-old murder. Even if Harbaugh was a dirty cop, he was still a cop. And no one wants to be caught for being a cop killer."

Ozzy shook his head. "No. No they don't. We're going to take him down, Dawn. We're getting closer every day."

"I believe you," she said, meeting his eyes.

Chapter Twelve

Pete picked up more work as the summer stretched out before them. There was plenty of it to be had. Summer always brought an increase in violent crime along with it. That increase in violent crime came with an increase in newspapers, magazines, and online outlets doing think pieces on the sharp increase in violent crime, as though it hadn't happened just last year and as though they couldn't just tie that same increase to rising temperatures and the lack of air conditioning in lower-income areas.

Pete was willing to take their money, although he'd given a few moments' thought to re-using old photos from previous jobs. That, in turn, gave him an idea, and he reached out to another freelancer who did amazing work. They put together a project that demonstrated the correlation between violent crime and rising temperatures, sold it to the *Times,* and made a pile of money that almost felt obscene for a feature piece. That article, in turn, became a reference piece for a number of other pieces, and got both Pete and his friend some recognition from such diverse groups as poverty reformers and climate activists.

Pete didn't think that was half bad, considering that he'd been confined to bed rest only a few short weeks ago.

Ruth was settling in nicely, too. She laughed and joked with both Pete and with Ozzy, and she was great with Marissa. She traveled with him on the occasions when Pete had to travel, although he was trying to keep that sort of thing to a minimum still. There weren't many people that Pete wanted to be stuck with for a long car ride, but Ruth quickly showed herself to be one of them.

Marissa was old enough to show her little personality now, and Pete fell more in love with her every day. She still didn't do much, just ate and slept and crapped, but she watched the world through her huge brown eyes now and seemed to be genuinely curious about things. She kicked at things on her play mat and grabbed at her blankets. She couldn't speak, of course, but she could express herself through her facial expressions just fine. A furrowed brow usually meant that a diaper change was in the near future. She would purse her lips just before demanding to be picked up and held.

And then there were the smiles. Oh, the smiles. Pete sometimes thought that he could die from the smiles. It didn't matter if he hadn't gotten a lick of sleep all night; one of her toothless smiles would have him awake and dancing with joy for the whole day.

Ozzy wasn't around enough to see many of those smiles. "We're getting close," he told Pete. "We're getting close, I can taste it. I know that it's hard, and I want to be there with you guys, but I'm trying to coordinate with two different departments and one other agency, and we know that some of them are dirty. I'm doing everything I can to come home as early as I can, babe. I promise."

"I know you are." The funny thing was, Pete did trust Ozzy. With almost any other alpha, he would have had to suspect that something was wrong by now, but Pete knew in his heart that Ozzy was faithful. That didn't make the long nights any warmer, or any better. And it wasn't always Marissa keeping him up at night, either.

He went to his six-week postpartum checkup. His doctor checked him out all over, let him get dressed again, and then asked him to sit down in his office. "Tell me, Pete," he said, "How are things with you?"

Pete shrugged. "They're okay, guess. Why?"

"The time right after a person has a baby can be challenging. Sleep deprivation alone can cause a lot of problems, never mind the hormonal changes. It's difficult for most parents—

people with partners, people without. People with a huge family with a big support network have just as much trouble adjusting to their new lives as lone wolves. You're not alone, however it's working out. I'm here to listen."

"Doc, it's fine. I have a healthy, beautiful baby girl. What could be better than that?" Pete spread his hands wide.

"Humor me, Pete. I know that you're used to doing everything for yourself, but this really is part of my job. Tell me. How are things with that alpha of yours?" The doctor leaned forward, looking at him expectantly.

"I mean, he's busy at work and everything." Pete rubbed his arm. "I don't really mind. I mean I do, but it's something that he needs to do. He's convinced himself that Marissa and I won't be safe until he deals with this one case. And he might be right, I don't know. This is his profession, I don't know enough about this kind of thing, you know?" He rubbed at his temples. "There's a part of me that's afraid he's never going to look at me again, which is ridiculous because he didn't know me before I got pregnant. But what if he's got unrealistic expectations, and I'm just not meeting them?" He pinched the bridge of his nose. "I'm being absurd. Ozzy's not that shallow. I know he's not."

"Well, I don't know about that, but I can tell you that you weigh less now than you did before your pregnancy." The doctor looked down at Pete's chart. "I think you need to sit down with your partner and have a little talk with him. You might be experiencing a bout of postpartum depression, which is perfectly normal and nothing to be ashamed of. I'd say that your symptoms are comparatively mild, which means that I don't think we need to medicate or ask you to seek counseling yet. I think we can take more of a watchful waiting approach and see how things go."

Pete blinked back at his doctor. "What does that mean?"

"It means just how it sounds. I want to see you back here in a couple of weeks. We'll weigh you and see how you're feeling, in general. We'll do this for a while until you're doing better. Okay?"

Pete buried his face in his hands. He wouldn't lose it, not here and now. "I'm a complete failure as an omega and as a parent." He rubbed at his face. "Awesome."

"Hey." The doctor grabbed Pete's hands. "You're not a failure. You're doing just fine. You showed me pictures of a happy, healthy baby. Like you said, your partner has a lot going on right now, and that's going to have an effect on your relationship. It happens. It happens in all couples, even mated couples, and you'll work things out. I promise. The important thing for you to know, Pete, is that this isn't your fault. It's just something that happens, the result of genetics and hormones affecting the brain. It's something that you can work through. Okay?"

"Yeah." Pete managed to force a smile. "Yeah, okay. Thanks, Doc." He shook the doctor's hand and left the office.

He cuddled with his daughter for a little while longer when he got home, and then he explained what the doctor had said to Ruth. He felt beyond humiliated to explain something so personal to her, but he didn't think that it was something he could exactly avoid.

She just nodded, her round eyes sympathetic. "I was kind of wondering if it might not be something like that, but I'm not a mental health professional so I didn't want to speculate. Not a lot of people lose that much of the baby weight that quickly, but then again I don't know you all that well." She indicated his still full dinner plate. "Eat up."

He huffed out a little laugh, but he ate.

He got called out to a photo shoot in Deerfield, for a project commemorating the Deerfield Raid of 1704. He didn't get a ton of historical work, although it was inevitable that he would get some given where he lived and he enjoyed it when he got it. He didn't want to subject Marissa and Ruth to such a long drive, so he went alone and met up with his colleague outside the Barnard Tavern.

They explored the historic district for a little while, taking photos of what there was to see, but the museums weren't what Edison Sumner was after. He wanted to see more of the background, the scars, the visual aspects of the raid and the lingering aftereffects.

There wouldn't be many. Pete didn't have to have a PhD in history to know that. There wasn't a building left in Deerfield that dated back to the raid. They might be able to find foundation stones for something from earlier, if they tried, but they would have to go outside of the main village and into the woods and farmland.

They decided to go pay a visit to the Old Burying Ground too, just to see what they could see. The day was hot, it being July already, and Pete had stripped down to a tee shirt already. So had his buddy, Sumner. When they saw the stranger in the cemetery wearing a full leather jacket in the hot sun, Pete had to sit up and take notice. After all, he might not have been dating a cop for long, but he'd been paying close attention.

He and Sumner wandered through the graves, searching for indicators of the deceased from 1704—or earlier. Pete took photos of those, but he made sure to get a few selfies. As they walked through the once-neat rows, he kept a watchful eye on the stranger. The unknown man watched him, and only half seemed to be trying to hide himself, but didn't approach.

Pete took a selfie with his phone and texted it to Ozzy. *This guy is following us around the cemetery in Deerfield. Seems odd.*

"Dude," Sumner said, leaning in. "What's with all of the selfies?"

"That guy's been following us through the cemetery." Pete smirked but kept his voice down. "Now we've got proof."

"Oo-oh." Sumner high-fived him. "I get it. What are you doing now?"

"Complaining to my state trooper fiancé about being followed. There's this thing going on." He rolled his eyes as the response text came in. *I'll have a unit there in twenty.* "All we need to do is hang out in a visible location for another twenty minutes and it should be okay." He used the phone's zoom feature to take a closer look at the stalker.

He didn't like what he saw. *Ew. I'm pretty sure that's the guy who passed us the note when we were on that date.*

You sure?

The hands are familiar.

I'll tell them to step on it.

They found some of the headstones they were looking for, and some from before. Sumner was looking to write a book about patterns of Native resistance to colonization during the settlement of New England, and Deerfield seemed like a fantastic subject for him. Not only was it the site of a disastrous raid in 1704, but it had also been the site of pitched and bloody battles during Metacom's War decades before. Finding the tombstones was a fantastic stroke of luck— although maybe not for those buried beneath them.

It did, however, give the two men something to do while they waited for the cavalry to arrive. Pete took pictures. Sumner took notes and tried to take rubbings, which was a bad idea and didn't work out all that well anyway.

Ten minutes after they set up for their activities, the strange man approached. "Hiya, Pete." He held out a spotted hand. "We weren't properly introduced the last time we met, but my name's Russ."

Pete could barely hear anything over the roar in his ears. He hadn't been all that afraid of this guy the last time they'd met, but that was before he knew what Russ was. Now that he knew that Russ was a stooge for one of the worst gangsters in Massachusetts, he couldn't shake the image of his own body laid out on the ground.

He didn't want to offend Russ and hasten that vision's journey into reality. He didn't want to get Sumner into trouble, either, or at least not worse than he already was. "This is Edison," he said, gesturing to Sumner.

"Pleased to meet you, Edison. My friend Pete doesn't work with sub-standard journalists. Pete, you're really looking well since your daughter was born. You're looking downright gaunt."

Pete fought back a snicker. "Um. Okay. Thanks. Not that it's not good to see you again, but I'm curious as to why you're hanging out in a cemetery in Deerfield in the middle of July."

"Oh. Right. I was hoping we could talk, just a little bit. Your boy, he's barking up the wrong tree with Sierzant." Russ smiled then, just a little bit.

"Okay?" Pete spread his hands out in front of him. "Listen, he's a great guy and everything, but I'm going to need more than 'A guy in the graveyard told me that he didn't do it.' Cops don't just listen to their partners, you know? I have to have evidence."

Russ nodded a few times. "Makes sense, I guess. Unfortunately, I have no way to give him the proof he needs. He's already got the evidence that he needs, if he thinks about it right."

Pete's mind raced, trying to sort through several thoughts at once. Could they get away? If so, how fast could they do it? He still had to keep the conversation going, too. It was no different from that night in the IHOP with Sierzant, except he no longer had a fetus trying to do chin-ups on his ribcage. What could Russ have meant by his comment that Ozzy already had all of the evidence that he needed? "Do you mean the gun that started the whole thing?"

Russ tapped the side of his nose. "You're a smart cookie, Pete. Yeah. The gun should still tell the whole story. I mean, nowadays you've got all kinds of testing, right? You can see the tiniest drops of blood, little bits of skin that get caught where little girls don't think to clean a weapon. That kind of thing." He winked. "In a very real way, Joe and your boy are on the same side. They both want the person who killed Tim Harbaugh to get what's coming to them. Your boy's just more likely to be able to do it in a way that's socially acceptable than Joe is, and your boy's involvement makes it harder for Joe to just take care of it."

"Yeah." Pete took a deep breath. "This many eyes, making Harbaugh look like some kind of martyr, makes it harder to just kill the one that did it. Brings in too much scrutiny and, assuming that he's telling the truth, it looks bad. Makes him look extra guilty."

"Exactly." Russ grinned, less shark-like and more genuine this time.

"What do you think?" Pete tilted his head to the side. "Who do you think killed Harbaugh?"

"Me? Who cares?" Russ huffed out a little laugh. "I just work here. I know exactly who killed Harbaugh. And I know it wasn't Joe. But you know what? I don't care. The bastard had it coming." He stuffed his hands into his pockets. "Any of us working for Joe, we all got it coming, okay?"

A siren wailed in the distance. "That's my cue, boys. It was good meeting you, Edison. Good luck with your project." Russ shook their hands again, and then he faded away among the trees at the edge of the space.

Two police cruisers pulled into the space one minute later. One of the officers ran off into the tree line to look for the criminal. Pete knew they wouldn't find him.

Chapter Thirteen

Ozzy wanted Pete to stop working after the incident with Russ. "It's too dangerous," he said, in a very earnest voice. "I can't keep you safe if you're out there throwing yourself into harm's way like that. I just can't; it won't be physically possible."

"I understand that." Pete sat on the edge of their bed that same night, Marissa in his arms, trying to calm Ozzy down. "I do. You're scared, I'm scared, we're all scared and that's perfectly normal under the circumstances. But my work is important to me and you can't just demand that I stop doing it because the world's dumbest dirty cop decided to act out. I could get hit by a bus tomorrow; do you want to ban buses?"

"Kind of!" Ozzy crossed his arms over his chest and pouted. "A bus isn't going to seek you out and try to harm you to get at me, Pete. This isn't a game. These are real people, bad people, and they don't mean you well."

"That's fine." Pete set his jaw. "It's not the first time I've faced down something ugly, either. I'm not exactly a wedding photographer, remember? No, I don't seek it out, but it's a reality that I have to accept. This is just one more aspect that I need to take reasonable precautions against and try to plan for. It's not something that I'm going to let scare me off."

"Pete, listen to me! This is not just a couple of guys playing with matches!" Ozzy pulled at his hair.

"You know, part of the problem with being what we are, of having that kind of instant and binding connection, is that we don't usually know one another well before we commit. Go look at my body of work, Ozzy." Pete got up and put his sleeping daughter in her bassinette. "I've done shoots in the middle of forest fires, epic floods, and even tornados. I've gone down to Peru, and Colombia to do jobs on the guerrillas there. I've covered the drug cartels in Mexico. I've covered the militias out in Montana and Idaho. I've covered religious extremists who think people like us should be burned at the stake to purify our souls before God, Ozzy." He remained standing as he turned back to Ozzy.

"This is different!" Ozzy massaged little circles into his temple.

"How? How is this different? It's my choice."

"It really isn't. Not anymore." Ozzy pointed at the bassinette. "You have her. You have me. You have people who depend on you now. You don't get to just turn your back and say *whatever, it's art* to us!"

Pete stiffened his back. "Actually I do. And that's not what I'm doing now." He closed his eyes. "I'm showing my daughter, *our* daughter, that I'm not going to live a life dictated by fear, or by anyone else. I make my own decisions. When she goes to school, and the teacher says, 'What do your daddies do?' she's going to say, 'One catches bad guys and one shows the truth to the world.' Not, 'One catches bad guys and one hides in the basement from his own shadow.'"

He took a deep breath. "And you don't depend on me. Marissa depends on me. You don't. You come crawling home at midnight, you leave before six, you don't even eat here on the weekends anymore. The house is just a place to store your stuff."

Ozzy staggered back. Pete could have stabbed him and it probably wouldn't have hurt that bad. "How can you say that? Everything I'm doing I'm doing for you, to keep you safe!"

"Except you could literally lock me into a closet somewhere and I still wouldn't be safe. This guy has a wide network that's going to take a long time to dismantle." Pete closed his eyes. "I think you must be pretty unhappy here, or else you'd be more interested in what's going on here than what's going on down at the station." He shook his head. "I'm sorry. I'm not looking to pick a fight with you. I know that you want this to work as much as I do. I just… I think that if it *was* working, you'd be here."

Tears rolled out of Ozzy's eyes. "Pete, come on. I know it's been rough, but it's just until we catch Sierzant. Once we get him, things will get better."

Pete sighed. Everything he'd said had just gone in one ear and out the other. "Sure, Ozzy." He headed for the walk-in closet and got changed into pajamas. "I'm pretty tired. It's been a long day."

"Oh. Yeah. Good night, Pete."

Ozzy didn't come to bed that night. Pete found a blanket on the couch when he got up the next morning.

Pete's family was falling apart, and there was nothing he could do about it. He'd tried to express his concerns, and might as well have saved his breath for all that Ozzy had listened. Ozzy hadn't even noticed the weight that Pete had lost, the way that Pete had been unable to eat much at all since Marissa was born. If Ozzy wouldn't even listen to Pete about staying in the workplace, or about Pete's need for him at home, he certainly wouldn't listen to him about how Pete was feeling about himself.

Ruth didn't say anything. Pete didn't expect her to. They worked well together, and he knew that she cared, but they didn't have that kind of friendly relationship.

Pete didn't completely discount everything Ozzy had said about Sierzant, just because they disagreed about the response. Pete knew that he wasn't safe, and he was less safe given that the alpha whose investigation caused him to be targeted wasn't paying enough attention to know what was going on. He made a point of being extra aware of his surroundings. He tried to avoid going alone into secluded locations for shoots.

And he made more of an effort to bring Ruth to Weston.

Ruth hated Weston. She didn't hide it well, getting tense and quiet as soon as they crossed the town line. She acceded to the plan more readily once Pete explained himself to her, though. "Look. Ozzy's right to worry, even if I don't think that he's right about how to handle it. If something happens, I want you to take Marissa and get to safety. My mom's got this giant gate around her property, and it's electrified when she wants it to be."

"I see." Ruth nodded. "That's actually kind of genius."

"I have my moments."

If Cynthia suspected the reasons that Pete insisted on bringing the nanny on visits, she didn't express them. When Pete insisted on leaving a cache of formula, diapers, and clothing changes at the house, she did raise an eyebrow. "Trouble in paradise, my dear?"

"It's not what you think, Mom." He stood up straight. "It's in case something happens to me or Ozzy, and one of us or Ruth has to run with Marissa. Your house is the most secure."

"Ah." She pressed her mouth together. "You know, I thought you'd have been claimed by now. How old is Marissa now? Nine weeks?"

He wouldn't react. He wouldn't rise to the bait. "Something like, yeah."

"Hm." She shook her head. "Well, I do hate to be an I-told-you-so. Is he still sharing your bed at least?"

"Mother!" His cheeks burned. Then he hung his head. "No. I don't... He doesn't want to. He's been on the couch."

Cynthia threw her arms around him, the first time she'd done that since Pete had been a small child. "Oh, Peter. I'm so sorry. Come home. Come home, and live here again. Don't live someplace where you have to be reminded of him."

Pete let the tears leak out of his eyes. Could he truly give up on Ozzy, and on their life together? Was there anything of that life to cling to? "I'll think about it," he promised, and he meant it.

"Excellent."

He cleaned himself up and even managed to have a civil conversation with Angus before he and Ruth packed Marissa up to go home. He felt a little bit better for having admitted to his mother that things were going poorly. Cynthia hadn't ever been the kind of mother that a person confided in, but she'd been supportive when he needed her just now. She hadn't judged him, and she hadn't really judged Ozzy either. She'd just offered him a space to go where he didn't have to be reminded, and if things were truly over that was what he needed.

When they pulled into the driveway, the house was dark. That wasn't unexpected. The house was usually dark when Pete and Ruth were both out. Pete sat in the driveway for a long moment, trying to figure out why something seemed amiss. The front door was closed, the window treatments looked as pristine as they always did, and there wasn't anything outward to signal what was wrong.

"The patrol car," he said, snapping his fingers.

Ruth twisted her body around to try and get a look behind herself. "The one that usually sits across the street?"

"Exactly. It's not there." He licked his lips. "Your phone is paired to the Bluetooth in this car, right?"

"Yeah." She nodded, eyes wide. "You made sure of it yourself. You don't really think there's a problem, do you? It's possible that he got called away by something major, like a big accident or a bank robbery or something."

"It's possible." He gripped the wheel for a moment. He should just turn the car back on, throw it into reverse, and head back into Weston. He didn't give even half a crap if he looked ridiculous. He cared about his daughter. He cared about Ruth. He wasn't a court of law; he didn't need proof right now.

If he spooked, though, he'd have to talk to Ozzy about it. He wasn't ready for that yet.

"Have 911 pre-dialed and be ready to run," he warned. "I hope that it's nothing, and I'm probably being absurd. Postpartum depression, right? But I'd rather be too cautious than not cautious enough."

They got out of the car together and headed toward the kitchen entrance, the one they usually used. Pete opened the door cautiously and inched into the house. He didn't smell anything different, or anything special.

The fact that the presence of his alpha now qualified as something *different* and *special* almost knocked him to his feet with grief.

He paused after a few steps into the kitchen. There weren't any new scents. He couldn't see anything special in the dark house, either. Not right away. He held up a hand, and Ruth froze in her tracks, creating perfect silence.

A floorboard creaked. Pete turned his face to look in that direction, and he saw a glint of metal.

"Run!" he barked to Ruth. "I'll hold them off!"

The door slammed as Ruth raced back out the door. A gunshot exploded, the muzzle flash bright and beautiful in the darkness just before searing pain ripped through Pete's arm. He cried out and clutched at the arm, ducking close to the ground before he raced for shelter.

Liquid, hot and sticky and bad, pumped out between his fingers. That wasn't good. He tried not to think about it as he duck-walked toward the living room. If he could make it out to the front door, maybe he could make it out of here alive.

"Ah, ah, ah!" called a voice that Pete didn't recognize. "I don't know if anyone ever told you, what the boss wants, the boss gets. And the boss wants you." Another gunshot echoed through the house. Pete heard it embed itself in the drywall. *I hate spackling,* he thought to himself with a semi-hysterical giggle. "Come out, come out, wherever you are!"

He heard the attacker's heavy boots stomp past him and into the living room. Well, crap. Maybe he could find his way to safety through the kitchen. He crawled out from hiding and made a beeline for the back of the house, staying as low to the ground as he could.

Blood loss was already making him dizzy, which wasn't good. Hopefully Ruth had gotten away. Hopefully she'd called 911, but the important thing was that she'd gotten away. Marissa being safe was the only thing that mattered right now.

He fumbled with the back door and stumbled out onto the deck. He'd almost made it to freedom. If Ruth had called 911, he'd be safe just as soon as the cavalry got here. Assuming, of course, that the cops who showed up were clean.

He didn't have time to be chilled by the thought. Russ stood at the foot of the deck stairs, shaking his head. "Your boy doesn't know when to quit, does he?"

Pete didn't know what else to do. He threw his head back and screamed.

A light went on at the house next door.

"Ah crap." Russ shook his head. "Here we go." He hefted Pete into his arms and made a face even as the other assailant ran out the back door. "Hey dumbass, shooting him was brilliant. He's bleeding all over the place. Our orders were to bring him in alive."

"Yeah, well, if we get him to the car I'll patch him up. I got a kit in there." Pete could see the attacker clearly now. He wore a state trooper's uniform. "If you hadn't run, I wouldn't have shot you."

Russ carried him, huffing and puffing the whole time, over to Pete's detached garage. When the assailant threw open the door, Pete's heart sank.

No one was going to save him. Not only was his attacker in uniform, he drove a state police cruiser. In fact, he was the guy scheduled to sit outside Pete's house.

The trooper opened the trunk and cut off Pete's shirt. Then he slapped a piece of gauze down onto the wound, pressing hard, and wrapped it in more gauze. He taped that gauze in place. Pete was already woozy from blood loss, which he could see now was substantial. When they tied his wrists and ankles, he didn't have the strength to resist them.

They folded him into the trunk and closed the lid. Ozzy's final thoughts, before pain, panic, and blood loss caught up to him, were about how no one would think twice about letting a cruiser through, in any direction.

...

After the fight about Pete staying home, when Pete decided to be a stubborn ass and then accused Ozzy of staying at work so late just to avoid him, Ozzy found himself at a loss. For the first time in his life, he had no idea what to do. He decided to sleep on the couch, so that he wouldn't wake Pete up. Obviously Ozzy waking up so early was having a kind of negative effect on Pete, making him overthink the whole thing with Ozzy's schedule. If he wasn't confronted with it, then he wouldn't think about it.

For a while, Ozzy thought that it must be working. At least, he didn't have any way of knowing that it wasn't working. He didn't see much of Pete, at all. At least before, he'd been able to see Pete when Pete was sleeping, to hold him close and breathe in his scent. Now he couldn't even do that, and he knew on some level that was bad. It was going to take a lot of work to fix their relationship, and to get some things through Pete's head.

God, but he missed Pete. He missed Marissa, too. He missed their alone time, those late night feedings. It would all get better, he told himself, once they'd nailed Sierzant to the wall.

Devlin was the one who first tried to clue him in that things might not be as great as he wanted them to be. He called Ozzy into a meeting, first thing in the morning because the guy was a sadist. "Hey. Is everything okay?"

"Yes, sir." Ozzy nodded. "The case is moving along. We've found what Parzych was hiding. He's been working for Sierzant for five years, helping him to run drugs from Springfield to Worcester. And I've got a full name for the guy who accosted Pete and his buddy in Deerfield." Mentioning his omega's name gave him a pang, but he pushed through it. "Russell Meyrick, formerly of the Massachusetts State Police and now the proud owner of a whole row of buildings in the Back Bay."

Devlin whistled. "Yeah, sure, that money's clean. But that's not what I called you in to talk about. You're here from six o'clock in the morning until well past eleven at night."

"Oh, that's okay, sir. I've never needed much sleep." Ozzy shook his head.

"That's fine for you. But you've got an omega now. You have to take care of him, Ozzy." He folded his hands on his desk.

"Oh." Ozzy blushed. "I haven't claimed him yet."

Devlin drew his brows together. "Oh. Well that's interesting. Can I ask why not?"

Ozzy frowned. "There's a case, remember? I have to focus on the case. That's my job."

"Sure, it's your job. But you're supposed to be in love with him, right?" Devlin sat back in his chair, waiting for Ozzy's answer.

"Of course I'm in love with him. I'm just waiting for the case to be over before I claim him." Ozzy bit the inside of his cheek. "He's not ever going to be safe until I finish this."

"Okay. But you do get that he has other needs too." He cracked his knuckles. "Did they talk to you about an omega's needs, postpartum?"

Ozzy stood up. "Sir, Pete's a big boy. He'd tell me if he were sick, if there was an infection. He'd go to the doctor."

"It's not like that. Pregnancy changes a body, and a lot of people feel very uncomfortable with their bodies after they've just had a baby. Those that have partners need to feel that their partners still love them, still want them, and are still attracted to them." He leaned forward. "I know this is a delicate subject, and I normally would never want to even briefly think about my subordinates in anything resembling a sexual context. Ever," he added with a shudder. "But here's the thing. The man I saw when he was here the other day did not look healthy. He's not taking care of himself. And there's no one around who's making sure that he eats or sleeps.

"If I didn't know that he has an alpha, Ozzy, I'd say that he was alone. I'd go so far as to suggest that he'd been abandoned by his alpha. Now I know that none of my detectives would abandon an omega."

Ozzy rolled his eyes and leaned on the wall. "Sir, with all due respect, I feel like you're overreacting a little. It's hard to be a parent. It's harder to be a parent when the other one's working overtime, okay? He's doing all the work, getting up for all of the late night feedings and everything, while I'm here. We've got a nanny; I'm not sure what she's supposed to be doing. But it's just until the case is over."

Devlin blinked at him. "Ozzy, there's always a case. We're detectives. When there aren't any more cases, we're out of a job."

He shrugged off Devlin's comments, moved on and kept working, trying to narrow down enough on Sierzant to get a warrant. They would have to move against the dirty cops all at once, and Amos was reluctant to do it now. He was sure they could catch more if they kept digging, and he wasn't wrong. The question was, was it worth it to keep digging at dirty cops or would it be better to go after the mud puddle that soiled them?

Robles tried to say something to him about Pete too. He came up to Ozzy about a week and a half after the fight and bent down at his desk, speaking to Ozzy in a low voice. "Hey, man, are you and Pete okay?"

"We're fine." Ozzy shrugged. "No problems. Why?"

"Because Ryan's freaking out. He says that you haven't claimed Pete, even though it's been eight weeks since Marissa was born, and now Ryan's scared that I'm going to abandon him too." Robles rolled his eyes. "I know, right?"

Ozzy scowled. "What the hell is this, *abandon* crap? I haven't abandoned anyone. I still live there. I'm sleeping on the couch so that Pete doesn't wake up when I come home or when I wake up. I haven't claimed him because I need to finish the case first. That's all. Did he use the word abandoned?"

"No, man." Robles held up his hands. "No. Ryan did. I mean, Pete's looking kind of bad, I think Ryan can be forgiven for thinking that. But it's between you guys. You still do want him, right?"

"Of course I do!" Ozzy thumped the desk. "Why do people keep asking me that?"

Robles turned bright red. "Um. Ryan asked him if sex is any different after the baby than it is before, and Pete told him that you haven't wanted it since Marissa was born." He held his hands up again, in a kind of warding gesture. "I mean, again, that's between you guys. Not my business, but hey, you asked."

"Why the hell is Pete talking about this with Ryan and not me?" Ozzy looked up at the ceiling.

"Um." Robles looked down at the ground. "Don't shoot the messenger, but according to Pete, he did."

Ozzy's mouth dropped open. "I mean we had a fight, but—" He clenched his jaw. "Damn it." He sighed. "Once this case is over, we're going to have to have a come to Jesus meeting, I think. It's obvious that there's a lot he just doesn't get."

Robles' eyes narrowed. "I think he gets just plenty, man. You're avoiding the house like it's the plague. Everyone can see it. Again, not our business, but it's not like we can't see it. What's going on that's keeping you away from him?" He tilted his head to the side. "Do you think that he's being unfaithful? Because I can tell you, buddy, he isn't."

"No!" He pounded his hand on the desk.

"He's not going to be willing to wait around forever, man. I get that the honeymoon couldn't last forever, but remember that Ryan did actually dump me. We loved each other plenty, and he still dumped me because I was being an idiot. Don't let that be you. He took me back and I'm still trying to figure out why. Don't think, even for a minute, that you'll be that lucky."

Ozzy closed his eyes. "Look. It's just a matter of finishing this case, okay? If he can't manage to hold out until we finish this case, then he's not cut out to be mated to a cop." The thought clawed at him. He only wanted Pete. He needed Pete. He didn't want to lose him, but facts were facts. He was a cop, and that wasn't going to change.

Another week and a half after that confrontation found Ozzy sitting at his desk, as usual. He was fairly certain that they had the evidence they needed to convict Sierzant of racketeering, drug running, and a host of other charges. He didn't have the evidence that they needed to convict Sierzant of Tim Harbaugh's murder, and that was what he needed. Once he had that, once he'd arrested Sierzant for that one crime, he could back off and work on things at home.

His phone rang. "Detective Morris, Cold Case." He didn't bother to look at the caller ID.

"Ozzy." The woman's voice dripped with ice, venom, and spite. "This is Cynthia Norris. You know, Peter's mother, back before you abandoned him."

Ozzy looked up at the ceiling. "Lord give me patience." He picked his head up. "I haven't abandoned anyone. I'm working on a very important case right now, Cynthia. One that happens to involve your son, and an organized crime organization that's threatened your son twice now. I'd think that would arouse your interest—"

"Three."

"No, it was just two. Unless there was something that Pete just didn't bother to tell me." Had things deteriorated to the point where Pete just wouldn't tell him that he'd been threatened again?

Cynthia gave a bitter little laugh. "He can't very well tell you anything, can he? He's been taken."

Ozzy's entire world narrowed to the telephone. "What?"

"His nanny, Ruth, got away with the child. She said she heard gunshots as she was fleeing. She wanted to stop, but she had to get Marissa to safety. That was their plan all along. A plan," Cynthia said, with a terrible emphasis, "that Peter came up with all by himself, because he had to."

Ozzy couldn't get enough air into his lungs. "Where are you?"

"I'm at home, silly boy. With Ruth and my grandchild, should anyone want to speak with her." She hung up.

Ozzy's hand shook as he dialed the only number that he could think of: Lt. Devlin.

Within moments, the empty office was alive with activity. Oliver had still been in the office; he rushed upstairs to assure Ozzy that he and his most trusted colleagues would process the house to within an inch of its life. Ozzy knew that they would miss nothing, the fact that it was dark notwithstanding. Devlin showed up at the office not long after that, with Ed Amos in tow. Amos, like Ozzy, had still been in the office.

The others filed in slowly, since they were all coming from different places. Robles brought Ryan with him, because when they found Pete he was going to need a friend. Ryan was as big as a house by now, but he was as alert and quick-reflexed as ever. Langer showed up a little bit after them, in civilian attire; he'd been at a rock show, and drove straight to the office when he got Devlin's text. Tessaro came next, carrying two boxes of Dunkin Donuts coffee. "No one sleeps until Pete is found," he declared, and then he jerked his head at Ryan. "Except Pretty Boy." He grinned as Robles bristled.

Nenci was the last one to show up, but he showed up with something important. He showed up with a scanner. "We don't often listen in on radio frequencies in here," he grinned. "It's distracting. But I figured that we could make an exception now."

It made sense. They were dealing with dirty cops. Dirty cops would be talking to other dirty cops on the tools that they usually used. "All right," Devlin said, taking charge after one look at Ozzy. "Robles, you and Langer need to go out to the crime scene and check it out from top to bottom. I know Oliver's already out there. I want detectives out there too, not just technicians. Ozzy, you and Tessaro are heading out to Weston. I want you talking to the witness. Take Amos with you, I get the sense that he's going to need to hear some of that.

"Nenci, I want you to be here with Ryan, manning the radios. Can you promise me that you won't shoot one another or do I have to take your guns away?"

"No promises," Ryan told him, with a glower at Nenci. "But considering that this is for Pete, and Ozzy, and Marissa, I'll only shoot him in the ass."

Nenci flipped him off, but it was casual, and Ozzy staggered to his feet to follow Tessaro and Amos to Tessaro's car.

When they got there, the gate was locked, and they could hear the telltale spark of electricity that suggested that it had been electrified. "Huh," Tessaro said, raising an eyebrow. "Grandma's not playing."

"Do you have a security code?" Amos asked him.

"I don't." Ozzy shook his head. "She hates me."

Amos took his phone and called Cynthia. After he held the phone away from his ear to receive her aggressive greeting, he spoke. "Sorry to reach out this way, ma'am, but I had no other way to reach out. My name is Lt. Ed Amos, I'm here with Ozzy Morris and Pat Tessaro. We're here to speak with Ruth Venalainen about the abduction tonight."

He paused, and the gate opened just wide enough to admit Tessaro's car. It closed just after the bumper closed behind him, and Tessaro winced at the close call.

They parked in the circular drive, and an armed guard let them in only after seeing all of their badges. Cynthia met them in the overly elegant foyer, along with the eminently useless Angus. "So. Now you care." She sniffed.

"Not the time, ma'am. We have multiple departments working multiple shifts. No one sleeps until Pete is found." Tessaro gave her a little smile—still authoritative, but sympathetic. "We love him too. Not as much, of course, but we love him too. Ozzy tells me that you knew this was a possibility, that you planned for it. When was the subject brought up between you?"

Ozzy wandered away in search of Ruth and Marissa. He found them ensconced in a small, cozy nook between the stairwell and the kitchen.

"Oh, Ozzy!" Ruth looked up at Ozzy and sobbed. Marissa started in too, and Ozzy took his daughter into his arms and held them both close. He needed to get Pete back, and that was his priority, but he was a cop. His job was to help people, and they'd just been through a deeply traumatic experience.

Besides, Marissa was his daughter. If Pete was missing, it was Ozzy's job to take care of her.

Chapter Fourteen

Pete woke up to two things. He woke up to pain, pain that was on par with giving birth—although it was nothing like bringing a child into the world. And he woke up to pressure, pressure that felt exactly like four grown men sitting on his limbs. When his eyes flew open, shocked into wakefulness by pain and misery, he could see that he felt that way for a reason. Four large men were, in fact, sitting on his limbs.

The pain had a logical source too. Russ knelt down on the dusty ground beside Pete. He had a sharp knife in his hand, and a pair of tweezers. A younger man crouched nearby with a Mag-Lite aimed at the wound in Pete's arm, and Russ was using the tweezers to poke around inside his arm. "Oh good. You're awake." Russ rolled his eyes. "This is going to hurt. Hey Moab, bring some of that vodka over here, would you?"

"Vodka?" Pete croaked.

Russ smirked. "You wouldn't want to have me digging a bullet out of you without any anesthetic at all, would you?"

Some guy that Pete didn't know held the bottle to his lips and turned his head to look back at Russ. "Drink up, buddy. This is going to hurt."

Pete thought about resisting. He'd been kidnapped. He needed to keep his wits about him. At the same time, there was no element of choice here. Russ was going to operate, whether Pete consented or not. Taking something to numb the pain would be in his best interests. He drank until Moab pulled the bottle away.

His stomach was empty—it often was these days—and he was more than a little dehydrated. It didn't take long for the vodka to hit. He watched as Russ took the bottle and took a healthy swig from it himself before turning back to Pete's arm.

"You know," Russ said, digging into the flesh of his arm again, "I don't like the way this bullet hit. I can't find it; I think it ricocheted off the bone. That's kind of weird."

"Is it?" Pete tried to remember his breathing exercises from the hospital. If he'd gotten through that, he could get through this.

"Trust me, I would know. I'm a professional. I was, anyway." He put his knife aside, on the dirty and dusty ground, and started to poke around at the wounds. "There we go. I was never a professional at this, of course. I was a cop. You do what you have to do as a cop, but field surgery isn't usually one of the job requirements."

"Mmm. Never hurts to be repaired. Prepared." Pete grunted as Russ used the tweezers to pull the bullet out.

"I guess you're not a big drinker." Russ chuckled.

"Not since I got pregnant, no." Pete closed his eyes. "Also I think I'm a pint or so low, maybe."

"Yeah. I think my genius partner over there might have nicked something important. Don't worry. We'll get you stitched up, you'll be good as new." He ruffled Pete's hair with his bloody hand. "We'll get you a sling for that busted wing, too."

"We will?" asked the guy holding Pete's right leg.

"Sure we will. We've got to hold him until the boss comes. There's no reason we can't make him a little more comfortable. I mean, his arm's fractured, Johnny. I could see the damn bone." Russ scowled at the man, and Johnny shut up.

Pete's gut tied itself into a knot. His arm was broken? A fracture was less awful than a full break, but it was still pretty bad. It would keep him from being able to pick up Marissa, or wash her, or change her. He'd have to hire a backup, temporary nanny to help Ruth, because it wasn't fair to Ruth to expect her to spend every minute of every day with the baby.

Who was he kidding? The chances of him getting out of this alive were slim to none. They might not intend to kill him now—otherwise they wouldn't have wasted the time and energy fixing his arm as best they could. Still, they'd cut his throat without a second thought if they thought it would get them something. He groaned and passed out just as Russ started the stitching.

When he woke up again, there was no more pressure on his limbs, and he wasn't lying on the floor anymore. He'd been moved to some kind of a beanbag chair. It was indifferently clean, but it was softer than the scuffed wooden floor he'd been on before.

He felt awful. He chalked the headache and vague nausea up to having consumed so much vodka the last time he'd been awake; he'd never been a heavy drinker and he hadn't drunk much at all since Marissa showed up. Drinking alone had never been his thing.

Would he ever get a chance to see Ozzy again? Would he have a chance to tell him that he loved him? Even if things didn't work out, even if Ozzy didn't love him anymore, he was still glad they'd been together.

Someone cleared his throat. Pete rolled over, only now realizing that his arm had been strapped into a makeshift sling, and saw Joe Sierzant standing near Russ. He struggled to rise, but found bracing himself to stand with only one arm to be more difficult than he wanted it to be.

Russ stepped in to help him up. Sierzant rolled his eyes. "I'm sorry my man shot you," he told Pete. "His orders were to bring you in alive and unharmed. He's being dealt with."

Pete did not want to know what that meant in the Sierzant organization. There were so many different possibilities. "Thank you," he said, squinting against the dim light pouring in through the dirty windows. "I appreciate that."

Sierzant grinned. "You're probably wondering why you're here."

Pete bit his lip. "My guess is that you're trying to use me to get Ozzy to back off. Because you didn't kill Harbaugh, and I'm inclined to believe you."

Sierzant pursed his lips a little. "Really? Why is that?"

Pete tried not to sway on his feet. "Honestly? Because you don't strike me as the kind of guy who would be ashamed of it if he had. Not that you'd go bragging about killing a cop in front of cops, that would be stupid. But you wouldn't spend as much time and effort on convincing Ozzy, or me, that you hadn't done it if you had. You're a very confident man, Mr. Sierzant. You're not ashamed of anything you do."

Sierzant laughed out loud. "Did I tell you that I like this guy or what, Russ?" He patted Russ on the back. "You're exactly right. How is it possible that you can be so right and your man can be so wrong?"

Ozzy. What was he doing right now? Did he even know that Pete was gone? Pete had no way to know how much time had passed, only that the vodka had burned its way out of his system. Was he looking for Pete, or had he delegated that responsibility to someone else in his obsession with Joe Sierzant?

"I don't know," he admitted. He met his kidnapper's eyes. "He hasn't been confiding in me about the case. I know he's found some things that he feels strongly about. You'd have to talk to him about that." He gave Sierzant a grin. "If you feel like giving me a ride back to Framingham, I could probably arrange something."

"I'm telling you, this guy, he's a pistol!" Sierzant laughed again. "You look tired. I'm going to let you get some rest. Russ, have someone find a blanket for my friend here, would you? The poor guy is shivering."

Russ winced and followed Sierzant away. Pete staggered over to the window. How could he be shivering? He didn't feel cold. He felt warm, uncomfortably warm.

The windows were the old-fashioned type, huge, heavy, and impossible to operate with one hand. Even if they hadn't been impossible to open that way, they had been nailed shut at some point when they put in air conditioning.

He stumbled back over to his beanbag. As near as he could tell, he was in an old school. The school clearly wasn't in use anymore; the desks had all been removed. When had the last class been taught?

He settled back into position on the beanbag. It wasn't big enough for his body, not being intended to be a bed at all, and he had to curl up like a dog to fit onto it entirely. Part of him was grateful just to be alive. They hadn't set out to hurt him, and seemed genuinely concerned about his welfare. The rest of him knew that it was all crap. If they were all that worried, they'd have brought him to a hotel or a motel instead of leaving him on a dirty beanbag in an abandoned school.

All of him could agree on one thing: he missed Ozzy, and terribly. Their last words to one another had been a fight, and that had been weeks ago. He didn't want to leave it this way. There hadn't been a chance to make up. They hadn't been around one another since then; Pete hadn't even seen his lover in passing. Maybe he should have gone into the office and forced Ozzy to pay attention to him. Ozzy would have been mad, but at least they'd have had that face off instead of fading away into nothing… and then this.

He wanted Ozzy. He wanted Marissa, wanted to see her tiny face staring up at him in wonder again. He wanted to feel her little fingers on his face, or grabbing at his clothes. He just wanted the warm comfort of family again.

Russ returned with a blanket. It was none too clean, and even stained here and there. He settled it over Pete with tenderness and a degree of affection that Pete wouldn't have thought he possessed. "Thanks," Pete whispered.

"Don't mention it," Russ murmured." He sat down beside Pete's beanbag. "I've got to say, Pete. I'm sorry about all of this. I wasn't on board with the decision to bring you in. I was worried about you getting hurt." He sighed and rested his head on his hands. "It's like this. I know that taking Joe up on his offer was the wrong thing to do, morally speaking. And I know that I've done a lot of things that I'm not so proud of while I've been out here, you know? But I never went after a cop. I never went after a cop's family. I get that it's extenuating circumstances, but there are some lines you just cannot cross, you know?" He tugged at his collar and looked away. "And I ain't the only one that feels that way." He sighed. "I'm not comfortable with your fever, buddy. I'm just saying." He got up and left the room.

Pete looked back up at the ceiling. Maybe Russ was feeling something about this whole mess, but if Pete had a fever why wouldn't he bring him some water? Or maybe some kind of recording device, so he could record a last message to Ozzy?

Pete knew what a fever meant. Fever meant infection. Infection was bad. The infection could get into his bloodstream and become systemic, killing him. The infection could get into his bones and… do bone things. He didn't know. He was a photographer; it wasn't his job to know these things.

He hunched in on himself even further. Everything was pain at this point, from his head to his toes. Now he knew that it wasn't a hangover. He'd been feeling the first symptoms of infection, which meant that he must have been out longer than he'd thought. That roughly jived with the sun starting to come up outside.

He tried to remember how infections progressed. How long did it take before they killed you? He guessed that depended on what exactly the infection was in the first place. He might have picked up the infection from the bullet itself, or from lying in the trunk of a car. It was entirely possible that this wasn't the result of hack surgery on the dirty floor.

His own blood still stained the floor over in the corner. He decided that he didn't need to check it out. He could see the puddle from here.

He didn't want to die like this. He didn't want the infection to kill him. He didn't want to go out the way that the infection would take him out, either. He'd heard enough to know that it would be bad, nothing resembling dignity to it at all. Not, he mused, that death carried much dignity to it in the first place. He'd been at enough crime scenes to know.

He tried not to think about it. He knew that there was at least one guard outside his door. In his condition, he couldn't get much of anywhere. Outside people drove past on their way to whatever the day held, but they had no way of knowing what was happening in the old abandoned school.

He wondered if Russ or Sierzant would shoot him before his own ravings started to get to be too bad. He hoped that it would be Russ. He thought that Russ was kinder somehow; maybe it was just the age spots on his hands, making Pete think of his own grandpa.

He drifted in and out of slumber. There wasn't anything else for him to do but fret, and he wasn't feeling up to fighting it anymore. Each time he woke up he felt warmer and warmer, and he wondered if when he woke up next he'd finally be in Hell.

...

Ozzy guzzled cup after cup of coffee. He didn't need the caffeine. Nothing was going to let him sleep until his omega was safe in his arms again. He drank the coffee so that he had something to do with his hands, so that he could avoid snapping something in half or punching a wall or otherwise being a destructive jackass.

His last words to Pete had been a fight. They'd been a damn fight. Everyone had told him that he needed to spend more time with Pete, that he needed to be there for his omega, but would he listen? No. They'd had a fight, and Ozzy had gone off and slept on the couch for three damn weeks. He'd assumed that there would be time to make up later. There was no more later. There might not be any more later, ever, if they didn't find Ozzy soon.

Everyone put everything else on hold to join in the hunt. If there had been any doubt in anyone's mind, it went out the window when Oliver showed up at the Cold Case office to tell detectives that Pete's blood, and no inconsiderable amount of it, had been found at the house.

"It wasn't enough to kill him," Oliver told him, back straight and head held high. "It wasn't. But it was enough to leave him weak and disoriented, and not able to fight back effectively. We also found a large amount of dust on the floor."

Ozzy shook his head. "I don't care if Pete has been depressed, he would never allow dust on the floor." He swallowed. "Even before Marissa showed up, he had this thing about keeping the house clean. It's a thing with him."

Oliver cleared his throat. "The dust is most conspicuous in the footprints of a male, wearing size ten work boots."

"But Pete's a twelve."

Tessaro whacked Ozzy on the back of his head. "Stop thinking like a family member and start thinking like a cop."

Ozzy rubbed at the back of his head. Tessaro hadn't held back much. "Ouch. Okay. So there was someone else in there, which jives with what Ruth told us and with what neighbors heard. They heard gunshots. The assailant came in from a very dusty environment. What does that tell us?"

"Could be anything," Nenci drawled, "but I'm thinking abandoned building. They get this level of grime to 'em, this deep dust, that never comes out no matter how hard you try. Plus, if it's abandoned, it's not going to have a lot of curious eyes."

"Considering the amount of blood, they couldn't have taken Pete very far if they wanted him to live. And they presumably want him to live." Ryan looked the worst out of all of them, because he was trying to solve a crime while growing another human. Pete hadn't done much but sleep at this stage of his pregnancy. "Kidnapping people you just plan to kill is an entirely different type of crime. I'm thinking abandoned buildings in Wayland, Lincoln, Concord, or Maynard. Marlborough is just a little too far out. Framingham is too close to here, too likely to run into one of our own."

Langer's fingers raced over the keyboard. "I've got a list of about a hundred buildings for us to check out."

"Pete doesn't have that kind of time!" Ozzy shouted.

"Hey," Devlin told him, grabbing his wrists. "Pete is strong. He can do this."

Ozzy's phone rang. He picked it up. "Detective Morris."

"Ozzy. I don't have much time, so put this on speaker."

Ozzy didn't recognize the voice on the other end, but he recognized the sense of urgency. He pushed the button to put the phone on speaker and gestured to his friends. "Okay. You've got the floor, buddy. Who are you?"

"My name is Russ Meyrick. Pete is being held in Room 206 at the old Roosevelt School in Maynard. Right now there's a guard of about ten, all ex-cops or current cops. Some are sympathetic to him. Some are not. You come in, you come in with your lights off and your cars silent. And I mean silent. They're listening for you. Don't trust anyone with a badge that you don't know. Got it?"

"Yeah?" Ozzy shrugged, stunned into helplessness.

"Good. He's sick. Get here fast." The line went dead.

Ozzy looked up at Devlin. "Do you think it's a trap?" His heart throbbed in his throat. Every instinct in him wanted to go after Pete, right the heck now, but he knew all too well the value of a well-baited trap.

"It's a possibility." Devlin stroked his chin. "Meyrick has shown himself to be friendly before, but that doesn't necessarily mean anything." He took a deep breath. "At the same time, Oliver said he'd lost a lot of blood. I think we have to risk it. SWAT is ready to scramble. Go suit up. I'll call Amos."

Ozzy had never put on his body armor so quickly in his life. He jumped into the SWAT transport with the rest of the guys and only briefly wondered if Amos had cleared them. He couldn't think about that now. When you went into a fight, you had to assume that the guys with you had your back. You couldn't sit around and twitch about it.

The trip up to Maynard passed in a blur. He couldn't see out the sides of the armored vehicle, so he had no idea what he was driving into. All that he knew was that the large, overstuffed vehicle was propelling him toward his mate.

The vehicle pulled to a stop, and the SWAT team rushed out of the back. Uniformed troopers, in conjunction with some members of Maynard PD, deployed around the perimeter. State troopers closed the road around the building, much to the anger of people engaged in their morning commute. It was time.

A cool calm came over Ozzy as they circled the building. The front door was boarded up, which made sense given that the building was abandoned. He could only assume that the kidnappers had gone through a rear door, not easily visible to the casual passer-by. He gestured to Tilson, and they circled around to the back.

They encountered their first guard, a denim-clad man with a stereotypical cop haircut and hooded blue eyes. He had dried blood on his clothes, and Ozzy could smell Pete in the stains. The cop held his hands up in surrender, even though he showed no fear. "I'm okay with a lot of things, boys," he said in a low voice. Ozzy figured that he was probably trying to avoid alerting anyone to the conversation. "I ain't okay with putting hands on a cop's family, man. That ain't right." He shook his head and let himself be pulled along to be formally arrested.

The next guard they encountered was not so remorseful as the first. He saw the black-clad SWAT team members heading up the stairs and pulled out his gun, drawing a bead on Ozzy. Ozzy didn't think twice. He shot the man in the shoulder that held the gun, knocking him down and forcing him to drop the gun. "So much for the element of surprise," he muttered, and ran. Someone else would detain the man. His first priority, his only concern, was Pete.

He and Wilson raced up the stairs to the second floor of the hundred-year-old school building. The sight of the old murals on the walls was jarring, reminding him of some of the old zombie apocalypse flicks he used to watch. He'd seen some similar places in Fallujah, "repurposed" schools, and he had to fight hard not to see Arabic graffiti on the colorful pictures.

When he saw room 206, his heart jumped. Two guards waited outside, and Ozzy brought his gun up when he saw them. They exchanged glances, though, and surrendered. "Dude's in bad shape," the one on the right told him. "He needs to be evacuated, pronto."

Tilson gestured, and he took the two prisoners down to find cops who could formally arrest them. Tilson was a smart guy. There was no way he was going to get in between Ozzy and his mate.

Ozzy kicked in the door to Pete's prison. The room was filthy, covered in a thick coating of dust. Pete wasn't hard to find. He lay curled up on a beanbag that had seen better days, under a blanket that had been used for God knew what in the past. His eyes were open but glazed over, and he shivered despite the sweat that shone on his face.

He turned his face toward Ozzy, and then he laughed. "Now the hallucinations," he said, speaking through cracked, dry lips.

Ozzy ran forward and peeled back the blanket. It wasn't hard to find the source of infection. Someone had sewed up a large wound in Pete's arm with black sewing thread, and big red streaks radiated out from the foul-smelling injury. "Oh, baby," Ozzy said, and dropped a kiss to Pete's burning forehead. "I'm going to take good care of you." He lifted his omega up into his arms. Maybe he should have waited for a stretcher and paramedics, but right now he didn't care. "We're going to get you to a hospital and we're going to get you healthy again, you'll see."

He couldn't help but wonder when Pete had gotten to be so damn thin.

He had to wait for Tilson before he could head out, but Tilson came back quickly. Then, Tilson covered him while Ozzy carried Pete down the back stairs and out toward the perimeter.

Pete had no idea what was happening. Ozzy had no way to know what was going on inside that fevered brain, but rescue wasn't part of it. He became combative as Ozzy tried to carry him out, which wouldn't have been a problem given Pete's weakness if Ozzy weren't trying to run with him through what was essentially a kill zone. Later, his heart would break that Pete didn't believe that Ozzy would come for him. Right now, he just had to hunker down and let his mind go blank.

Bullets exploded around him, but none hit him. He was lucky. He knew that. Cops on the ground fired back at cops in the building, and there was a part of Ozzy's brain that screamed in pain at the thought of firing on cops at all. It didn't matter what they'd done, shooting his brother officers was wrong, and he knew that every other officer on the ground and firing had that same voice screaming.

He made it out of range and screamed. "I need a truck!"

Tessaro was at his side in half a second. He holstered his weapon and reached out, not to take Pete from him but to share the burden. "Come on, there's one over here." They carried the struggling omega over to a waiting ambulance near the roadblock.

Paramedics opened the door and recoiled at the sight of Pete. Maybe it was the stench, Ozzy didn't know. "He's in bad shape," one said. He reached down to take Pete's head and shoulders.

Ozzy helped him to get Pete onto the gurney. "I know there's a gunshot wound that looks like a bad home surgery job."

"We'll get him to Emerson," the driver told him with a smile.

"Oh no," Tessaro told them with a shake of his head. "Pete's already been put in danger once today, by people we should have been able to trust. Do you really think his alpha's going to let him out of his sight?"

The paramedics swallowed and looked at each other. "Good point," the first one said and strapped Pete to the gurney. "Buckle up, officer."

"Thanks, Tessaro." Ozzy grinned at him, just a little, as the doors slammed closed.

The ride to Emerson Hospital should have taken five minutes. It took two. The first nurse to see Ozzy almost screamed when she saw him in his SWAT team get up, but the paramedic assured her that it was necessary. "Apparently there were dirty cops that took the guy, and the patient is this guy's omega, and it's fine. He didn't even try to shoot us."

"Close quarters," Ozzy shrugged.

They got Pete into a treatment bay right away. No one wanted to give him any nonsense about insurance or waiting to see a doctor, which told Ozzy that this was a dire emergency indeed. Doctors, nurses, and other people in scrubs and masks flooded the treatment bay, shouting out orders and demands for medications and equipment until Ozzy started to feel distinctly out of place.

Finally a doctor, a tiny woman who looked like she was probably of South Asian descent, turned to him and pointed. "Out. That gun is not sterile. A gun is never sterile. Out. Go call someone or something. We'll take it from here."

Ozzy had never been given an order with such finality. He left the treatment bay and went to the waiting room as the adrenaline slowly melted from his body.

He took off his helmet and his gloves. His phone was somewhere in his equipment, silenced for the mission so it couldn't be a distraction or give them away. He turned it on now, and stared at it for a long moment before finding the *recents* tab. Then, before he could chicken out, he dialed Cynthia Nolan's number. She deserved to know.

She picked up on the first ring. Had she been waiting by the phone all night, just hoping for a call? "Osmund?"

"Yeah. Yeah, Cynthia, it's me." He sounded awful, even to his own ears, and he didn't care. "We got him. We got Pete."

"Oh thank God," she said, her sobs obvious even over the phone. It was the most overt display of emotion that he'd ever seen from Cynthia, and for a moment he wanted to scream. Now she showed concern for Pete? But she came from a time and place and class that didn't reward outward displays. Ozzy was too emotional right now to be judgmental.

"He's in bad shape. The bad guys shot him, and the wound got infected. We're at Emerson Hospital. Still at the ER. We literally just got here." He let himself chuckle. "I wanted you to know."

She hesitated. "What about the miscreant behind all of this?"

"The other guys can take care of him. They've got him locked down inside the building. I don't give a crap about him. All I care about is getting Pete well again." He closed his eyes.

"We'll be there as soon as we can." Cynthia hung up.

She showed up not half an hour later, with Ruth, Angus, and Marissa in tow. Marissa barely seemed to recognize Ozzy, which brought tears to his eyes. He knew that he deserved it, though. He'd gotten so blinded by his drive to keep her and her daddy safe from Sierzant that he'd been a ghost in her life.

Cynthia seemed to be content to put their differences aside. In full view of the rest of the waiting room, she helped him to remove the heavy body armor that went with his SWAT identity. Then she put her arms around him and hugged him. "Thank you for rescuing my boy."

All of the adults clustered together for another two hours before the tiny South Asian doctor emerged from the treatment area. Her face was grave, and she'd changed her clothing. "I'm Dr. Sudhakar. I'm Mr. Nolan's physician while he stays with us." She looked around. "Are you all his family?"

Ozzy nodded. "I'm his alpha. This is his mother, his brother Angus, and our housemate Ruth." He decided to describe Ruth that way so that Dr. Sudhakar would let her stay; she didn't deserve to be excluded just because she was an employee.

"Okay then. If you'd like to come with me." She led them into a private consultation room. "I'm not going to lie. The infection is very bad. We're throwing everything we can at it. We've admitted him now; he's in the intensive care unit. He'll be there until we can reduce the effects of the infection and make sure that he doesn't lose the arm, or anything else."

Cynthia gasped. "In only a few hours?"

"Like I said, ma'am, it's a severe infection. The paramedics reported a gunshot wound, but what we found was a bad home surgery job sutured with sewing equipment. Any of the above could have caused the infection, and it could have been exacerbated by unsanitary conditions. He was already in a weakened state, thanks to slight malnutrition and dehydration.

"The person who did the bad home surgery might have caused the infection, but they also saved his life. He'd lost a lot of blood. You can go up and see him now. We have him sedated for his own safety. Oh—his right arm has a fracture of the humerus. It seems almost minor at this point, but he'll have a recovery time of four to eight weeks."

Ozzy nodded. "We'll take good care of him."

She gave him a hard look, but then softened. "I'm sure you will. Go be with your omega now, Mr. Morris."

She left the room, off to save another life.

Chapter Fifteen

It took Pete a few days to drift toward full consciousness. He had very few memories of the time in between recognizing that his wound had become infected and the time when he woke up, and the memories that he had didn't make sense. He remembered the scent of Alpha but also the sound of gunfire and of being carried off yet again. He remembered poking and prodding, and he remembered a lot of screaming.

He didn't think that remembering more than that would do wonders for his psyche, so he pushed the memories away from his brain and focused on his return to consciousness.

He didn't feel great. The first thing he noticed was the pain in his right arm, which only made sense. He'd been shot, and then Russ had pulled the bullet out with tweezers. Wasn't that how everyone's bullets got removed, on the floor of an abandoned factory covered in grime and rat droppings? Or had it been a school?

The scent of Alpha hadn't gone away. Pete had almost forgotten what Ozzy smelled like, and for a second he wondered if one of the nurses had just popped some popcorn. Then a hand touched his, and he heard the heart rate monitor pick up the pace a little. No, Alpha was really here, really with him.

That same hand stroked his face. "Hey, no need for tears." Ozzy's lips brushed across his forehead. "How you feeling?"

"Um. Confused. Embarrassed. Thirsty?" He blinked his eyes open and gave them a moment to adjust. "Why can't I move my right arm?"

"It's broken. Fractured, anyway. It's immobilized. It's going to stay immobilized so that you can eventually pick up our amazing daughter all by yourself. They're bringing her by a little later, by the way." He stroked Pete's cheek, like he couldn't get enough of touching him. Pete didn't mind. It had been a long time. "Do you want to sit up a little?"

Pete nodded, and his alpha pushed the button to move the top of the bed up. Then Ozzy brought a cup of water over and held it to his lips so that he could drink. "So," he said, when he was done. "How's Marissa?"

"She's as well as can be expected. She wants you. She cries a lot, and when she sees you and can't play with you she cries even more. Sometimes they just put her in your arm and she falls right to sleep, all happy and contented. It's amazing. I got some pictures with my phone." He paused. "She didn't remember me."

Pete looked away. "I'm sorry."

"No, Pete. I am. I was so obsessed with keeping you safe that I let it keep me away from the two of you. It was awful of me. I had no idea that you were going through postpartum depression."

"That's not your fault." Pete reached out for his alpha. "It would have happened anyway."

"I sure as hell didn't help." Ozzy hung his head. "I promise to try to do better, if you'll let me. I mean, I'll probably still screw up sometimes. And there will be times that you still try to do everything on your own. Neither one of us is perfect."

Pete held Ozzy's hand. "We're perfect for each other, though."

Pete didn't have to stay in the hospital more than a couple of days after he woke up. The antibiotics were doing their thing, and once they'd gotten the infection down to a dull roar he could take oral antibiotics instead of intravenous antibiotics and go home to shower and such.

The biggest problem was defining home. Ozzy had a house that he still hadn't sold, although he wasn't comfortable using it because it wasn't large enough to be comfortable for so many and because he was still nervous about security. Neither of them wanted to return to the Sudbury house, which was still technically a crime scene and still included a lovely pool of dried blood in the kitchen.

Cynthia provided them with an excellent interim option. She'd already purchased a crib, changing table, and baby supplies for Marissa during Pete's hospitalization, and the house was large enough that they could have an entire floor to themselves if they wanted. She simply insisted that they all move in with her while they looked for someplace else, and if they didn't find anything else suitable she would be more than happy to live with it.

Pete and Ozzy were uncomfortable taking her up on her offer, but they accepted at the end of the day. Pete couldn't take care of a house, even if it didn't mean scrubbing blood from the floor, and it was a secure facility from which to operate while Ozzy tried to grapple with his need to keep his family safe.

When Pete was released, they headed to the Weston house. Ozzy had already gotten permission to retrieve their personal effects from the property, and his friends had already brought them over, so Pete didn't have to try to deal with moving or unpacking. He just got in the car and got out at his childhood home.

Marissa was more comfortable with her daddy back, or so everyone told him. He couldn't pick her up by himself, but everyone was more than happy to take that on for him. All he had to do was to cuddle her and play with her. Cynthia seemed to be enthralled with her granddaughter, who laughed and giggled for her. "I sometimes feel like I missed out on something when I didn't do this myself with you boys," she confessed with a sigh. "Of course, it was a different time, and I was in a different place. Maybe it would have been different."

Marissa got more comfortable with her dad, too, which seemed to cheer Ozzy up considerably. She liked to play with his ties, which led to his new interest in organic cotton ties given her interest in putting things in her mouth.

By the time that Pete had been home from the hospital for a week, he was feeling much better. His right arm was still immobilized, of course, but the effects of the infection were gone and he was just finishing up his course of antibiotics. He got out of the shower one morning only to come out and find Ozzy standing by the bed, with two packed bags. "What's going on?" he asked, panicked.

"I got leave," Ozzy told him. "I got family leave. An alpha officer gets that when he makes a claim, or is going to make a claim." He looked down, and then he looked back up and met Pete's eyes. "If you still want that, I booked us a good, long weekend at a bed and breakfast in Concord. We've got a very private room. Ruth, Cynthia and Angus have things here, with Marissa. I want to be yours. I want you to be mine. I just wanted to wait until you were in good enough shape to do this. So, uh, let's do this. If you're up for it."

Pete pinched himself. Was this part of some fever dream? Was it a hallucination from the infection? "I… I want this." He swallowed. "But only if you do too."

Ozzy walked toward him with a green polo shirt to help pull onto his body. "I want this." As he helped him with the shirt, he let his hand creep up to Pete's nipples, where they teased them to a point. "I want this, and I want you. Are you with me?"

"I'm with you." Pete gasped the words out as his mate worked his nipples. It felt too good to be touched after so long.

Ozzy helped him to get dressed. They went downstairs to give some extra attention to Marissa before they left. Pete had a few qualms about leaving Marissa again, but they were only a few towns away. She would be fine, and they could get back if they needed to.

They checked into the bed and breakfast and got a tour of the facility. The place was owned by an alpha and omega couple, and Ozzy had told them why they were coming to the inn. They were extra accommodating to the pair, and made sure that they had everything that they could possibly want before leaving them to their own devices.

Pete needed help undressing, but not as much as he did getting dressed. He took another quick shower, not because he'd done all that much to work up a sweat but because he wanted to present himself as cleanly to his alpha as he could. As he sluiced the soap from his flesh, he gave a little smile. He wouldn't have to fight with his clothing for the rest of the weekend.

Ozzy was already waiting for him when Pete emerged, naked and beautiful. Pete's breath caught in his chest. How could Ozzy want him—scrawny and wasted him?

Ozzy approached him with his brace and helped him put it on. "I know what you're thinking, Omega. None of that. We're the only ones for each other, and that's enough. Come on. Let's make this happen."

Pete let his alpha lead him to the bed. He liked this bed. It was antique, like everything else in the bed and breakfast, but it was also solidly constructed. He smiled, and then he saw the discreet bottle of lube on the nightstand. Had Ozzy put it there, or had their hosts?

Whatever. It was there, everything that they needed was within reach. He got into the bed and lay down on his back. The claiming was usually done from a rear-entry position, but

Pete couldn't brace himself properly with his arm the way it was. They would have to be a little less traditional in their act, but that was something that they could certainly handle.

He lay down on his back and looked over at Ozzy, pulling the comforter aside in invitation. Ozzy looked him up and down, eyes dark with lust. His cock stood up tall, dark, and proud from his thatch of hair, demanding and eager already. "Look at you," he purred. He stalked over to the bed like a predator. "All laid out for me like Thanksgiving dinner. You want it, don't you?"

"Take me, Alpha." Pete opened his legs, leaving no mistake as to his intentions. "Don't make me wait."

"Oh, you'll wait all right." Ozzy chuckled. He bent down and kissed Pete's ankle. "You want my bite? You're going to have to wait for it." He nibbled his way up Pete's leg, moving carefully along the inner part of his leg until he got to the fork. Then he carefully turned around and nibbled all the way around Pete's abs, moving around his cock without letting a single part of his skin touch his aching member, and moved down the other end until he got to the other ankle.

Only then did he show any interest in Pete's cock. He reached for the lube with one hand and slicked up his fingers. As he teased Pete with kitten licks up the underside of his hungry cock, he slipped a finger into his hole. Pete let out a little whine. It had been so long, months, since he'd felt this.

Ozzy added another finger right away, and took Pete into his mouth. He knew that Ozzy wouldn't let him come, not yet, but it felt so good to have his alpha touching him like this that he wondered if Ozzy could stop him. He groaned and bucked his hips, just enough, and Ozzy laughed. The laughter created deep vibrations in Ozzy's throat, which felt amazing, and Pete had to close his eyes and try to think of anything but where he was right now.

Ozzy added a third finger. He seemed to want to stretch Pete thoroughly, but he was moving through it pretty quickly too. Pete didn't mind. They'd been waiting for this for a long time. When Ozzy finally slicked himself up and eased his way into Pete, Pete didn't mind the stretch at all. It felt right and good. It felt perfect.

"Alpha," he murmured, and wrapped his legs around Ozzy's waist.

That seemed to be the signal, because Ozzy snapped his hips back and let loose.

Ozzy had apparently been holding a lot in. He set up a vigorous pace. Pete tried to match it at first and then he just held on. It felt great. It felt amazing, and he cried out in his pleasure over and over again. Almost as good as the way Ozzy's pounding cock made him feel was the look on Ozzy's face. His eyes were wide, and his lips had rounded into a little o, like each thrust was some kind of a revelation. Pete had put that look there, Pete and the chemistry between them.

Finally, Pete recognized the signs. Ozzy was starting to lose the rhythm. It was only a matter of time until he finished, and Pete wasn't far behind. Ozzy met his eyes, the question unspoken but understood. Pete nodded, and Ozzy bent his head and bit down on the space where Pete's shoulder and clavicle joined.

They both cried out as their orgasms took them at once. The bite had hurt Pete, but only a little. He didn't care. He could feel everything right now. He could feel his alpha pumping into him. He could feel his own blood flowing into his alpha. He could feel his alpha's heat, his need, his warmth and reassurance.

When it was over, Ozzy pulled out of him gently and rolled him over onto his good side. Then he snaked an arm around his waist. He didn't bother to clean them up, and that was fine by

Pete. They were going to get a lot dirtier than this over the weekend, and that was fine by him.

He was with Alpha, forever now. He was home.

...

Ozzy wasn't the most religious guy in the world. People often found that surprising about him, given that his father was a minister and all, but that was just the way he was. He knew, however, that someone had been smiling on him. He'd survived an attack that had killed all of his men. He'd survived multiple assaults while on SWAT that should have gotten him killed, to include the one that had allowed him to meet Pete.

And he'd almost lost his omega, twice now, but he'd still come out on top in the end. He knew that he owed his thanks to someone, and whether that someone was God, Fortune, or even some ancient Greek god, he didn't know, he was grateful. He had Pete, and they had a beautiful daughter together. He vowed never to lose sight of his good fortune again.

Living with Cynthia wasn't as bad as Ozzy had thought it would be. They had plenty of privacy when they wanted it, and they had the comfort of being close to family when they needed that too. At the same time, Ozzy knew that Pete chafed at not having his own space, or having things cleaned his way and to his specifications. He didn't quite realize that Cynthia realized it too.

She sat them down one evening, just after Pete had been given clearance to take the brace off, and poured them glasses of wine. "I've been thinking," she told them, and smiled, "that while it's been an amazing experience having you and your family here, that you might be happier if you had a place of your own again. But I like having you here in Weston, and of course I want to have you close by. So I thought it might be a good idea if I bought you a house."

Ozzy's jaw dropped. Homes in Weston didn't come cheap. "We couldn't ask that, Cynthia. We can both afford to get places of our own."

"Of course you can." She sniffed. "You both have places of your own, and you can rent them out or sell them, it makes no difference to me. But it isn't as though I can take the money with me, and I want you all close by. I want to be able to come for a visit without making a big production out of it, and I want to have you over without a big hassle on your part. I want to get a security setup for you like the one I have for myself. And I want to say, when I meet up with your father after my time is up, that I contributed to your happiness instead of frowning from the distance."

Pete hugged her then. They'd been doing a lot of that lately. They hadn't been given to many open displays of affection but now they seemed to be making up for lost time. He looked over at Ozzy and nodded, and Ozzy squirmed. "Okay. Thank you. We'll take you up on that."

They settled on a lovely old place from the 1870s. It was bigger than they'd ever planned on, but it had enough bedrooms that they could have as many kids as they wanted and not run out of room. As soon as the security people finished setting up the fence, they moved in and hosted a little gathering to celebrate.

Ozzy didn't take time off from work to deal with the move. In fact, once he'd gotten back from his long weekend with Pete, he had a lot on his plate. Sierzant was in custody, which was a load off of Ozzy's mind, but there was plenty of work left to be done. They still had to track down the rest of Sierzant's network of cops, and they had to deal with the rest of the guy's criminal empire too.

Oh, and they had to find a way to nail him for the murder of Tim Harbaugh, the murder that had started this all.

That, at least, would prove difficult. Oliver approached Ozzy about two weeks after he returned from his claiming and cleared his throat. "So, I've got the DNA back from the gun used in the bank robbery and the Harbaugh murder. I tested it where Meyrick said. The killer caught her hand in where she inserted the magazine into the gun. It ripped a piece of her skin off, and it's remained inside the gun ever since."

Ozzy frowned. "Her?"

Oliver nodded. "Her. Testing has given us a match. The donor entered into the system when she was convicted for heroin possession. Her name is Dawn Moriarty."

Ozzy closed his eyes and bowed his head. He'd been a fool. He'd been lured in by a sad story and distracted by the dirty cop angle. "All right. I'll get a warrant. We'll bring her in. Thanks, Oliver."

"You're welcome, Detective Morris."

Ozzy ran the case by the prosecutor, who agreed to bring Moriarty in. "I'm not sure that it's enough to sell a jury, but it's worth bringing her in and talking to her." He made a face. "When I look at all of this evidence, I'm not liking the picture of Harbaugh that I see, Ozzy."

"Me neither," he sighed. "But we've got a job to do. Might as well do it."

He sent uniformed officers to pick her up, and he met up with her at MCI-Framingham. On a whim, he called her probation officer and invited Mary to meet them there. Dawn seemed to trust Mary. Maybe Ozzy was still too sympathetic toward Dawn, considering that she'd murdered a man, but he wanted to give her someone she trusted.

Mary agreed to join him, and they met up with Dawn in a monitored visitor room at the state's only women's prison. Dawn hung her head when she was brought in, and she didn't pick it up when she sat down across from them. "You want your lawyer here, Dawn?" Ozzy offered. "We can call her."

"No." She swallowed and scratched at her arm. "I'm good. It's been a long time. I should talk about it, I think. I'm not ashamed of what I did. It was him or me."

Ozzy didn't doubt it. He nodded, but he still felt like he needed to say something about the situation. "You were sixteen."

"Still him or me." She shrugged. "He'd picked me up a few times, legally. He knew what I was, and he knew who I was. He knew where I lived. Turned out he was working for Joe. When Joe decided that he wanted to bring me *in house*, he sent Sierzant to bring me in.

"He used to do that with a lot of folks. If you said no, a cop would pretend to arrest you. Either you accepted that you had a pimp now or no one ever saw you again. I said no, and we went for a long drive. He dragged me out of my car by my hair, and he threw me up against the trunk. He started grabbing at my skirt, saying that at least someone might as well get some use out of me before he put a bullet in me."

"So you shot him." Ozzy looked down.

"I wrestled to get him off of me. When I got the gun out of his hand, I saw the opportunity. I pretended I was throwing it away and he fell for it. When he turned around I shot him in the back of the head. I'm not sorry. I'd do it again. It might not have been much of a life, and it still might not be much of a life, but that doesn't mean it was okay for him to just take it, you know?" She wiped at her eyes. "It wasn't right for him to shoot me, or to force me."

"No." Ozzy shook his head. "It wasn't. And I don't know…" He trailed off, at a loss for words. If she'd come forward at the time of the attack, no one would have believed a teenaged hooker over a decorated cop. As it was now, she would best be described as a "non-credible witness." Her only saving grace was the huge network of dirty cops being unearthed, and the emerging notoriety of her ultimate tormentor. "I don't know if things could have gone any other way. I'm going to bring your confession to the prosecutor. I don't know what he's going to decide. I'm hoping that he'll go for a lesser charge, if anything."

She wrinkled her nose, taking years off of her appearance. "Why? I killed someone."

"You did. I've killed people too, in war. It's not a fun decision to make, and it's not always something you have a lot of time to think about. But Dawn, I think that Sierzant has made you suffer enough. I'm not making you any promises, okay? I'm just one guy. But I'm going to do what I can."

She stared at him for a long moment, and then she nodded. "Thank you."

Ozzy went back to the prosecutor with Dawn's confession. He brought the crime scene photos, the autopsy report, and the testimony from Balsalmo and other people caught in Sierzant's web. Together, he and the prosecutor called up Dawn's defense attorney. She was surprised to hear from them, but got together with them over dinner. Together, all three of them approached the presiding judge in the case.

The case didn't get a lot of publicity. Most of the press was, quite reasonably in Ozzy's mind, much more interested in following the dirty cop story. There weren't many people in the courtroom when Dawn's hearing was held. Ozzy was there, though, sitting right behind Dawn at the prosecutor's table. Mary sat beside him, and Pete on his other side.

They all rose for the judge's entrance. The judge sat down and cleared his throat as the docket was read. "All right. This is a highly unusual case. I received a visit not only from the prosecutor, and not only from the defense attorney, but from both of them at the same time, in conjunction with the lead detective on the case. This doesn't happen, my friends.

"But it did happen. They took the time to explain to me the facts of the case in full, right down to minor forensic details that put me to sleep faster than three glasses of Cognac. It was all very useful information, but the fact of the matter is that Ms. Moriarty has confessed to killing Officer Harbaugh. She has pled guilty, and I therefore must find her guilty of first degree manslaughter no matter what the extenuating circumstances." He held up his hand to forestall the outrage he no doubt saw on everyone's face.

"However," he continued, "the crime was committed when the defendant was a juvenile. While Ms. Moriarty's record hasn't been exemplary since the incident, her issues haven't been violent, and her record for the past five years has been pristine. I do declare that the crime will be entered into her *sealed* juvenile record. No custodial sentence is ordered. I might recommend an extension of her probation, since reports seem to suggest that this is a helpful and supportive relationship for Ms. Moriarty to have. Is this agreeable to all parties?"

The prosecutor rose, looking stunned. "The Commonwealth is satisfied with this judgment, your Honor."

The defense attorney rose. "The defense agrees to these terms, and we thank your Honor."

It was the fairest possible outcome. Dawn was released, and she shook Ozzy's hand afterward. "Thank you," she said, with tears in her eyes. "I mean it. Thank you. No one's ever done anything for me before, but this… this takes the cake."

"We're supposed to be about justice," Ozzy told her, blushing. "All of us." He gestured to the courtroom. "Good luck, Dawn. If you need anything, you've got my number."

Dawn let Pete do a photographic essay about her afterward. They made some money off of the project, but that wasn't the purpose. The project had two goals: to boost employability of previously convicted people, thus reducing the stigma and helping people get back onto their feet, and to help boost the image of the state police in the wake of the scandal.

Sierzant wasn't saved by the DNA. He hadn't killed Harbaugh, but he'd ordered the killing of countless others. He was convicted on racketeering charges within two months of being taken. The time to trial seemed almost absurdly fast to Ozzy, but he guessed that the judicial system wanted to wrap up the case and throw it into the landfill too. He was sentenced to life. When he appealed, he was sentenced to consecutive life sentences, and he gave up appeals after that.

Pete visited him in prison. Ozzy thought that was weird. Ozzy tried to forbid it, which led to a loud fight and more couch time, but they made up. Apparently Pete liked the guy, in spite of the whole kidnapping and near death thing. Furthermore, he didn't think that leaving Sierzant to twist would bring the good guys any more information, or bring Sierzant any kind of epiphany.

So he visited, and Ozzy fretted. Sierzant soon started up a little empire behind bars, which didn't surprise anyone. He was charismatic. He could sucker anyone into doing anything that he wanted. It wasn't long, though, before the warden was calling Ozzy. "I think your omega's missed his calling, Pulitzer prizes be damned. You want to know what Sierzant has his little band of miscreants doing?"

"Let me guess. They've all found God." Ozzy had a dim view of jailhouse conversions.

"No. No, as a matter of fact. They're trying to intervene in inmate disputes. Some of them are getting hurt doing it, but they keep trying. Some of these guys are probably doing it for brownie points with the parole board, but some of these guys aren't going anywhere, you know? They're here until Gabriel blows his horn and all that. But they keep trying. And it's working, some of the time."

"Okay." Ozzy pulled the phone away from his ear and stared at it for a long moment. "What does any of this have to do with my Pete?"

"None of it was happening before he started showing up for visits with Sierzant."

Huh. Ozzy wasn't sure what to make of that. He didn't trust Sierzant, and he was sure that he had an ulterior motive. But the idea that Pete could be having a positive effect on these guys warmed his heart.

Massachusetts had 2,300 state troopers. Ten percent of that force wound up getting spatter on them from the scandal, although not all of it related to Sierzant. The highest concentration was in Troop C, the troop in the middle part of the state, with a healthy dose in Troop B, which covered the western part. Worcester didn't emerge unscathed, either. They had 417 officers. Thirty-five turned out to be working for Sierzant, all patrolmen. None of that took into account retirees.

The union barked about the first couple of cops who got prosecuted. When they saw the evidence as it mounted, aided by those officers who changed sides when Pete got kidnapped, they changed their tune. They demanded to see actual hard evidence for any union members implicated, which only made sense, but they admitted in the press that those cops who had gone bad only made the job more dangerous for the good cops.

As fall rolled around and families started to prepare for Thanksgiving, Ozzy let himself into his car one evening only to find it occupied. He recognized the spotted hands on the back of the passenger seat. "Well, well, if it isn't Russ Meyrick."

Meyrick chuckled. "I'm impressed."

"I've been wanting to talk to you," Ozzy said. "Been wanting to talk with you for a few months now, actually."

"I'll bet." Meyrick sighed. "Look. I'm sorry that I ever said yes, okay? My folks were going to lose their house, and I got greedy."

"Thank you."

Meyrick fell silent for a long moment. "Excuse me?"

"The doctor, when we got Pete to the hospital. She couldn't say what caused the infection, although she did say that your surgery skills needed work. What she did say was that you saved his life, when you stitched him up. Yeah, he got an infection, but he'd have bled out if you hadn't. And you made sure that he got to help in time. So, thank you."

"You're welcome." Meyrick went quiet for a moment. "Look. I know you're supposed to bring me in."

"Never saw you."

"I'm glad he's okay," Meyrick said. "I liked him. He has spirit. He's got a lot of strength, that one."

Ozzy knew he must be glowing. "Yeah. Yeah he does." He smiled into the rear view mirror. "You take care, Meyrick. You know how to find me."

"I do."

Ozzy closed his eyes and listened as the last part of that chapter of his life faded away. Then he started up his car and drove home to his omega.

<<<<>>>>

Bonus Chapter 16

Pete held Marissa's tiny hand and balanced Adrian on his hip. They'd just finished a picnic out on the back patio and were now ready to come in and wash off the remains of said picnic. Adrian the one most in need of washing. He was new to solids and preferred to explore texture by smearing it onto his face rather than ingest it. Marissa was no innocent. Mustard made a kind of grotesque mask spread across her pretty little face.

Sometimes Pete wondered about her biological father, but not often. He wouldn't have appreciated the wonder that was Marissa. He'd have been horrified by the way she'd come into the world, and he'd have been appalled by her spirit. Her real father adored her.

They headed into the house. Ozzy had just gotten home from the Police Unity Tour. Ozzy was a fit guy. No one could take that away from him. The muscles used to cycle from Framingham to Washington, DC, were different from the ones he used to heli-ski, or to rock climb, or to charge at suspects while carrying a hundred pounds of equipment or whatever it was. He was tired, and he was sore, and he was not feeling up to sitting on a blanket on cold fieldstone.

All of that was fine. Pete could do it alone. He didn't resent it, not when he knew that he had backup. His mom was down the road, and Angus was with her. They'd both learned how to handle the kids over the years and had proved adept caregivers in a pinch. "Gamma," in particular, was a favorite. Ruth was around, even though it was her day off. She wouldn't mind pitching in if things really hit the fan.

For that matter, Ozzy would rouse himself and push through the pain if things truly went pear shaped. Pete just didn't want him to have to.

He got the kids upstairs and into the bath. They were both sweet natured kids, and cooperated with the washing-up pretty easily. This was a good thing, considering that both of them seemed to delight in situations that got them grimier than he'd have thought possible before becoming a father.

Once he got them dressed again, and found dry clothes for himself, he brought them both downstairs. Ozzy found it comforting to be with his kids, even when he couldn't necessarily chase after them as much as he liked to do. Pete settled Adrian in his father's arms and let Marissa climb into Ozzy's lap with a book. She opened the book and proceeded to read it to him, which still delighted Ozzy to no end even though she'd read it to him every day for a week before he left for the Police Unity Tour.

Adrian, though. Adrian looked at his big sister like she'd hung the moon. For him, she had.

Pete headed toward the kitchen. It wasn't too early to start dinner, and this early in the season it still got cool enough that he could still serve the stews and casseroles that he loved. He got out the ingredients that he needed, and he wasn't surprised to see Marissa push her Learning Tower closer to his workspace so that she could climb up and watch. She loved her parents equally, but she was fascinated by the alchemy of the kitchen and loved to watch meals take shape under Pete's capable hands.

Pete wouldn't lie. He found the whole thing pretty flattering.

He chopped up some onion and measured out milk, butter, and flour for the béchamel. He thought hat a vegetarian lasagna would be nice for dinner tonight, something good for spring but still hearty for the chill in the air that came with May. He let his daughter crush up the garlic; he hated the thought of her getting hurt, but there wasn't much she could do to hurt herself with a garlic press.

The buzzer at the gate rang through the whole house, just as it had been designed to. Pete frowned and went over to his tablet, first wiping his hands on his apron. "Hello?" he said, after pressing on the app.

"Hi." The face on the screen was distorted from looking into the camera, which gave a weird sort of fish-eyed image back to the viewer. "I'd like to see my son, please." The speaker was an older male, probably in his sixties, and wore a clerical uniform.

"Well, you're not my father, so I'll have to check with my Alpha." He beckoned Marissa down silently from the tower and carried the tablet into the TV room, where Ozzy was watching the Sox on TV.

Ozzy frowned when Pete muted the TV. "I've got a guy here looking for his son?" Pete said, and passed the tablet over to his alpha.

Ozzy took the tablet, his eyebrows drawn together. When he saw the face on the screen he froze. "Dad?"

"Would it be all right to drive up?" the stranger asked. "I think four years is long enough don't you?"

"Can you be civil?" Ozzy pressed his lips together.

The man on the screen paused. "I can only do my best, son."

"I will not hesitate to throw you out." Ozzy swiped right on the app, opening the gate long enough to admit the one car.

After a few moments, the stranger appeared at the front door. Pete wasn't sure what to expect, and he knew that his anxiety transmitted itself to his children. Marissa was uncharacteristically silent, and Adrian was chewing on his pacifier like there was no tomorrow. Ozzy had passed both children off to him while he got up to attend to his father.

Gary Morris turned out to be a moderately tall man. He was attractive, if one were into older men, with loose gray curls down to his earlobe and a little goatee. He was thin, and his eyes were only for his son. "Ozzy," he said. "I've been thinking about you."

"Glad to hear it, Dad." Ozzy's jaw clenched. "Let me introduce my omega, Pete. These are your grandchildren, Marissa and Adrian."

Gary's pupils constricted, just a little, but he kept his mouth shut and shook Marissa's hand. "I am very pleased to meet you, young miss. How old are you now? Nine? Ten?"

Marissa giggled. "I'm three and a half. I'll be four in August!"

"Well that's a good age." Gary straightened up. "Ozzy. It's been four years. Don't you think it's time to come home?"

"I am home." Ozzy clenched his jaw. "You can be a part of my family, or you can chose to not do that, but I am home." He gestured to the sofa. "Sorry for the disarray. I just got back from the Police Unity Ride yesterday. I'm a little frazzled."

"Was it down a cliffside?" Gary asked.

Pete snickered.

Ozzy pretended to glare, but wrapped an arm around him. "No. It's to commemorate the officers who've fallen in the line of duty, and raise money for the memorial. Don't trivialize it. So. How's Mom? And Zack?"

"They're well. You know, living their lives." The pair fell into silence again, and Pete wondered if he shouldn't get the children out of the way. Then Gary spoke again. "Son, I'm sorry."

Ozzy's eyes bulged. "Sorry?"

"I should have accepted your choices from the beginning. You're an adult. You have the right to be treated like an adult. Not like a child. I might not always like the choices that you make, but then again, you had a lot of good points to make. I was acting badly. I was acting without compassion, without understanding, and without knowledge. Please forgive me."

Ozzy was on his feet in a heartbeat. He all but tackled his father, wrapping him up in his strong arms tightly enough that Pete almost felt jealous. He understood the arrears, though, and tried to keep his angst to a minimum.

When the pair parted, he stepped in, and invited his father in law to stay for dinner. Gary accepted, much to the surprise of Pete and apparently of Ozzy. Pete left his alpha and his father-in-law to chat n the TV room while he and the kids hid out in the kitchen, preparing dinner.

Gary met Ruth over dinner. The meeting was cordial, and Gary even bought a piece of art for the church offices before he left. All in all it was a successful visit, for all that it was unplanned, and as Pete cleared the dishes he smiled to himself. The surprise visit could have gone so much worse.

After Gary left, they got the kids changed and put to bed. Then they retreated to their master suite, their personal retreat, and shared a shower. Showers always made Pete frisky, and he found himself mouthing at Alpha's jaw and neck more than he'd planned to.

Ozzy chuckled at him and playfully smacked his ass. "Someone's eager tonight."

"Can you blame me?" Pete laughed. "I've got this amazing alpha, who by the way rode a bicycle from here to D.C. How impressive is that?" He calmed down a little, even though having Ozzy's hands on hm was about the least calming thing in the universe. "Are you okay?"

Ozzy didn't have to ask what he meant. He just knew. He was like that. "I'm good," he decided. "It's a little weird. I might not be as good tomorrow, but right now? I've got the most beautiful omega in the world in front of me, a big bed behind us, and we've been apart for days."

Pete let his alpha turn the water off and grabbed a owe for him as they stepped out into the steamy bathroom. He didn't pass it over. Instead, he devoted himself to towel drying every inch of his alpha, from the top of his head to the tops of his ankles. The little gasps and choked back moans from Ozzy told hm that he was on the right track, that his ministrations were shaving an effect.

He didn't dry off Ozzy's cock until he'd dried off every other inch. Only then did he move his cloth-covered hand to stroke the water off of his beloved, stroke after stroke. Ozzy groaned. His knees buckled, just a little bit, and be braced himself up against the wall so that Pete could dry him off completely.

When Ozzy was fully erect, cock purple and almost painful to see, Pete backed off. He toweled himself off quickly and efficiently so that he could get into the bed. He didn't need any teasing, any buildup to get himself in the mood. The mere scent of his alpha, after several days apart, was enough to get him going. He climbed into the bed and peeled the covers back in invitation.

He wasn't being subtle. He wasn't trying to be.

Ozzy strutted toward the bed and rummaged through the bedside table for the lube. "Huh. I wonder what my omega wants." He nipped playfully at Pete's jawline.

"Please, Alpha." Pete hated to beg, absolutely hated it, but he would do it if he got what he wanted. "I need you to touch me."

Ozzy picked up the lube. His hot, hard, insistent cock was already pressing at Pete's hole, but it wasn't a demand. It was more of a gentle rocking, a "hello, I'm here," kind of signal. Ozzy would never hurt Pete, and Pete could relax and trust his alpha because he knew that. He wrapped his legs around Ozzy's waist, another invitation that he knew Ozzy would have a hard time ignoring.

Ozzy gave a low laugh and caught his mouth in a kiss. He knew what Pete needed, all right.

Ozzy stretched him out quickly, and entered him as though his life depended on getting inside quickly. Pete didn't mind. H loved the feel of his mate inside of him. He bucked his hips to meet Ozzy's thrust, and cried out when Ozzy dragged across his sweet spot.

Ozzy set up an athletic pace. Pete could keep up, although he knew that he would feel it tomorrow in all of the best ways. He could live with that.

Ozzy's thrusts became more erratic, and Pete reached in between them to stroke himself to completion. He could see the veins standing out in Ozzy's face. He was trying to hold himself back; he hated to come before Pete. Fortunately for both of them, Pete was close. One, two, three strokes and he was done, spilling hot and messy over his hand. Ozzy followed soon after, and he pulled gently out.

After, when they'd had another shower and gotten back into the bed, Pete encouraged Ozzy to roll over. Usually the alpha was the big spoon, but sometimes they needed to feel held and cared for too. Pete could offer that to his mate. He wrapped an arm around his waist and molded himself to his back. "You doing okay, there, Ozzy?"

"Well, I'm better now." Ozzy gave a little chuckle and held Pete's hand. "I think I'm still in shock that he showed up, you know? I've got so many questions. Why did he show up alone? Why now? Why not years ago? I don't know how to feel about this." He closed his eyes. "I don't… I know that he means well. He's always meant well."

"A lot of people mean well, or think that they mean well." Pete kissed his mate's hair. "That doesn't mean that they always have great motives. In this case, I don't know him at all. But you… well, I mean he's a man of God, right? He's supposed to be willing to accept that he was wrong. He seemed sincere. Your hurt is sincere too."

"What should I do?" Ozzy asked after a moment. His muscles released their tension as he accepted Pete's embrace.

"I don't think there's really an answer for that. I think it's good to try to reconnect, but only as far as you feel comfortable. Take it slow. Maybe we can invite him to dinner sometime. Don't stretch past where it's a good stretch, you know? And maybe you'll both feel a little more comfortable taking it a little farther next time, maybe not." He gave a little laugh. "Maybe he'll want to come to Land's Sake Farm with us sometime soon. That's not too confrontational, and everyone likes a hayride."

Ozzy snuggled back into his embrace. "That's a good idea. I'll give him a call and set something up for maybe next week."

"Sounds good. I love you."

"I love you too. You're the best."

Pete buried his face in the crook of Ozzy's neck and let himself drift off to sleep. Life was pretty good, he had to admit. He and his alpha were pretty solid. He had two amazing children. He had friends who cared for him, and he had a fulfilling career. His family life had improved since he'd gotten together with Ozzy, and now it looked like Ozzy's family might finally be coming around.

Pete had thought that this kind of domestic bliss was out of reach for him. Getting there might have taken a little bit of a roundabout path, but he wouldn't trade any of it.

Preview Chapter: Omega's Kiss

Doug removed his belt, his shoes, and his briefcase. He put them onto the table for the guard to search and turned his pockets inside out. Then he stepped through the metal detector. When he emerged on the other side, he received his hand stamp and signed the visitor log.

The guard looked up at Doug and wrinkled her nose. "How many times have you been here this week, Doug?"

"Twice, Katie." Doug smiled at her. The guards weren't bad people. He had to try to remember that. They were just trying to do a difficult job, with very few resources. "But those visits were different. Then I was his son."

She raised an eyebrow. "Any big news you want to share with the class?"

"Today I'm his attorney." He passed her the document. "It's taken a while, but I filed the paperwork yesterday."

Katie scanned the document and clicked her tongue ring against her teeth. "Well I'll be damned. I didn't even know you were a lawyer."

"I've been cleverly disguised as just another family member for months, right?" He gave a little laugh. "But hey—now you know who to call if you ever need a lawyer." He passed her a card.

She rolled her eyes. "Do you have any idea how many lawyers I get through here?"

"Yeah, but I'm different. I'm good. And I actually like you." He winked and she laughed, buzzing him into the visitor waiting room.

He had to wait his turn to be allowed into one of the confidential visiting rooms, so he sat back and took a good look at the other visitors. Most of them were family members, all looking tired and not terribly happy. Shirley wasn't exactly easy to get to, especially if you lived in one of the more remote parts of the state. It was also the only maximum-security prison in Massachusetts.

Doug saw young mothers carrying fussy babies. He saw a couple of anxious-looking omegas in the mix, and he winced when he saw their claim scars. He wouldn't wish this kind of life on his worst enemy, to have to come all the way up to Shirley for conjugal visits or die. There were a few young people who were there without other family members. They might have been there to see siblings, or parents, or friends. None of them made eye contact with anyone else.

Then there were the lawyers. There were four of them there today, Doug included. They stood out like sore thumbs. They were well rested. They were well dressed. Their eyes were sharp and keen, not filled with despair. They nodded at Doug like they saw a kindred spirit in him, and he supposed that they did.

He glanced at the family members, and then he went to sit with the lawyers.

They made small talk as they waited to be called. The guy defending a double homicide got called first. Then went the woman defending a guy who'd gone on a violent spree down the Cape over the summer; he hadn't even bothered to deny what he'd done, but she was trying to appeal based on mental incompetence and get him sent to a secure hospital instead. She was replaced by a dark-skinned man in a gorgeous silk suit, who was defending one of the alleged dirty cops that had kidnapped a state trooper's omega last month.

Doug wished him all the luck in the world. He was going to need it.

They called Doug next. He got up and followed the guard into a confidential visitor room, where he sat down and spread out his documents. Then he waited.

Five minutes later, three guards escorted his father into the room. Orange was not a good color for Larry Morrison, or for any other pale person really, and Larry had only gotten paler in prison. He blinked at Doug owlishly through his thick glasses and smiled broadly. "Dougie!" he said, as the guards pushed him gently into his chair. One of them watched him carefully while the other shackled him both to the chair and the table. "What is this, the third time this week? And what's with the funeral director get-up? Did you just come from work?"

Doug huffed out a laugh, even though he had to blink back tears. "I'm at work, Dad. I filed a motion for a new trial yesterday." He smiled, broad and happy. "I managed to find proof that you were in Maryland when Melina Bonnaire and Ada Alumi were killed."

Larry's green eyes widened. "Are you serious? That's great news! That's fantastic news!" He laughed out loud. "I didn't even know them!"

"I know you didn't, Dad." Doug closed his eyes and hung his head. "I am so, so sorry that I didn't find this before your first trial, but we're going to make it right. We are. I promise."

"I know you are. You're the best son a father could hope for. I know it wasn't always easy growing up. I wasn't always around as much as I wanted to be, but Dougie, you turned out amazing. You made me so proud. I'm telling you, I'm so proud to call you my son." He chuckled and shook his head. "And my lawyer, now, too. Seriously. Who would have thought it?"

Doug glowered at the walls. "Who'd have thought that you'd need a lawyer? Seriously, dad. Maximum security? Shackled to a chair? You don't need that. That's not you."

Larry shook his head. "Son, they think I'm a serial killer. If it were anyone else—if I were a serial killer—you'd be the first one to tell them that they needed to keep me as secure as possible. I don't really mind, son."

Doug crossed his arms over his chest. It was funny how being around his father could reduce him to a sulky twelve-year old again. He was a successful attorney, on the partner track, and here he was pouting. "Well I mind. How are things?"

"They're things." Larry shrugged, making his chains rattle. "They gave me a cell mate about my own age. He's a guy from Worcester. He's still on trial, but I guess he's a special case. His name's Joe. Seems nice enough for a mobster."

"That's something. Do you have a job yet?" Doug tapped his pen on the table, beating out the drum part to an old Muse song.

"Oh sure. I'm working in the prison library. It's not so bad. At least I'm using my degree." Larry sighed and gave Doug a smile. "That lawyer look, it's a good one for you, son. You look all smart and stuff."

Doug blushed. "I am all smart and stuff, Dad. I've got a lot of wins. And I'm going to get this one, too. Is there anything else you can tell me that will help me out? Anyone that you can think of who will corroborate where you were when the victims were killed?"

Larry laughed and shook his head. "Son, I'm going to need a list. The real killer murdered an awful lot of women, and I can't really go ahead and tell you where I was every minute of every day for twenty years, now, can I?"

"Good point." Doug chewed on the end of his pen. "I'll get that list. And I will be back. You can count on that."

"I know you will. Dougie, you're something special. I know you'll do whatever you need to, okay?" Larry leaned back. "Tell me. We haven't talked about you in a while. Are you still seeing that guy, what was his name, Liam?"

"No." Doug made a face. "Liam, as it turned out, was really into unhealthy polyamory."

Larry mouthed out the words *unhealthy polyamory*. "What does that even mean?"

"It means that he had three other omegas that he was messing around with, Dad. He firmly believed that this was not a problem, and that I was just being *uppity* for objecting." He rubbed the back of his neck. "The upshot is that now he has no omegas, and I have three new very good friends. So there's that."

"Okay then." Larry grinned. He'd lost a few teeth while inside. Doug wondered how he hadn't noticed before. Had he just been too busy looking at his own shoes? "Hey, want me to make a few calls? You know us convicts, we all got connections." He laughed at the absurdity of his own joke.

Doug chuckled. "Thanks, but I'm good. Liam's out of my life now, let him go pester someone else. The guy had a personal hatred of toothpaste anyway. He always had bad breath. You going to be okay in here for a while, Dad?"

"You bet, son." He smiled up at Doug. "You going to go give 'em Hell?"

"It's what I do best, Dad. I love you. I'll see you soon."

Doug signaled to the guards and left the room so he wouldn't have to see them treat his father like a dangerous animal. A guard escorted him back to the visitor processing center, where he signed out and was searched yet again. He was prepared to simply head back to his car, but as he headed to the parking lot he noticed a woman struggling with a baby carriage. She wasn't walking toward the lot, but toward the road.

He glanced at the sky. Ominous dark clouds lurked overhead.

Doug cursed. He had a plan, and a direction. He wanted to set it in motion right away. At the same time, this woman wasn't much different than he was, and she had a baby with her. He raced to catch up with her. "Are you trying to catch the train?"

She blinked at him and bit her lip, clearly afraid.

He tried again, this time in Spanish. She nodded, still not trusting. "Look," he told her, speaking as gently as he could. "It's going to rain. I'll give you a ride wherever you want, okay? I'll even drive you home." He gave her a little smile. "My dad's inside. Folks like us, we have to stick together, help one another out."

She hesitated, but when they heard thunder in the distance she decided to take a chance. They ran for Doug's car and she strapped the bucket carrier into the back seat, turning it into a car seat. She folded down the stroller and put it into Doug's trunk and slid into the passenger seat just as the first raindrops fell.

When she told him that she lived in Framingham, he wouldn't hear of her taking the train. "That'll take you more than three hours," he pointed out, "and I'm going to Framingham anyway for work. Seriously. I'll just bring you straight there. It's not a problem."

She blushed, but accepted, and they hit the road.

Her brother was in jail, she explained. He'd absolutely done the crime. She had no problem admitting that. He'd made a lot of mistakes in his life, but he was still her brother. She still loved him, no matter what he'd done. That was what family was all about. It was just hard for her to get to see him more than a few times a year, since she couldn't drive and the train took an entire day.

"I hear that." Doug sighed. Before his father's arrest and trial, he'd been concerned about the effect of incarceration on families, but only in an abstract sense. Now it was personal. "Look. If you want, I'll bring you up there once a month, okay?"

She gave him a suspicious glance. "Why?"

Doug laughed. "Because I'm going there anyway, remember? My dad's in there for something he didn't do. I'm his lawyer now, so I'm going to be there even more often. It's not a hassle. Like I said, we're in the same boat. We have to stick together."

Her eyes softened. "Thank you. I feel like I probably shouldn't take your help—but I will. I really appreciate this."

They pulled up to her apartment complex, and he helped her get her stroller and her baby out of the car. He gave her a card and wrote his cell number on the back. "If you need anything at all, whether it's a ride to Shirley or even just a hand with the baby, give me a call." He smiled and shook her hand, and then he headed back to the car.

His next destination wasn't going to be nearly as pleasant. He aimed his car toward the Massachusetts State Police Headquarters. It wasn't far, and before he knew it he was parked in their visitor lot.

Before he went inside, he ran through his notes. He could just file a formal motion and force them to give him the list, but he didn't want that. He always preferred to do things the nice way whenever he could. That didn't mean that he was foolish enough to think that he was going to be able to saunter inside, say, "Hi, give me all of your notes for my dad's case," and have it happen. No, he was going to have to be on top of his game here, even more than he was when he was in court.

He grabbed his briefcase and made a beeline for the front door. Once inside, he walked up to the front counter and gave his most professional smile to the young trooper on reception duty. "Good afternoon," he said. "Would it be possible to speak with Detective Raymond Langer from the Cold Case unit?"

"Do you have an appointment?" The trooper was not moved by Doug's charm and smile.

"I don't. I just filed a motion yesterday and I was hoping to speak with him about it."

The young trooper didn't seem to care. "Whom should I say is calling?"

"My name is Douglas Morrison, with Findlay, Allison and Jones." He passed a card to the trooper.

The officer picked up the phone. "Detective Langer? Yes, sir. I've got a Mr. Morrison from a law firm called Findlay, Allison and Jones here to see you? I don't know, sir. Yes, sir." He looked back over at Doug. "Detective Langer will be right out."

Doug retreated to one of the hard plastic chairs, eerily reminiscent of those in the prison waiting room, and held his briefcase on his lap. He had no idea what to expect here. He had probably seen Langer at least once, but he couldn't remember him from the trial. Either he'd had a commitment he couldn't escape, or he'd faded back into the background.

When Langer emerged from the troopers-only area, Doug knew that Langer could never have faded into the background. He stood tall, with short and curly black hair and a long, aristocratic nose. His wide green eyes scanned the waiting area until they found Doug, and his basil scent made Doug's mouth water.

Doug bit back a curse. This was going to be harder than he'd expected. No one had warned him that Detective Langer was an alpha, and a hot one at that.

...

Ray didn't have to work too hard to pick out which of the visitors in the waiting area was Doug Morrison. The rain-spattered lawyer suit was a giant clue, for one thing. Even if he hadn't been wearing the suit, Morrison's scent would have marked him out.

Ray tried not to squirm, or to drool. Maybe he shouldn't have used terms like *marked*.

He breathed in for four seconds, paused for one, and let it out slowly. He could do this. He was an alpha, but alphas weren't animals ruled by their baser instincts. Alphas, like all humans, were strong and intelligent people. They could control themselves and their urges. They could be men of peace and understanding, even around omegas.

Even around omegas who smelled like cotton candy. Ray bit back a whimper.

He stepped forward and held out his hand. "Hi. I'm Ray Langer. You must be Doug Morrison."

Morrison gave him a thin, small smile. It completely belied the surge in cotton-candy scent that signaled his arousal. "That's me. I'm here to talk to you about Lawrence Morrison."

"I kind of figured." Ray shot the lawyer a sheepish grin and stuffed his hands into his pocket. He knew it probably looked unfriendly, but it helped him to keep his hands to himself. "Come on with me and we can sit down and have a talk someplace a little more comfortable. Only a little. They don't waste taxpayer dollars on conference rooms, I'm afraid."

The corners of Morrison's mouth twitched. "They're probably a lot more comfortable than the ones where I see a lot of my clients." He followed Ray back toward Cold Case, shoes squeaking on the linoleum. "About half of my caseload is appeals."

"For real?" Ray turned his head to look at the attorney and decided to walk by his side. It made conversation easier, even if it didn't make it easier to keep his mind on his work. "How's that work out for you?"

"Pretty well, actually." Morrison smirked, a little glint of light coming into those narrow green eyes of his. "I have the advantage of only taking on cases that I think I can win."

Ray nodded slowly. "I can see where that would be an advantage, I guess. Here we are. We'll just go right into the first conference room on your left. Careful; all of the detectives are alphas. It might be a little intense." He held open the door to the Cold Case unit.

Morrison gave no indication that he noticed the intense concentration of alpha scents, but he did pick up his pace as he walked through the bullpen. It gave Ray an opportunity to get a good look at his ass, which he both appreciated and kind of resented. After all, he needed to not be thinking these kinds of thoughts about Lawrence Freaking Morrison's son. He was supposed to be above this sort of thing.

Ray closed the door behind them and sat down across from Morrison. It felt strange, having his back to the door like this. It felt like he was the visitor. "All right, Mr. Morrison. Let's talk. I can probably guess why you're here today."

Morrison was unfazed by Ray's tone. He folded his hands on top of his briefcase. "The court has already notified you of my request for a new trial."

"It has. I'm not entirely sure why you think it's a valid request." Ray leaned forward. "Look, I'm really sorry that you have to come to grips with the fact that your father is a serial killer, but the fact of the matter is that the evidence was overwhelming. That conviction is solid. It's hard, to find something like that out about your own flesh and blood. I get that."

Morrison's jaw tightened, but he nodded. "Exhibits A and B." He reached into his briefcase and pulled out photocopies of credit card receipts.

Ray picked them up. The receipts were from a hotel in Annapolis, Maryland, and dated to April of 2002.

Morrison pulled something else out of his bag and passed it to Ray. It was a printout with two pictures, both with date and time stamps. "Library Studies Convention, Annapolis, 2002," Ray read aloud. "That's Morrison, right there. One from April 3, one from April 5." Ray's heart sank. "There's no way he could have gotten back and forth from Annapolis in time to kill Bonnaire or Alumi."

Morrison didn't grin. He didn't smirk, or give a shout of triumph. "That is the preliminary basis of my request for a new trial. How many more victims am I going to find, where my father has an ironclad alibi?" He shook his head.

Ray's hand shook. "Okay. This is… this is bad. It's very bad. I'll take a copy of this and bring it back to you—"

Morrison held up a hand. "Keep it, Detective. I have lots of copies. Trust me."

"Okay then." Ray swallowed. Of course the guy had multiple copies. His father's freedom depended on it. "But here's the thing. The case of these two women is bad. I'll grant that there's no way that Lawrence Morrison killed those two women. And I'll do what I have to in order to make sure that those two women are stricken from the list of his victims, but Mr. Morrison, I'm sorry. They got caught up in the rest of the victimology because they fit the profile for his usual victims and because he has a pattern. I stand by those convictions." He swallowed. "All twenty-two of them."

Morrison did smirk now, and he turned his head away. "I can't say that I'm surprised. You're the one who sent him up in the first place. The person who did kill Melina Bonnaire and Ada Alumi is still out there, somewhere. Serial killers don't just stop killing. Are you honestly ready to have that on your conscience?"

Ray clenched his jaw. He didn't mind helping out a grieving man. While Morrison's father was still alive, he was going to spend the rest of his life up in Shirley. That created real grief, and Ray could respect it. At the same time, he didn't have to tolerate someone impugning his commitment to the job. "I'm convinced that I have the right man. What exactly is it that you want from me?"

"I want the name, date, and time of death for each of my father's alleged victims." Morrison wasn't intimidated, not in the slightest. He met Ray's eyes squarely, without hesitation. "I can do the rest without your help."

"What rest?" Ray threw his hands up into the air. "I was wrong about those two, and I admit it, but Morrison, he's guilty. He killed twenty-two women. That includes your mother, for crying out loud. Doesn't that bother you?"

"It would bother me." Morrison shrugged. "If he'd done it. He didn't. I know my father. I know killers. My father is not a murderer. I'm not exactly new to this game, Detective."

Ray stood up. "All right. Do you have an email address?"

Morrison chuckled. "I thought carrier pigeon would suffice." He produced a card and passed it over to Ray. "They look so festive with a long line of dot matrix paper tied to their little legs."

Ray had to laugh at that, even though he was still furious. "All right," he said, hanging onto the card. "I'll get that data for you and send it out within the next day or so." He shook Morrison's hand and ignored the little jolt of electricity that arced through his body when their skin connected.

Ray left the room immediately. He figured that a guy like Doug could probably find his own way out. Ray had never met an omega who affected him so strongly before, and of course he could do nothing for him. He needed to get away.

He saw his friends all turn their heads to watch the slender, small omega walk out the door. Then all of those heads turned back to stare at him as his boss, Lt. Devlin, walked out of his office. "So," Devlin said. "That's the son, huh?"

Ray slumped down in his seat. "Yeah." He picked up a pen and twirled it in his fingers. "Yeah, that was the son. Apparently the son is a big shot lawyer whose practice consists mostly of appeals."

"I hate appeals." Nenci screwed up his face and glowered at the door Morrison had just walked out.

Tessaro flipped Nenci off. "You hate everything, man. Just go drink some tea or something." He turned to the rest of them. "I mean I feel bad for the guy, you know? How much must it not suck to have your dad kill your mom?"

"Right?" Ray leaned back in his seat. "Although I wouldn't recommend saying that in front of Morrison. He's already found two victims that the senior Mr. Morrison couldn't possibly have killed. We'll have to take a look at the evidence and make sure that the time of death is really correct, but I'm pretty sure that he's right on those cases. It just gives him false hope."

Devlin cleared his throat. "What makes you so sure it's false?"

Ray looked up at his boss in shock. "Sir, you're kidding me, right? I mean you were right there with me, the whole time. Larry Morrison was the last person to see his wife alive. His behavior after the discovery of the first part of Mrs. Morrison wasn't that of a grieving widower; he seemed more likely to be bidding good riddance to bad rubbish. And then there's all the circumstantial evidence."

"All of which has been wrong before." Devlin grinned at him. "I'm pretty confident that we got our guy too, but I'm not going to pretend that people don't get wrongly convicted. We're supposed to be here for justice, not vendettas. It can't hurt to take the time to look back over the case and make sure we got it right." He grimaced and rolled his shoulders. "Not that we're going to have a choice, considering that Morrison Junior petitioned for a new trial. And given what you found, I think he'll probably get it."

The entire squad groaned. Ray had been the lead detective on the case, but they'd all pitched in once they realized that they weren't dealing with a single cold murder but a long-term active serial killer. The case had been grueling, and when they'd finally closed it and gone to trial Ray had personally paid for champagne for the entire squad.

He got up from his chair and walked over to the nearest empty whiteboard. "Hey, Camille, would you mind terribly asking the records department to send up the boxes from the Morrison case?" he called over his shoulder, and picked up a dry-erase marker. "Okay. What do we know?"

Robles' fingers flew across the keyboard. "Okay. Emiliana Romola Morrison, of Lakeville, was reported missing by the priest at her church when she didn't show up for a church group meeting in February of 1998. According to Detective Wilson of Lakeville PD, Mrs. Morrison never missed group." He tugged at his collar. None of this was new to him, but the details were still chilling. "According to her husband, Lawrence, they'd had a difference of opinion and she'd gone 'for a walk.' She often stayed out all night to pray about their 'differences of opinion,' so he hadn't called it in."

Ray put the date on the far left of his timeline. "Okay. What's the last murder?"

"Clarissa Baldovini, age forty-five, in 2014. Body dismembered and scattered just like the others, with the remains found in Massasoit State Park and in various lawns and bush sites in Lakeville and Taunton." That was Morris, who was finally starting to look a little more with it since his omega had almost been killed.

One by one, the other guys on the team read out the names of Larry Morrison's victims while Ray plotted them out on the timeline. They hadn't done this the first time they'd investigated Morrison; they'd been looking into the cold case of Emiliana's death and discovered the serial killer almost by accident. Now that they were looking at the crimes together, and thinking in terms of serial killers, one fact became glaringly obvious. "We're missing victims," he said, staring at his timeline.

"Right." Devlin wiped at his mouth. "Between 1998 and 2000, assuming that the wife was the first. There should be more victims in that space."

Morris jumped to his feet. "Do you think that he maybe got scared off by the blood or something? Or that maybe there was another triggering incident?"

"It happens sometimes." Tessaro shook his head. "Not often. More often, there will be some kind of a gap, but not like this unless they leave the area. Morrison ran the town library. He just went about his daily life. The only change that was made was that he and his son left the Church."

Nenci poked at his keyboard, but his eyes were far away. "If I remember correctly, I think that the priest there was a member of the Order of Lot. Really not a fan of alphas, omegas or anyone else who likes the company of their own gender. That would have been around the same time that the younger Morrison would have tested for the omega gene, so it's not unreasonable that they should leave."

"I wonder if that's what the fight was about?" Ray scratched his head. "Doug doesn't seem at all bothered by the fact that his father killed his mother, but if she bought into that way of thinking it's possible that he just doesn't care."

Robles bobbed his head from side to side. "Maybe. I mean maybe he's just kind of numbed himself to it, too. I don't know. Remember he doesn't accept that his father *did* kill his mother. So we have that to contend with." He rubbed at his cheeks. "Man, I am so not looking forward to having to comb through all of this again. Especially if we might have two of these guys out there, you know?"

Ray did know. It had taken police so long to put the pieces together because the killer had struck all across the southeastern part of the state, making it difficult to put any kind of pattern together. If the crimes belonged to more than one perpetrator, that would make teasing out the reality even more difficult.

Devlin put his hands behind his back. "Well, you boys know what to do. I'm confident that you'll prove your case."

Tessaro elbowed Ray. "Well, it could be worse."

Ray turned to his friend with a bleak look. "How?"

"The guy's omega son could look like a boot. At least you've got someone nice to look at while you two butt heads."

Ray couldn't argue with that. He sat down to compile the list that Morrison had asked for. It was a lot of work, but it would be a good tool for him and the rest of the team too.

<<<<>>>>

Made in the USA
Columbia, SC
12 January 2018